The Fierce Highlander

Donna Fletcher

The Fierce Highlander

Cover art
The Killion Group

Visit Donna's Website
www.donnafletcher.com
http://www.facebook.com/donna.fletcher.author

Chapter One

"Do not waste your breath, Elsie," Leora warned before her sister could say a word. "He is no husband of mine. Not now. Not ever. I will not have a husband chosen for me. I choose who I will wed."

"Perhaps that was possible at one time, but no longer," Elsie said, joining her sister to sit on the end of her bed. "I wish it could be that way for you, truly I do, Leora, but Da wed you and me to Gallowglass warriors to keep us safe and our sister Sky to the brother of a Gallowglass warrior, and it is a good thing he did. That warrior now protects Sky, his brother's widow.

"I would never choose a husband from a fierce group of aristocratic mercenaries," Leora argued and raised her hand to still her sister so she could finish what she had to say. "I do understand Da's reasoning for doing what he did. He and Mum inadvertently caused this situation out of nothing more than kindness and love by accepting three newly born bairns, in danger, as their daughters and never telling anyone about it. I love them even more for saving us from dire circumstances, but I do not want to be forced into a marriage with a man I have never met, let alone a fierce Gallowglass warrior." She silenced her sister again with another abrupt raise of her hand when she went to speak. "I know what you will say. Your marriage turned out wonderful. You love your husband and

Cavell loves you, and I am happy for you, believe me, I am truly happy for you both. But Da spoke with you about the arranged marriage and you agreed to it. I was not given such an opportunity."

Elsie hurried to speak before her sister could stop her again. "And why do you think Da did that?"

Leora threw her hands up in the air as she hurried off the bed. "It is obvious. He knew I would reject such an outrageous and ridiculous proposal."

"So, Da did what any good father would do. He took it upon himself to save you whether you liked it or not," Elsie said and remained where she was and watched her sister's lovely face scrunch with annoyance.

"It is easy for you to say when things turned out so well for you. What if my husband, Noble, turns out to be nothing like his name. What if he is cruel to me and beats me?"

Elsie rushed off the bed to her sister's side, gripping her arm. "You will tell me right off and I will help you poison him so you will be rid of him."

Shock held Leora's tongue captive but only for a short time. "You would do that?"

"Without hesitation," Elsie confessed. "I would not see you suffer such a horrible fate."

Leora smiled softly. "You finally found your courage, Elsie, and I am so pleased you have. But I would never risk having you do such a dangerous thing for me." She grinned. "I would kill him myself."

Elsie smiled at her sister's bravado. "You always could look after yourself, far better than Sky or I could."

"Determined," Leora said. "I have a determined nature."

Elsie laughed. "Stubborn. Da would call it stubborn."

Leora laughed as well, though it faded. "Presently, I am more perplexed than stubborn. I am aware of the wisdom of Da's decision, yet that wisdom has determined my fate and I find that difficult to accept."

"I understand perfectly, Leora, and perhaps it would help for you to know what Cavell told me about Noble."

"Aye, do tell me," Leora said anxiously and tugged her sister to the bed for them to once again sit.

"My husband said that he is the fiercest of all of Slayer's warriors and tracks better than Slayer's hounds. He follows Slayer's command without question and expects obedience from the warriors he commands." Elsie hesitated to continue.

"Tell me everything, Elsie," Leora urged.

"Cavell told me that Noble will take this marriage seriously and commit to it."

"Leaving me forever trapped with a husband who expects obedience at every turn," Leora said and shuddered. "Not a future I favor, and what if I cannot abide his features? What if he is sloven and has a God-awful odor about him?" She scrunched her nose as if she could smell it.

"Why don't you seek the solitude of your room for the remainder of the day and give the situation thought," Elsie suggested, hoping Noble would be to her sister's liking and that time alone would help her come to terms with the situation. She was surprised when her sister's face brightened.

"That is a good idea, Elsie. That will give you time to meet my husband, since he has arrived here without prior notice, and return to my room and tell me what you think of him."

Elsie was not so sure about that, though she could not deny her sister's request. "I will—"

The door burst open, admitting Cavell. "Help your sister gather her things, Elsie. She leaves immediately with her husband."

Leora stood. "I most certainly will not."

Elsie was not surprised when Leora fell back to sit on the bed, her husband descending on her so fast he caused her to instinctively retreat. She also knew he would not issue such a demand if it was not necessary.

Elsie got quickly to her feet and pressed a hand on her husband's impressive chest when he stopped in front of them. A few scars on his face had almost healed and those left did little to distract from his fine features. But that did not matter to Elsie, scars or not, she loved her husband beyond reason.

"Why the sudden departure, husband?" Elsie asked.

"A small clan that doesn't sit far from Lord Slayer's clan and is one he protects, Clan Skirling, is in need of help and he has ordered Noble to proceed there immediately."

Leora regained her courage, slipping off the bed and moving away from Cavell. "Why doesn't he see to it himself?"

"No Gallowglass warrior questions Lord Slayer's command," Cavell said with a slight scowl.

"Lord Slayer can order his warriors all he wants, but he does not order me. I will not be leaving here today."

"Aye, you will, wife."

Leora turned and was struck with surprise at the man standing in the open doorway. Not only were his features striking but the determination in his powerful voice left no room that he would have it any other way than as he ordered. And the way the muscles in his body shifted and grew taut as he took a step into the room warned her that he was prepared for battle.

Leora's chin went up with her determination. "Nay, I will not."

She stood her ground as he approached her, though the closer he got, the more she thought it would have been wiser to retreat. Cavell had described Noble to her sister perfectly... the fiercest of Lord Slayer's warriors. There was a fierceness in his every step, every movement, and more so in his deep blue eyes. She imagined that his foes would run in fright before lifting a weapon against him, though his striking features and his gorgeous deep blue eyes might have women melting in his arms... but not her. Her chin went up even higher.

"There is one thing you need to know about me, wife—"

"There is something more important you should know about me, husband. I will not be dictated to," Leora said, not letting him finish.

"You will learn."

The man constantly sounded as if he commanded, and Leora would not have it. "I think not."

He stepped closer to her, so close she caught a whiff of him. For an instant she thought she stood in the forest when spring was at its most potent, the earth releasing a slightly damp aroma reminiscent of freshly turned soil and burgeoning life. It was a scent she favored.

"Then let me give you a choice, wife. You gather your things and ready yourself to leave posthaste or I will throw you over my shoulder and physically remove you, and your belongings will be left behind."

"You wouldn't—"

Noble planted his face close to hers. "Challenge me! I love a challenge."

Cavell tried to stop his wife from going to her sister's aid but failed. Though he was proud of how fast she was learning to move. It kept him on his toes in catching her.

Elsie took hold of her sister's arm. "Let me help you get your belongings together."

Leora went with her sister, though stopped after only taking a few steps and turned to glare at her husband. "Since you love a challenge, I will make sure you get a challenge."

She could not believe her husband had the audacity to smile.

"I have yet to lose a challenge."

"There is always a first time," Leora said and turned her back on him.

***

Leora watched Elsie fade in the distance as she left the only home she had known since birth. Tears threatened her eyes, but she refused to let them fall. She kept a soft smile on her face and her chin up as she waved to the clan members seeing her off with cheers of well wishes and a fruitful union while riding through the village directly behind her husband.

She had had no intentions of leaving with him but when she and Elsie had been left alone to pack her belongings, her sister pointed out a far better reason why she should go with her husband. She recalled their conversation that had changed everything.

"I know this is not what you want but there is a much more important reason for you to go with your husband," Elsie said.

"Nothing could be more important," Leora argued.

"Our sister Sky."

"What does Sky have to do with me submitting to this marriage and leaving with my husband?"

"Did you not hear what Cavell said about Clan Skirling being not far from Lord Slayer's clan?"

"Aye, and it is the very reason Lord Slayer should see to the problem himself," Leora insisted.

"You are angry and thinking only of yourself," Elsie warned.

Leora went to argue again and stopped, realizing what her sister meant and grew annoyed at herself for not seeing it. "I could get to Sky and make sure she is safe."

"And see if you can get Lord Slayer to send her home, here with those who love her," Elsie said tearfully. "We both told her we would return for her, and we have failed her. Please, Leora, this is a chance for us to see that our sister is returned home, where she will be loved and kept safe."

"You are right. We have failed Sky and I foolishly stand here thinking of myself while we do not truly know what Sky suffers. I will go with Noble not because he is my husband but to secure our sister's safety and her return home."

"And along the way see if this marriage may benefit you," Elsie urged.

"And if it doesn't benefit me?"

"We will find a way out of it for you that doesn't involve poison," Elsie said with a gentle smile.

Leora had brightened seeing her sister's soft, teasing smile. She was glad to see how much Elsie had flourished since she had last seen her in Dundren Abbey. She had always known Elsie possessed a strength that she had yet to discover, and she was thrilled she had finally discovered it and that she had discovered love as well. She could leave Elsie without worry, knowing that she had a husband who loved her and would protect her with his life, but also that she had the strength and courage to protect herself if necessary.

Leora also recalled Cavell's parting words to her.

"Noble is a good man and will make you a good husband if you are not too stubborn to let him."

She was determined not stubborn, and it was born out necessity. Her da was a strong man, but her mum was stronger, and her strength was there for all to see if they but took notice. Her mum had seen that her husband never made an important decision without consulting her. And she had seen how her mum had helped settle disputes in the clan better than her da. When her mum had taken ill, she had asked Leora to be there for her da when needed. She had realized that her mum had asked her to take her place in guiding her da when necessary. She had not minded since helping her da make good decisions had come easily and after a while, he told her to do what she thought was best and she no longer consulted him on clan matters. She had enjoyed her leadership role in the clan and did not like the prospect of having to follow orders instead of issuing them.

How she would deal with her husband was a matter yet to be determined. What was more important to Leora was to get to her sister and see that she was safe and to make sure she got her returned home as soon as possible.

There was one fault she possessed that she had agreed with when her mum had told Leora that at times, she could be… impatient. She did her best to keep that in mind and not let it interfere when patience was called for. Right now, she worried that she would fail at being patient.

Her husband had yet to speak with her since leaving her home, and he had barely said a few words to her that had not been a command while at her home. He should at least have had the manners to properly introduce himself and discuss their marriage that she had not known about until recently. That he ignored her, riding just ahead of her and speaking with a warrior who she assumed was his second in command, annoyed

11

her. Was that how he intended to treat her, as if she did not exist?

After they were a good distance from home, her patience worn far too thin to ignore it, she directed her horse to ride alongside her husband's.

"Whatever it is you want will wait until we stop. Until then, you ride directly behind me," Noble ordered.

"Nay, I will not," she said and went right on speaking. "You barely spoke to me when at my home and you have spoken not a word to me since leaving there. You have yet to properly introduce yourself to me or discuss this marriage I have yet to accept. So, nay, I will not ride behind you or wait until we stop to speak with you."

That his expression did not change surprised her. She thought he would at least turn a scowl on her, or she would see anger in his deep blue eyes. His expression did not change, which told her that he was secure in his command. Also being this close to him, she could not help but be struck by his handsome features. They could distract, if one let them, but she had no intention of being distracted even if she felt a strange tug to her stomach when looking at him which, of course, she blamed on her irritating husband.

"It is not a request, wife," Noble said and turned to the man beside him. "You know what to do." The man rode off, and Noble turned to speak to his wife. "While I need not offer you an explanation, I feel it is only fair I give you one for not paying mind to you since leaving your home. I am presently more concerned with your safety than introducing myself properly to you. Our marriage was conceived for your safety, and with Cavell having informed me that someone searches for a woman with your description and that one woman has already been killed because she bore your striking reddish blonde hair color, I am making plans to see that you are kept safe. Cavell may have minimized part of the threat by killing the man hired to see you dead, but there are others who will gladly take his place. So, wife, you can be reasonable and do as I command, or I can force you to do as I command."

The man who had ridden beside Noble approached with two warriors and Leora had no doubt they were meant to flank her sides, forcing her to obey her husband's orders and remain behind him.

"Do you always command with every word?" Leora asked, annoyed at seeing reason in his explanation.

"Aye, I do, and you would be wise to grow used to it."

"I doubt that will happen, just as I doubt this marriage will be permanent, but I understand your reasoning and will do as you say… this time."

Leora went to turn her horse around to resume following behind her husband when he grabbed the reins, halting her.

"Only death will end this marriage," Noble warned and released the reins.

Chapter Two

Noble glanced at his wife where she sat by the campfire. He had had little time for her today, his orders from Slayer having been urgent.

Get to Clan Skirling posthaste and settle the mess there.

He did not know what mess he would face but he was prepared for it. He had not been prepared for the kick to his senses when he met his wife for the first time. He had heard she was beautiful, but she was beyond beautiful, if that was possible. Her face was flawless, not a blemish on it, and while she wore her reddish blonde hair piled on the top of her head, more stands fell in waves around her face and neck than looked to be secured. But it was her bold green eyes and her infectious smile that captured a man's attention and refused to let go. Her body held its own appeal, full and luscious with curves that ached to be stroked. One look and a man would believe her a perfect wife… until she opened her mouth.

She was stubborn to a fault, and worse, she thought to command. He had thought that he would be forced to carry out his threat about physically removing her from her home. He still wondered what or who had turned her agreeable. He wondered if it was something her sister Elsie had said to her. Cavell had a good and wise wife, holding her tongue when necessary and speaking when necessary. She had plain features, but her eyes lit with love every time she looked upon her husband, and you could see the same bold love in his eyes when he glanced at her. It was rare to see such a strong love as theirs, and Noble could not help but envy it.

Love or not, Leora was his wife, and they would make the most of their marriage. This was not a temporary arrangement. It was a commitment, and he would honor it… no matter how difficult. That meant protecting his wife and keeping her safe, and he had a feeling that she was not going to make it easy for him to do.

"I do not envy you, Noble."

"And why is that, Finley?" he asked, turning to face the man that had been his second in command since the Gallowglass troop was formed several years ago and knowing what the man would say.

"Having a wife can be difficult enough, but having a beautiful woman for a wife is far too hard of a task to bear." Finley shook his head. "Look at the way the men stare at her, though they try not to, but it cannot be helped. Her smile, which is more constant than not, is like a ray of sunshine from heaven and her bold green eyes glow with—" He stopped abruptly and shook his head again.

Noble tilted his head, a glare in his blue eyes. "Do finish what you were going to say."

Finley continued shaking his head. "It was nothing. Nothing at all."

Noble did not force a response. He knew what Finley was about to say. He had recognized it himself. *Passion.* It flared in her eyes when she smiled, spoke, argued. That she was a passionate woman was obvious and if she was that passionate about life itself, he could only imagine the passion she possessed when coupling.

"Warn the men to keep their eyes off my wife," Noble ordered.

"I already have, and you can see how much good it did," Finley said, looking around the camp at the glances men were sneaking Leora's way.

Noble stepped forward, the strength of his voice carrying throughout the camp. "Eyes off my wife!"

Every head turned, not daring to look at Leora, and Noble caught his wife shaking her head directly at him as if chastising him. He could not recall the last time he had been chastised by anyone.

"We leave at dawn," Noble said without looking at Finley and went to join his wife.

He lowered himself to sit on the ground beside her in front of the campfire.

"I am too tired to talk now," Leora said, not looking at him. "It will wait for another time."

"Then you can listen to me talk, wife," Noble said, giving her no choice and annoyed at the command in her tone. "First, don't ever shake your head at me again. My word rules among my men and I will not have my wife undermining my rule. Second, as I said before, only death will end this marriage."

Leora was unable to hold her tongue. "Do not tempt me."

His smile caught Leora by surprise and once again she felt a strange tug in her stomach. The thought crossed her mind that she was either feeling unwell or her husband irritated her since there was absolutely no way the tug had anything to do with finding her dictating husband appealing. The thought alone was laughable, though his response was shocking.

"I thought the same myself."

"You wouldn't dare," she said, her eyes narrowing.

"Then shall we agree not to kill each other, so neither of us need to worry about that?"

"Is it a truce you seek from me?"

"When it comes to killing each other, aye," he said with a chuckle.

He might be fierce, but Leora was caught off guard by his lighthearted laugh.

"No killing," she agreed, not having the stomach for it anyway, even with all her earlier bravado of poisoning him if necessary. Life was precious and she did not truly know if she could rob someone of it unless she was left with no choice. She continued, needing to have her say. "I only learned of our marriage. I was never given the opportunity to agree or to reject it. I dislike very much that it was forced upon me, and I have yet to decide if I wish to remain in it."

"I am afraid that is not an option," Noble said. "We all have our duties and yours is to accept the marriage your da arranged for you. I will be a good husband—"

"Describe what you think makes a good husband," she said, annoyance in her every word.

"A man who provides for his wife, protects her, keeps her safe, and gives her many sons and daughters to look after."

"And you think that pitiful explanation makes for a good husband?"

Noble could not understand how her annoyed smile could be attractive, though the spark of passionate anger in her eyes was what really caught his attention. It was a fiery green that held an invitation of even more passion.

Again, she continued talking, not giving him a chance to say a word. "A good husband trusts and respects his wife. He is there for her when needed, to talk with her, comfort her, hold her close so she can feel his strength, feel that he cares. He also seeks her counsel on matters, knowing her wisdom can benefit him, and he shares all clan matters with her. A good husband does not work separately from his wife, he works with her as one. That is what makes a good husband and a good marriage."

"And what makes a good wife?" he asked, thinking over her words.

Leora looked at him strangely. "Isn't it obvious? A wife gives the same in return. She does for him as he does for her."

"And how did you reach this conclusion of a good husband and wife?"

"I saw it with my parents. They worked together as one—"

"So, they both decided it would be wise to take newborn bairns, not belonging to them, and raise them as their own?"

Leora was quick to defend the only parents she had ever known. "And glad I am they had the courage to do so, or I would not be alive today and be able to tell you that you are a horse's arse."

"I but stated a fact. A fact that now presents a danger for you, and I would advise you not to call me a horse's arse again."

"I will take it into consideration," she said dismissively. "And that fact only proves that my parents risked much to accept and welcome a newborn bairn they knew nothing about into their home and hearts. I am safe and much loved because of them, and I am forever grateful that they had the strength to be so courageous."

"But they were fools in never learning your true origins since it could cause future problems and present a danger to you and the other two women."

"You mean my two sisters, Elsie and Sky, for we may not share the same blood, but we are sisters of the heart, a bond that can never be broken. As far as why my parents never learned the truth of our origins, I can only imagine that someone thought it wise, safer, a secret to always be kept."

"If more than one person knows a secret, it will not remain one," Noble said. "Now the secret is out, and the problem is… we are not privy to it."

***

Noble glanced at his wife now and again the next morning as they made their way along a well-traveled path. She kept a pleasant smile on her face as she took her surroundings in with interest, and he wondered if her smile was deceptive. Was she contemplating ways to sabotage their marriage? She was not as committed to their union as he was and understandably so. At least he had been given a choice, Lord Slayer having proposed the arrangement assuring him it would prove beneficial for him, and Lord Slayer was an honorable man whose word could be trusted. He had planned to wed one day and if the marriage would benefit him, he would have been foolish to reject the offer.

If his wife was wise, she would see the wisdom of her father's decision in marrying her to him. She was in danger, and he could protect her, keep her from harm while more was learned about who was searching for her, if indeed she was the woman they searched for and—

His head went up just a fraction, having caught a sudden scent that wasn't there a moment ago. His sense of smell was strong, which was what made him an exceptional tracker, though it could be a blessing or a curse. He had learned to tolerate the more potent scents. He was glad his wife had a gentle, sweet scent about her. He would liken it to stepping into a field of wildflowers when the blooms were most fragrant.

He caught the scent again, growing stronger and there was no mistaking it, the pungent sweat of warriors and with it growing stronger rapidly meant only one thing.

He turned his horse toward his wife and let loose with a roar. "Attack!"

His men drew their weapons ready to fight as they quickly directed their horses to form two circles around Leora.

Leora barely got to glance at her husband when a group of warriors emerged from the dense woods that surrounded them, roaring like banshees bent on destruction. Fear gripped her, seeing what looked like a herd of madmen rushing at them. Some were on foot and some on horses. The first circle of Gallowglass warriors were off their horses in a flash and fought the warriors who were on foot while the warriors on horses that followed attacked the remaining Gallowglass warriors who circled her.

She was shocked to see how easily her husband fiercely battled his way through warrior after warrior raining down on him. He swung a double-sided axe with great skill. The only thing she could do was to keep control of her mare and maneuver the animal when necessary. She had heard endless tales of the Gallowglass warriors, aristocratic mercenaries who fought to keep their clans free of rule from the Lowlands and from the Northmen who believed certain isles and lands still belonged to them. It was claimed that they were fearless men who would die fighting rather than surrender and seeing them now, she believed it.

Warrior after warrior fell to the Gallowglass, but not one of the Gallowglass fell, not that they did not suffer injures but they kept fighting as if invincible. That the warriors were after her was obvious, trying to break through the circle of men who surrounded her. Her husband kept on the outskirts of the circle taking down any who attempted to break through the formation.

Though fearful, Leora remained strong, knowing fear would do her no good. She did not think she would ever get the sound of clashing weapons, cries of pain from the wounded or moans from the dying out of her head or stop seeing wiser warriors flee rather than die today. Even when the battle finally ended, she still heard it in her head like a tolling bell that refused to stop ringing.

"Secure the wounded," Noble called out, "and toss the dead into the woods."

His orders roiled her stomach at the thought, though more so at a memory she preferred to keep buried. A memory she feared she would never forget, just like the horrific sounds of battle.

"I can help tend the wounded," she offered, knowing that keeping busy would help ease her mind.

"The men are used to tending their own and others' wounds," Noble said, directing his horse over to her. "Are you all right?"

She was pale and whether she realized it or not, there was a slight tremble to her hands that held a death grip on her reins.

"Of course I am. I am not a weak woman, husband, though I will admit to being fearful during the battle and relieved for the Gallowglass who protected me, and for that, I thank you."

"It is my duty and I never fail to do my duty," Noble said and gave a nod beyond her shoulder. "Follow me to that tree. You can sit and rest under it while I speak to those who are still able to respond and find out who is behind this attack."

"I will remain with you and hear what they have to say," Leora said eagerly.

"You will sit by the tree and rest while I see to this," he ordered sternly.

Leora cast a quick glance at the tree. "What if there are more warriors in the woods or a warrior or two who fled waits to sneak out and snatch me away and you do not realize it until it is too late to find me?"

"I am an exceptional tracker."

"Then why were you unable to find me after my escape from Dundren Abbey?" Leora asked with a pleasant smile. "Elsie told me how you searched yet failed to find me."

He had never failed when tracking someone until his wife and he was in no mood to discuss his failure with her. Though he did intend to find out how she had avoided his tracking skills.

With no desire to debate the issue with her, little time to spare, and eager to continue their journey and carry out Lord Slayer's command, he said, "Stay close to my side."

"As you say, husband."

"Words I wish to hear more often," he said.

She turned her horse ready to take the lead. "You will, when necessary."

Noble's hand shot out to grab hold of her arm and reminded, "You will follow beside me."

"Then hurry. It is not wise for us to linger too long here. Those who fled may have done so to alert a larger group of mercenaries."

Noble was impressed that his wife realized that possibility. He already sent two trackers, he had taught the skill to, to find out if more mercenaries lingered in the area, whether behind them or ahead of them. He was prepared one way or the other and part of that was leaving here as soon as possible.

Leora was off her horse before her husband could help her dismount. She had watched her mum do much on her own and she had asked her one day why she sometimes did things that were her husband's duties.

She had smiled and taken hold of Leora's arm, hugging her close, and spoke softly as had been her way. "Because, dear daughter, a time may come when I only have myself to rely on and I must have the skill and knowledge needed to do so."

After that day, Leora emulated her mum and began learning and doing things she had never given thought to. Surprisingly, she enjoyed gaining both knowledge and skills and continued to do both.

She was adjusting her garments when her husband approached from around her mare.

"You will wait for me to help you dismount," he ordered.

"Why when I am capable of doing it myself?"

"It is my duty and I do not want to see you injure yourself."

"Why would I injure myself when I know what I'm doing?" she asked, scrunching her face as if his response had made no sense.

"Regardless, it will be my way," he ordered once again.

"We are wasting time on a nonsensical matter," she said and went to walk past him.

His hand once again settled on her arm. "You are wed now, and we both have duties. I will see to mine, and you will see to yours. Do you understand?"

His deep blue eyes fascinated her. She wondered what lurked in the deepest depths of them and after being captured for a moment by them, she said, "I understand." She expected him to release her arm and when he didn't, she asked, "You have more to say?"

"I am waiting."

Again, her brow scrunched in confusion. "For what?"

"That response I wish to hear more often." Her sudden brilliant smile startled him, though he did not allow it to show. He kept his stoic expression.

"This is not the occasion when that response is necessary," she said, and with her smile still brilliant but her voice low, added, "now release my arm."

Noble smiled this time and Leora was stunned by his splendid smile and how it heightened his already fine features. And she was prepared for his retort and to yank her arm free, if necessary, but she was not prepared for his reaction.

His hand clamped firmly around her arm like a shackle, and she realized she would not be able to break free of him. He hurried her to keep pace alongside him as he walked to where the captured mercenaries had been herded and were being held.

"Remain by my side and speak not a word," he ordered just before they came to a stop in front of the group.

He released her arm after coming to a stop and she stood by his side, though wasn't sure if she would be able to do as he said and hold her tongue. This concerned her since she had questions that she wanted answered.

There were about half a dozen men exhibiting various wounds. None were serious from what Leora could see. Some of the men trembled in fright while others displayed a forced bravado.

"Who is in command here?" Noble demanded.

"You killed him," one man answered.

Noble continued to question, focusing on the man who was thick in the waist and lacking in height. "Who pays for this mission?"

The few there all shrugged while the man who had responded to the previous question spoke up again.

"We are not privy to that information."

"Who is?' Noble asked, though he knew the answer.

"The fellow you killed," the man said.

"What was the mission?" Noble demanded.

"To kill the woman from Clan Murdock with the reddish blonde hair," the man said.

"Why?"

"Who knows?' the man shrugged indifferently. "A mission is a mission. The reason matters not as long as we get paid."

"Now we don't get the coin, Hayes, and we lose our lives to the Gallowglass, who you never informed us we would be fighting," another man called out.

Other men echoed similar sentiments.

"This mission is an open one?" Noble asked, taking advantage of the quarreling among the men.

"Aye, it is," one man said.

"You idiot," Hayes snapped. "You just condemned us to death. You all but told him that if set free, there are other mercenary groups that we can join up with to finish this mission."

Silence followed, the captives' eyes wide and focused on Noble.

"You lie and play the fool."

All eyes turned on Leora, including her husband's eyes that sparked with annoyance that she had spoken when he had ordered her to hold her tongue.

"You know more than you say," Leora accused.

"Not true," Hayes argued.

"Then tell us why you knew that it was the Gallowglass you would battle while the others did not?" Leora asked and shook her head. "And do not waste your breath with more lies. You are privy to more information than you say, and no doubt if released, you will take it back to whoever is truly in command, which is the reason you got so annoyed with the man who responded when asked if this was an open mission. He squashed any possibility of you being freed."

Noble intended to silence his wife, but that she realized what he had assumed himself and her commanding tone had him holding his tongue to see what she would say next and what they could possibly learn.

"It would be much wiser of you to make a deal with the Gallowglass and tell him," —she nodded to her husband— "a Gallowglass warrior only too anxious to be rid of you all since you can offer him no help, everything you know so your lives might be spared."

"Tell him what he wants to know, Hayes," one man said.

"Aye, I did not sign on to fight the Gallowglass," another man said, and other men cried out the same.

"Fools!" Hayes spat. "He's not going to free you. We are all as good as dead. The Gallowglass frees no one who attacks them."

"Hayes is right. We don't free those who attack us. But since you did not know you would fight the Gallowglass, I see room for leniency, except," — Noble's eyes went to— "Hayes."

The men could not offer what they knew fast enough even if it had no connection to the present situation. Noble listened and he saw that his wife did as well, taking everything in that was said.

Hayes grew more annoyed with how easily the captives capitulated and he attempted to interrupt and dispute what was being said, but they shouted him down.

Noble watched as Hayes grew more and more annoyed, especially when Leora asked question after question and some he had not thought to ask. He listened and asked his own questions, but the discussion taught him one thing about his wife… she was more astute and knowledgeable than he expected.

"I am far more skilled at fashioning a weapon than using one, sir," a man into his years said. "I never chose the life of a mercenary. I would fashion exceptional weapons for you if you would allow me to serve you."

"You're a traitor, Atworth," Hayes yelled at him.

"I would say he finally sees his worth and offers it to someone who will provide him with a home and safety rather than constant battle and most assuredly an early death," Leora said as if what she saw was obvious to all.

It happened so fast that Leora was left speechless and breathless. She lay on her back on the ground looking up at the cloudy sky, thinking it was not gray enough for rain, while shouts and scuffles went on around her.

Though she did obey her husband's order when he shouted, "Stay down!"

It wasn't long before he stood over her, leaned down, and slipped his arm beneath her waist to scoop her up onto her feet, and tuck her against him. She was glad his arm remained around her waist and that she had him to lean against since she felt a bit lightheaded, although it might have been that she shackled her hand to his arm that forced him to keep hold of her.

She stood stunned to see Hayes on the ground lifeless along with a few other captives. "What happened?"

"Hayes lunged at you, and I pushed you out of the way, and disposed of him quickly enough, which is how you landed on your back. A few of his men joined him, the ones who I suspected would, and my men saw to them while the others who wanted no more part of Hayes and the mission removed themselves from the fray," Noble explained. "Are you all right?"

"It would be foolish of me to deny it when I feel a bit lightheaded," she said and was surprised to hear actual concern in her husband's voice.

"I am glad you speak the truth to me, wife," Noble said, pleased that she trusted him enough to do so. "Unfortunately, I had no choice if I was to keep you safe. I had to push you out of the way."

"I understand perfectly, and thank you for that."

"I am here for you, wife, it is my duty, and I will always honor my duty," Noble said, though realized that it was not duty that had him keeping hold of her. It was that he enjoyed the feel of her close against him, and he especially enjoyed the feel of her perfectly curved waist where his hand rested.

"Aye, duty calls, and one must answer," Leora said, not quite understanding why his response annoyed her.

"You will sit and rest while all is finished here," he ordered and with his arm firm around her waist, walked her to the tree whose branches he had ordered her to rest under not that long ago.

He eased her to sit on the ground and rest against the thick trunk, then summoned one of his men with a crook of his finger.

"Dyle will remain here to watch over you." A slight smile peeked at the corners of his mouth. "This way no one can snatch you away."

That he had not only recalled her words in a playful manner but also made sure she was kept safe, brought a gentle smile to her face. "You are a thoughtful husband."

"A dutiful one," he reminded and turned to walk away when he stopped and turned his head. "You will be riding with me when we leave."

She bristled at such a ridiculous idea. "I most certainly will not. I am more than capable of riding my own horse."

"Not after that fall. You will ride with me and that is an order you have no choice but to obey, wife."

Chapter Three

"I am not riding with y— OH!" Leora cried out when her husband grabbed her around the waist and hoisted her up onto his horse.

Noble swung himself up to settle with ease behind her and, with his arm around her waist, adjusted her to sit comfortably against him, trying to ignore how close her firm backside nestled near his manhood.

"I need not ride with you," Leora protested, though surprisingly found herself comfortable braced against her husband.

"I will not chance you feeling lightheaded and falling off your horse. You will ride with me until I am sure you are well enough to ride on your own."

His firm command left no room for her to argue and, besides, her head had a slight fuzziness to it. If she was to help Sky in any way, she had to remain strong in body and mind. She could not fail her sister. She had given Elsie her word and Sky as well before escaping the abbey, and she would keep it.

The gray skies followed them overhead as they traveled, and a cool breeze rustled through the multitude of trees. There would be a chill in the air tonight and she shivered, recalling the chilled nights she had spent after escaping the abbey. She had wondered if her bones would forever remain chilled.

"You're cold?" Noble asked, feeling her body shudder against him.

"A slight chill, nothing more," she said and nodded to the three mercenaries flanked by Noble's warriors as they walked, keeping pace with the plodding horses. "The three are all who are left from the attack? You spared their lives?"

"For now, we shall see how they fare and if they say what they mean or they think to play us for fools while I learn more from them."

Leora was impressed with her husband's strategy of allowing time to gather more information. "That is wise of you, and I look forward to speaking to them myself."

"You will do no such thing," he ordered sternly.

"I will—" She stopped and locked her lips together briefly, keeping herself from speaking, then briefly shook her head. "You are right. I failed to consider that one or more of them may still want me dead."

His wife's quick mind continued to impress Noble.

"You will, though, keep me abreast of all you find out."

And there went her commanding tone again and Noble's tone was equally commanding. "I will consider it."

Leora's brow shot up. "Consider it?"

"Were you not taught well the duties of a wife?"

"Duties composed by men who wish to rule their wives. I do not intend to be ruled—"

"And I don't intend to have a wife who believes she can do whatever she wishes regardless of what I say or command."

"If you would have let me finish," she said, a flair of annoyance shimmering in her green eyes, "I do not intend to be ruled... though I will respect my husband's wishes and opinions as long as he respects mine. A partnership, not a dictatorship."

Noble lowered his head until his face nearly touched hers. "I rule, wife, and my duty dictates that I do, so get used to it."

"Duty is what we make of it. It adjusts and changes with life. I suppose that means you are not a horse's arse, but rather an old, stubborn horse's arse."

"Did I not advise you not to call me that again?"

Leora feigned surprise, adding a slight smile to it. "Have you begun to lose your memory already, husband, that you do not recall what you said to me?"

"Watch your words with me, wife, I have been patient with you so far, but that patience is wearing thin," he warned.

Leora moved her face closer to her husband's, their noses almost touching. "Then I suggest you grow a thicker skin."

His hand grabbed hold of her chin to squeeze it. "Learn to hold your tongue, wife."

"Or what?" she challenged.

"Or you will regret the day you met me." He released her chin after giving it a firm squeeze. "And do not bother to tell me you already regret meeting me since that was obvious when I entered your bedchamber. Your beauty could not hide the fury in your eyes, and that brings me to a question I have been meaning to ask you. Why did you concede so fast to honor the marriage and leave with me when at first you made it clear that you had no intentions of doing so?"

A conundrum. Did Leora confide in him her reason for leaving willingly with him or did she lie to him?

"Lies do not help a marriage," Noble advised, seeing her hesitation and assuming she was searching for an excuse rather than the truth.

She waited, thinking he would point out how the lies of her and her sisters' births had brought them danger, but he said nothing more. He waited for her response. She gave the problem quick thought. Would she be wise to engage her husband's help in visiting her sister and getting her home? He was well acquainted with Lord Slayer and could very well be of great help in getting her to see Sky.

She decided to take the chance and tell him the truth. "I agreed to leave with you because of my sister Sky. Elsie reminded me that Clan Skirling is not far from Clan Ravinsher, Lord Slayer's clan where Sky is now. I will be able to see how my sister is doing and hopefully have her returned home to family."

"And you along with her?" Noble asked.

"I will not deny I am unsure of our marriage and whether I will embrace it or see it ended. Presently, I am more concerned with my sister Sky than my own problems. I promised her before I escaped from the abbey, as did Elsie, that I would return and free her and we would go home. Elsie and I both failed to free her. I cannot fail to see her returned home."

"Lord Slayer commands with a heavy hand. It is the reason for his endless victories. I do not know if he will allow your sister to leave since I know he would feel it is his duty to protect his brother's widow, but I believe there is a chance he will allow you to visit with her."

Thrilled to hear such good news, she squeezed her husband's arm. "That would be wonderful, and I would be forever grateful for your help."

"I doubt that since now it is your memory that fails you, wife," Noble warned. "As I have told you and will continue to remind you… we are wed. You are my wife and will remain my wife. We will have children, raise them to be fine men and women, and, Lord willing, we will grow old together. Nothing, absolutely nothing will change that."

His voice held such strength that he sounded as if he commanded it, and a chill ran through Leora thinking he had just sealed her fate.

***

They stopped briefly for a rest and for the horses to water at a stream, then they were on their way again. With nightfall settling late this time of year they could travel longer than usual, and Leora sensed that her husband was eager to reach their destination.

Leora did not bother to argue with him when once again he hoisted her up onto his horse. It gave her time to speak with him and learn more about him and to find out where they would eventually settle if she decided to remain wed to him.

She wasted no time in asking him. "If I should decide to remain in this marriage, where would we call home?"

"Where *we* will reside *permanently* will be Lord Slayer's decision," he said, emphasizing that there was no debating the issue.

"Why his decision?" she asked, her brow scrunching in question, then suddenly shot wide along with her eyes. "He promised you a clan of your own if you would agree to wed me." She nodded as if confirming it for herself. "Of course, he would. He had to make sure you would not refuse and what better way than to offer you your own clan." Her eyes widened again. "Clan Skirling. He intends to give you Clan Skirling."

The thought had crossed Noble's mind. It wasn't a large clan, but it bordered Clan Ravinsher, which meant Slayer would be well protected if Noble was made the clan's chieftain. He had not received any word on such a proposal but knowing Slayer, he was probably waiting to see how Noble handled the situation at Clan Skirling.

"What of your own family clan?" Leora asked, growing more curious about her husband.

"I am the youngest of three brothers. There is no future at Clan McCalgan for me."

Noble wondered if she purposely left her hand resting on his arm or if she had forgotten it was there. She had gripped his arm when he had adjusted her to sit comfortably against him after mounting the horse, as if worried she might fall. Not that he would let her. He had a good hold on her and he did not intend to let go of her, in more ways than one.

He liked that she did not think twice of touching him as if they were familiar with each other. He

36

enjoyed the touch of a woman, and it was a good sign that she touched him without hesitation or question.

"You have three brothers?" she asked, her curiosity about him continuing to grow since he truly was a stranger to her.

"Aye. Blake is the oldest, Dugald follows, then Charles, and I am last. So, when Lord Slayer presented the offer of an arranged marriage with the benefit of leading my own clan, I accepted it without hesitation. I would be grateful for any clan Lord Slayer offers me, for leading my own clan was something I never thought possible."

"And you cared not who it was you wed, it was the benefit of leading a clan that only mattered to you?" she asked, annoyed at the thought that the woman he wed had not mattered at all in his decision, but that was the way of arranged marriages so why should she care?

A smile tempted the corners of his mouth. "I told you I like a challenge. I knew I could tame any woman I wed to be a good wife."

His smile broke wide seeing her green eyes blaze with fiery anger, and realized just what a stunning green color they were, and he felt a pull in his gut. He found his wife appealing and that was not a bad thing.

The fiery blaze remained in her eyes, but a smile broke out on her face. "We shall see who tames who first."

Noble laughed, he couldn't help it, and he hugged her waist with his arm. "You do know I am known as the fiercest Gallowglass warrior, don't you?"

"You will get no advantage from me for your disadvantage," she warned, annoyed at his confidence.

"Disadvantage?" he asked, his smile remaining.

"Aye, if you think this challenge has anything to do with fierceness then you may as well surrender now since you have already failed."

His smile vanished and he yanked her tight against him and lowered his head until their noses almost touched. "I never fail, wife. It will go no other way but my way. But do feel free to challenge me. I thrive on challenges."

She pressed the tip of her nose to his and said, "As I said when we met... there is always a first time."

A shout from Finley ended their discussion and Leora watched him and another rider approach.

She was relieved by the interruption. His voice not only held the power of command, but his touch did as well. She felt it race through her and take hold as if taking possession of her, and she silently warned herself to be careful. Her husband was fiercer than she thought.

"What have you learned, Penn?" Noble asked before the barrel-chested warrior brought his horse to a stop.

Leora was surprised at the contrast between the warrior's sheared head and his bushy red beard and moustache that appeared to devour his mouth. He had more hair on his face than his head. She thought for sure both would stifle his voice, but he had a strong, distinct voice that was easily heard.

"Two men claim to call themselves Chieftain of Clan Skirling, neither are fit to do so, and neither are from Clan Skirling. And there are none in Clan Skirling fit or wise enough to lead the clan. The people themselves seem to be a good lot but suffering, their chieftain having been unwise. Much help is needed there. As you know, the land does not sit far from Clan Ravinsher, and the people there worry that Lord Slayer will take over their clan and Clan Skirling will exist no more."

"Our men remain where they cannot be seen?" Noble asked.

"Aye, sir, they do, and are prepared for your arrival," Penn said. "Also, Lord Slayer sent a small troop of warriors to wait with us for your arrival. Ross leads them and he has a message for you from Lord Slayer. They expect you in about three or four days."

Leora had sat silent, listening to them, though excitement surged through her hearing that one of Lord Slayer's warriors was at Clan Skirling. She would see if he knew anything about Sky and if he could possibly take a message to her to let her know that Leora was close and would see her soon.

"Did you come across any mercenaries on your way here?" Noble asked.

Penn shook his head. "None, but then I took a quicker path that is less traveled." He nodded toward the prisoners standing together, the troop having been brought to a halt with his arrival. "I see that you came across a few."

"Some claim they did not know it was Gallowglass they would face," Noble said.

"Foolishness is not an excuse," Penn said.

Leora had a good idea those were not Penn's words. It was more something she would expect to hear her husband say. Her husband was rigid about obedience, and she wondered why. She had time to find out just as she had time to decide what to do about their marriage. Her only concern now was her sister Sky, all else could wait.

They were soon on their way again and both she and Noble remained silent. She had much on her mind, and she imagined Noble did as well. It was quite a while later when Noble finally broke the silence.

"If Clan Skirling is offered to me, it would mean you would remain close to your sister Sky."

"That would be selfish of me to want her nearby. Sky needs to return home and be with family," Leora said, a tightness settling in her chest when she thought about what Sky had gone through at the abbey.

She wondered how her sister was after having lived with a hood over her head and chained to the wall for a few weeks. It would drive any sane person mad and yet the abbey supposedly had taken on the task of helping the insane. Leora had seen firsthand that had not been true.

"I have my doubts that Slayer will allow your sister to leave his care. Knowing him, he would feel it was his duty to see his brother's widow kept safe."

"Perhaps Penn heard something about my sister, I could ask him," she suggested.

"You will say nothing to him," Noble ordered.

"Why?"

"Because I command it." He pressed his finger to her lips to silence any protest. "No more. It is done."

Maybe for him but not for her, though she held her tongue since arguing would get her nowhere. When she got a chance, she would speak with Penn.

It was hours later that they finally stopped for the night. Leora had to admit that her husband was well organized. He sent men ahead of them to hunt and set up camp so that food was ready to eat and campfires were ready to keep the chilly night at bay.

Leora was exhausted from the long day, and she ate little, more interested in sleep than food. She stretched out on the blanket on the ground provided for her and secured her cloak around her. The heat of the campfire drifted over her, and it was not long before she fell asleep.

Noble watched his wife from where he sat talking with Penn. He did not like that she barely ate or that she looked like she would topple over from exhaustion at any moment. He was glad when she finally laid down and fell asleep. She would need her strength since he intended to hurry their pace tomorrow so they could reach Clan Skirling sooner than planned.

"What else have you to tell me, Penn?" Noble asked, the message having been clear when he mentioned Ross. There was more to tell but not in front of others. It was the way of the Gallowglass warriors to speak in a code of sorts that only they understood.

"Ross has a message for you from Lord Slayer. It is imperative that you hear it before you arrive at Clan Skirling. Do you think this could be it, sir?" Penn asked, hope in his voice. "Could Lord Slayer be offering us a permanent home, a clan of our own?"

"It is a possibility, Penn, but we will still serve him, serve the Gallowglass."

"Will we?" Penn shrugged. "Ross seems as tired as many of us who have fought for so many years. Do not think I would not fight for the Highlands. I will always do that. It is just that I would rather fight more often to protect a wife and gaggle of bairns than fight others' senseless battles."

Noble understood, he had been feeling the same lately, more so since he had accepted the marriage proposal Slayer had put forth. He would not mind hearing the laughter of children rather than the sounds of battle.

"If not Clan Skirling, then another clan," Noble said.

Penn nodded. "I hope sooner than later."

"Get some sleep, Penn, tomorrow will come fast enough as will a faster pace," Noble said and left the warrior to stretch out and sleep like all the others except those who guarded the camp.

His eyes remained on his wife as he circled the camp. He slept little, always had. He had always been too eager to start the day, learn something new, accomplish several tasks, talk with those knowledgeable. His mum had warned him that he would burn out one day and collapse. He disliked it when she would force him to sit, just sit and do nothing. She had insisted it was good for him to be still for even a short while. To him it had been pure torture. Even now his mind was going with endless things that would need immediate attention once he arrived at Clan Skirling.

He stopped walking, seeing that his wife had turned restless, her body jumping in her sleep as if startled and he wondered if she was suffering a nightmare. He walked toward her, her restlessness growing. He had nearly reached her when she suddenly sat up, breathing heavily, her eyes wide with fright and scanning the camp as if she did not know where she was.

He hurried to her side just as her eyes found him and her hand rushed out to him. He locked his hand with hers, her grip strong. He lowered himself down beside her and instinctively wrapped her in his arms.

"Don't let go. Please don't let go," she pleaded in desperation that had her grip growing stronger.

"Never will I let go of you, wife, you have my word on it," he assured her, locking his hand tighter with hers, and after a few moments her body fell limp against his.

He realized she was asleep or perhaps she had never woken from her nightmare. He kept hold of her as he lowered them both down on the blanket and remained there with her, though he had not planned to sleep just yet. He had given his wife his word and his word was his honor. He would not break it. He would not let go of her... not ever.

Chapter Four

Leora was not surprised when her husband deemed her fit enough to ride her horse the next morning. She expected it since she believed he would set a faster pace and the added weight of two people would not help the horse or the pace. She did not mind. She was as eager as he was to reach their destination. It brought her that much closer to Sky.

The thought of Sky had her looking around for Penn. She hoped to speak with him and find out if he had heard any word on the woman who Lord Slayer had rescued from the abbey or for that matter why he had had Dundren Abbey burned down. Something she had found out from Elsie and was curious as to why he would do such a thing.

She spotted Penn not far from her. She also spotted her husband riding several paces ahead of her with Finley on his right. They were busy talking as they rode. He would not notice if she shared a brief exchange with Penn, and if he did? She mentally shrugged. Her sister was more important than any consequences she would face.

Leora maneuvered her horse closer to Penn's and the warrior turned to her and she smiled, seeing a gap between his beard and moustache, his mouth having fallen open in surprise.

"A word, Penn," she said with a pleasant command to her tone, so he understood it was not a request. It did not matter though since he stared at her besotted as most men did when she smiled at them and had them answering any question she asked without hesitation. "Did you hear anything about the woman Lord Slayer rescued from Dundren Abbey? Her name is Sky."

His brow narrowed in thought, his bushy eyebrows almost connecting. He finally shook his head. "Nay, mistress. I know about the abbey burning but I heard nothing about a woman named Sky."

Since he responded easily, she continued to question him. "Do you know why Lord Slayer would burn the abbey?"

"Lord Slayer does what he does, and no one asks why," Penn said.

She sighed a bit heavily. "I was just wondering why he would do such a thing. Haven't you wondered?"

"It is not for him to wonder why Lord Slayer does anything and you, wife, should not be asking Penn such a thing."

Penn looked repentant as if he had done something wrong, not so Leora.

She turned as best she could to see her husband riding behind her. "How did you sneak up behind us without either of us seeing you?"

Penn looked stunned at her and turned another repentant look on Noble, as if he was somehow at fault.

That the warrior was shocked that she questioned her husband was obvious, but Leora was not about to offer any apologies for it.

45

"Leave us, Penn, and next time do not let my wife's beauty besot you into answering questions without giving any thought to them," Noble ordered.

"Aye, sir," Penn said and hurried to ride off and trail further behind them.

"You disobeyed me, wife," Noble said sternly, directing his horse to keep pace beside hers.

Her chin went up. "I did and I will do so again if you prevent me from finding out about my sister."

"I have no intentions of keeping you from finding out about your sister, but it will be done my way."

"And why is that?"

"Because I know Lord Slayer well and know how to approach him on this so that he is receptive to you visiting with your sister."

Leora hated to admit it, but his reasoning was valid. "I can see the wisdom in that. But you must also understand how worried I am about my sister."

"Aye, I do, which is why I will not punish you for disobeying me."

Leora was unable to stop the burst of laughter that spewed from her mouth. "Punish me? I will not tolerate a husband who thinks he can punish me. Our marriage is done before it can start if you think you will punish me for not obeying you. And if punishment is the way you think to tame me, then you failed the challenge and you definitely failed at being a good husband."

His wife reacted as he thought she would and that gave him more insight into her, more ways that he could tame her. He learned something else he had not expected to learn. Her laughter filled him with joy, even if it was directed at him. It was robust and genuine, and he could feel the humor in it and, strangely enough, it lightened his spirit.

"I have not failed yet," he said. "I may be some points behind, but I will pass you soon enough," Noble said confidently.

That got Leora's attention and it made her realize that her husband used battle tactics in this challenge, setting her up to fall exactly where he wanted her to. She would have to be more vigilant if she were to claim victory.

"I doubt that," she said and laughed again, letting him think she was easy prey.

"I wanted to ask you about last night," Noble said.

She turned silent, recalling last night, her nightmare, and how she had turned to him for comfort. She could pretend she did not remember, but it was not the last nightmare she would suffer, and lies would not help her.

Noble waited, seeing her silently debate what to tell him. He hoped she would choose to trust him with the truth, but nightmares could frighten one silent and he would not hold it against her if she did not choose to discuss it with him, at least for now.

"I should have thanked you earlier for being there for me last night. Your presence brought me great comfort and I do appreciate it," she said and hesitated a moment before she continued, though was grateful her husband waited and did not demand she confide in him. "I have suffered nightmares since returning home from my time at the abbey and my escape."

"You need not suffer them alone any longer. I will be there to give you what comfort I can."

47

"I appreciate that," Leora said, and that he cared enough to do so had her feeling a gentle squeeze to her heart.

"It is my duty as your husband."

And the gentle squeeze turned to a twisting pain, and she snapped at him. "You are definitely a horse's arse." She directed her horse away from him or else she feared she would punch him.

Her abrupt departure did not let her see Noble's slight smile. Another well laid battle strategy that would have him seeing victory soon enough. The only problem was that it troubled him since it was a lie and he had cautioned her about lying. He had not comforted her out of duty. He had comforted her because it had hurt him to see her suffering. Was victory that important to him that he would lie?

He rode after her and came up alongside her.

"I do not want to talk to you," she said without looking at him.

"Good, since it is I who has something to say to you." When she still refused to look at him, he continued talking. "I live by a code of honor, and I would fail that honor if I did not live by my own words. I told you that lies do not help a marriage and I meant it. I just lied to you. I did not comfort you out of duty. I comforted you last night because I did not like seeing you suffer."

Leora turned her head quickly his way. "You cared that I suffered?"

"I did. It hurt me to see you in the throes of a nightmare and unable to do anything about it and when

48

you reached out to me for help, it made me only more determined to do what I could to ease your suffering."

"It was instinct, my reaching out to you. I knew I could depend on you and your arms wrapped protectively around me allowed me to sleep peacefully. I truly appreciate what you did for me."

"And I will do it again most willingly and not out of duty," Noble said, and his heart nearly stopped when she turned a brilliant smile on him. Good Lord, but she was a beauty. He had never known a woman with such astonishing features. It was no wonder men melted when she smiled.

"I thank you for that, husband, and I apologize for calling you a horse's arse even though you deserved it," she said with a teasing twinkle in her eyes.

He smiled, thinking that life with his wife might be good just the way she was.

He heard the hiss of the arrow before it struck but he had no time to react or to know where it would land. He barely had time to catch his wife around her waist, after the arrow struck the side of her head, and stop her from falling off her horse.

***

"FIND HIM NOW!"

Leora cringed upon hearing the powerful roar, it sending a sharp pain shooting through her head.

"The bleeding won't stop."

Who was bleeding? What was going on? Was she caught in another nightmare? Nay, that was her husband's voice she heard. *Husband.* Aye, she had a husband and he sounded worried.

"It is a head wound and minor at that. Head wounds always bleed a lot."

"Finley," she said, recognizing his voice.

"She knows my voice, a good sign," Finley said, sounding pleased.

"Leora, open your eyes!" her husband demanded.

"Must you always command?" she asked, cringing from the pain that radiated in her head.

"Please open your eyes, wife," Noble said and got a stunned look from Finley since please was not a word Noble spoke often, if at all.

She struggled to open them. "It is not easy with this vicious pain in my head."

"The arrow caught the side of your head an—"

Her eyes shot open, and she cringed at the sudden pain that hit her again. "I was struck by an arrow? Am I bleeding?" Her hand rushed to her head.

Noble grabbed her wrist. "Leave it be. There is a cloth there to stop the bleeding."

"Does it still bleed? Is the wound deep? Is the cloth clean? Is—"

Her husband interrupted her. "Finley has treated many battle wounds. He has good knowledge of how to treat wounds."

"*Battle wounds,*" she emphasized.

"*Arrow,*" Noble snapped.

Leora stared at her husband as she finally realized the severity of the situation and in a whisper as if speaking to herself, she murmured, "Someone wants me dead."

Why it had only now become real to her, she couldn't say. Perhaps it was because the person had come so close to succeeding in killing her that she realized how dire the situation actually was. Instinct had her gripping her husband's arm, and only then did she realize she was nestled in his arms. Her head rested in the crook of his arm and his other arm fell across her waist.

"You didn't let me fall," she said, somehow instinctively knowing he had caught her before she tumbled off her horse.

"He moved fast, he did," Finley confirmed. "And shielded you with his body with more than one arrow nearly missing him.

Finley's praise seemed to annoy Noble, and he ordered, "We cannot linger here. Make sure the men are ready to leave and find out if the culprit has been found yet."

Finley stood. "A quick pace will not serve her well."

"Neither will remaining in this area where more marksmen may linger," Noble warned. "And find out why he was not spotted."

Finley nodded and shouted orders as he walked away.

"Did duty have you catching me?" Leora asked, though that he caught her was all that mattered, and yet she had asked anyway.

"Instinct," he said, which was true. Instinct played an important part in a warrior's skills. It often saved a warrior's life. What he didn't tell her was how his heart felt as it slammed against his chest when he saw the arrow skim her brow and blood begin to pour from it. "I would prefer to camp and give you time to rest but that would not be wise."

"I agree. The sooner we are on our way the better. Is there a stream nearby?"

"An hour or more away," he said, the slower pace he planned on setting keeping them from reaching it sooner. But that depended on whether his wife could tolerate the ride or if they would have to stop sooner.

"Good," Leora said. "The stream will provide an image for me to see the wound, then I can clean it and apply a clean cloth and a dab of honey as well, if Finley has any. Though anyone who treats wounds would have honey." She tried to sit up.

"Stay as you are. There is time yet before we leave."

She did not argue with him since her head spun when she struggled to sit up straight. She let herself relax in his arms, finding an unexpected comfort there.

"Noble," she said softly as he adjusted the cloth around her head.

His eyes met hers and he saw the worry there. "Something troubles you."

"I did not take the threat to my life seriously until…"

"Until you almost died today," he finished when she was unable to.

"I think part of me thought the whole thing foolish or a mistake. It was difficult enough finding out that my mum and da were not my true parents, but then to discover that there was someone who wanted me dead while it is possible another person sent warriors to search for me seemed nonsense to me. And it still could be so since I could be the wrong woman they search for. Sky has similar hair coloring to mine if that is what they are going by to identify the woman. This could all be a colossal mistake."

"The thing you must realize, Leora, is that the search is focused on you and your sisters. Word probably already circulates that it is not Elsie they search for so the mercenaries will turn their attention to you and Sky. To make sure the mission is a success, they will kill you both. Slayer will have thought the same and it is probably the reason he keeps your sister under his protection. No doubt whoever the woman is with a substantial price on her head is a threat to someone, while to another person the woman holds importance. This mystery must be solved if you and Sky are to remain safe."

"Sir, he has been found," Finley called out as he approached.

Leora caught the flare of fury that rose in her husband's eyes upon hearing that and she feared it would not bode well for the man.

"I am going to leave you to rest beneath the branches of that tree," Noble said with a nod toward a towering spruce. "While I go talk with this man."

"I will go with you," she said, latching onto his arm, making it clear she intended to do just that and explaining why. "He must see for himself that he failed. That I remain strong and suffered nothing more than a minor wound and that he will now suffer the consequences for his failure."

Her courage ran strong but so did her foolishness. She needed rest to heal, not have a confrontation with the man who almost killed her. He also didn't want her to see what he intended to do to the man when he was done getting what information he wanted from him.

She could see that he was considering it and offered more reasoning as to why he should agree to her request. "It will not take long to see this done since you wish to be on our way soon and I will at least have found my footing by then and be aware of any limitations the wound might have caused me."

She made sense, he couldn't deny that. It would be a good way for him to judge if she was truly fit to travel.

"A short time only, then you will sit and rest until we are ready to leave," he ordered.

It was better than a complete refusal, and she smiled softly. "Help me to my feet."

"Please, husband, would sound nice."

"To save time and future annoyance, know a please comes before anything I ask of you," she informed him and eased herself up, with the help of his firm hand to her back to sit before she attempted to stand.

"I would prefer to hear you say please," he said, holding her steady as she sat and seeing that she had paled some.

Her head spun more than she expected, and she feared she would not make it to her feet without losing her balance, so she remained as she was allowing the spinning feeling to pass.

"I don't know anything, nothing at all," a voice called out.

"Get me to my feet before he gets here," Leora said, tugging on her husband's arm.

"Please," he reminded.

"Oh good, you said what you heard in your head. That works perfectly."

Noble shook his head. Even a bit disoriented from a head wound and she still had a sharp wit about her. She was like no woman he had ever met and one he probably wouldn't have wanted to meet, and yet... there was something about her that he favored.

Leora was relieved her husband kept a firm hold on her, his arm tight around her waist. Her head spun again but not as badly as when she had first tried to sit up.

"A few moments and that is all," Noble reminded, though was surprised she had remained steady on her feet and color was beginning to return to her face.

A man medium in height and skinny stumbled out of the woods, a warrior having given him a hefty shove. He righted himself and walked with bravado toward Noble.

"Step too close and I will see you gutted," Noble warned in a calm yet strong command.

The man stopped a distance from them.

"Who hired you?" Noble demanded.

The man stared at Leora, ignoring Noble. "I missed. I can't believe I missed my mark. I never miss."

Noble heard the words in his head before they left his wife's mouth."

"There is always a first time," Leora said with a smile.

"At least I scarred you," the man said with pride.

"Your name," she ordered.

The man stuck out his chest. "Tavish."

With a lift of her chin, Leora said, "I will wear the scar proudly and tell everyone how I was the only person that Tavish the marksman failed to kill."

Noble's men burst out laughing and Tavish's face grew red with rage, and he went to lunge forward. Two sword blades were slammed flat against his chest stopping him.

"Who hired you," Noble demanded, "and I will not ask you again."

Tavish shrugged. "It doesn't matter. I can't tell you what I don't know. The leader of a mercenary group offered coins to anyone who would kill the reddish blonde-haired daughters of the chieftain of Clan Murdock and more coins would be given with proof of their deaths. No one would take on the task once it was discovered that the Gallowglass was involved, so I was offered more than a generous amount of coins since I never fail at a task."

"Until now," Leora reminded.

Tavish scowled at her. "I may not get to finish the task, but someone will since someone badly wants you and your sister dead."

"Who is the mercenary who offered this to you?" Noble asked.

Tavish spat on the ground before saying, "Why should I tell you? You are going to kill me anyway."

"It is the difference between a quick, easy death or a brutally painful one," Noble said.

Tavish laughed. "I choose my death, not you."

It happened so fast that Leora stared, trying to comprehend that Tavish lay dead, blood pooling beneath him, his throat slit by his own hand. She turned her head away, her cheek brushing her husband's chest and she rested her cheek against the thick muscle beneath his garment relieved to feel his strength.

He tightened his hold on her and lowered his head to rest his cheek to the side of her head and kept his voice low as he said, "You need to sit and rest until we are ready to leave." He didn't give her a choice. He walked her to the spruce tree, lowering her gently to sit beneath the wide branches. "Stay here until I come for you."

She did not argue with him since he was right. She did need to rest and let her wound heal. She had to make sure to keep strong so she could get to Sky and make sure she understood the danger she was in and that she was to take the threat seriously. Also, to see that Lord Slayer was keeping her sister safe.

This was a nightmare and one she wanted to wake up from before it grew worse. The thought barely finished in her head when her husband returned.

He leaned down and with an arm around her waist brought her to her feet. "We leave immediately. More marksmen have been spotted."

Leora was on his horse and in his arms and she saw as they rode away that not all his men rode with them, and the prisoners hadn't left with them either. She thought of asking him about it, but exhaustion had taken hold of her, and she found her eyes growing heavy.

She slept on and off as they traveled, the pain in her head lingering but subsiding. However, she was relieved when they finally stopped.

"You are tired, you will rest before we continue," Noble ordered once he lifted her off the horse and gave a quick glance at the cloudy sky that promised rain.

"There is just enough light that lingers for me to get a quick look at my reflection in the stream to see my wound. Then I will rest but not too long. The clouds overhead foretell of heavy rain, " she said, knowing rest was necessary if she were to regain the strength the wound had robbed from her, but heavy rain could prove challenging.

"A few minutes, no more," he said and walked her to the nearby stream. He had no intention of leaving her there alone. She was unsteady on her feet, and he could almost feel her exhaustion.

Leora was relieved he helped her to sit on the bank close enough to the water that she could lean over and hopefully catch enough of her reflection in it to see her wound.

She went to unwrap the cloth from around her head when Noble stopped her.

"I will remove the cloth for you." And he did not wait for a response from her, he eased the cloth from around her head.

His touch was so gentle that her eyes drifted closed as he slowly relieved her of the cloth.

Noble was glad to see the cloth come away from the wound easily and was even more relieved to see that the wound was minor as Finley had said. But he was also wise enough to know that even small wounds

58

could cause problems and even death. So, it was better to remain cautious.

Leora extended her head over the gentle stream and was glad to see it caught her reflection.

"It is not bad at all," she said staring at the minor abrasion on her brow near her hairline.

She scooped up a handful of water to scrub away the dried blood the wound had left on her face and neck. Another dab of honey and the wound would probably do fine. She turned to tell her husband when she saw that the water was no longer still but rushing past her.

It took a moment for her to realize it wasn't the water rushing but her head spinning. Before she could reach out to her husband, she felt her head tipping closer to the stream and before it hit the cold water, she managed a weak cry… "Noble."

Chapter Five

Noble rushed to snag his wife around the waist and stop her from falling into the stream, though her face skimmed the water. The shock of the cold water brought her quickly out of her faint, and her eyes opened as he patted her face dry with the edge of her cloak.

"I fainted," Leora said, shocked. "I never faint."

Noble could not resist. "There is a first time for everything."

Her smile came naturally. "For a fierce warrior, you do like to tease."

"It is difficult not to with you," he admitted, surprising himself since levity was foreign to him, until he met Leora. There was no humor in battle or in planning a battle or when on a mission for Slayer. Duty required awareness, determination, and tenaciousness. He had no time for levity, yet with Leora it couldn't be helped. Her abrupt, commanding nature and unexpected remarks often forced a humorous response from him. "So, you find me amusing?"

"At times, most definitely," she said, "though I suppose that is not the worst thing for a marriage. Smiles and laughter are far better for a husband and wife to share than angry words and constant disagreements and arguments."

Noble patted dry the few strands of her hair that got wet, thinking how right she was. His mum and da had been forever locked in battle and still were, the reason he saw little of them. His brothers had adopted the same fiery temperament, forever arguing amongst themselves or with their women. When his da had spoken about the Gallowglass to his sons, Noble had jumped at the chance to join the elite fighting force. He preferred a battlefield rather than his chaotic family. So, while he found levity with his wife surprising, it was also welcomed.

"On that, we are single-minded, wife," Noble said.

Leora's eyes lingered on his face. That he had fine features could not be denied by anyone with eyes. But that wasn't what she focused on. It was his honorable nature she saw in him that got her attention. He had not hesitated to keep her safe since meeting her, and though he had good reason for doing so, receiving a clan of his own for wedding her, he honored his word, his commitment to their marriage. Though there was that point of him thinking he could tame her, and yet it would not matter to him if he did or didn't since their marriage—to him—was not debatable. They would remain wed and spend the rest of their lives together.

"Are you all right, Leora?"

His strong voice yet gentle tone nudged Leora out of her musings. "I find myself forever in your arms. You keep saving me."

She was expecting to hear the usual, *it is my duty*, but it wasn't his words that shocked her as much as the force he spoke with, as if he declared it an edict.

"And there is where you will stay, for I will not lose you." He pushed the last few lingering, damp strands of hair off her face, his fingers stroking along her cheek as he did.

A strange sensation, a flutter of sorts, ran through her and she realized that she liked his touch, and she liked being in his arms. The thought caused her a moment of fright. Why she couldn't say, but it did. She wished Elsie was here with her. She was wed and had knowledge of the intimacies of marriage that Leora was not privy to. That thought also reminded her of Sky and her reason for remaining in the marriage. Sky came first, then she could decide on her marriage.

"I need to tend to the wound," she said, needing to focus on anything but her husband.

"I will help you and do not bother to argue with me," he said, seeing her about to protest.

"I think a dab of honey will suffice. The quick reflection I caught of the wound confirmed what you told me. It was minor," Leora said.

Noble summoned Finley with a quick wave and in no time the wound was seen to, and they were ready to be on their way again.

"I can ride my own horse," Leora said when her husband insisted that she ride with him again.

"This is not debatable, wife," Noble said, then turned to Finley. "Stay with her until I return."

Leora watched him walk off to talk with several of his warriors.

"I am feeling well enough, riding with him is not necessary and will only slow us down," she complained to Finley.

"He does it to protect you," Finley said. "He can shield you better when you ride with him, making it more difficult for an arrow to strike you."

"But not him," Leora said, realizing the danger he intentionally placed himself in.

"As I have said, Noble is an honorable man. He will suffer an arrow before he allows one to hit you. Tavish was wise in taking his own life, for Noble would have made him suffer horrendously for what he did to you."

Out of duty, she thought and startled when a whispery thought struck her, *he does so because he cares.*

The skies soon began to darken and there was no denying that heavy rain would fall soon. Noble returned to his wife and Finley. "A rainstorm approaches. We need to take shelter. You know where we need to go, Finley. It will take us off our intended path, but it will grant us the shelter we need."

"Aye, I will inform the men," Finley said and hurried off.

They were soon on their way and not long after veered off the path, traveling more slowly, the woods denser and the path not as clear. A crack of thunder startled Leora, but not one of Noble's warriors. It was as if they were impervious to the sudden noise.

"It could cost a warrior his life if he reacted to every unexpected sound he heard," Noble said, his wife having jumped in fright at the thunder.

"I envy them. It can be quite unsettling."

Noble heard fatigue in her voice. "You are tired."

She did not want to admit it, but she would be foolish if she didn't. She feared the wound had affected her more than she realized. "I will not lie. Fatigue is fast taking hold of me."

Noble grew annoyed at himself. She needed rest, not endless time on a horse. "We are not far from where you can rest easily."

She let her head gently fall on his shoulder. "I am glad to hear that, for I fear traveling much longer will not do me well. I need to rest."

He was glad she was honest with him even though it worried him. She had been strong since meeting her so for her to admit that she needed to rest worried him. He had hoped to reach the abbey so the nuns could tend to her and make sure she was fit for travel before they proceeded to Clan Skirling. The dark clouds had changed all that.

Noble took the reins in one hand and reached behind him to snag the rolled blanket tied there.

Leora, seeing what he intended, took the blanket from him, and untied the straps that held it closed in two places. Their hands worked together to unwrap it and wrap it snug around her.

"It is not much but it will at least offer some protection against the rain if it should start before we reach our destination," Noble said.

"And you? You have no protection against the rain."

"I have survived worse weather," he said, surprised to hear concern in her voice.

Leora sighed softly, his shoulder offering the comfort her head needed. "Where do we go?"

"An abandoned croft," he said glad to feel her relax in his arms.

"A croft will not shelter us all."

That she thought of others besides herself surprised him, and he was pleased to know that she did.

"It has more places to shelter than a usual croft," he said and tightened his hold around her waist when she jumped, another crack of thunder piercing the silent woods.

Thunder never bothered Leora but then she was always safe in the keep with her parents and sisters during a thunderstorm. Here, in the woods, wounded, and in the arms of a husband she barely knew, she was more vulnerable, and she did not like that. She had to remain strong if not for herself, then for Sky. And yet her strength felt like it was waning, and she wanted nothing more, at the moment, than to rest comfortably in her husband's arms and rely on his strength.

Noble grew concerned when her body grew far too limp against his and the sky continued to grow dark. She was fast losing her strength and he needed to get her to safety from the storm so she could rest. To do both, he would need to set a faster pace, which could worsen her already waning strength, but he had no choice.

He signaled Finley to pick up the pace and his men appeared relieved. They had had their fair share of getting stuck in a thunderstorm and it had been no pleasure. Everyone would be pleased to reach the abandoned croft.

A clash of thunder woke Leora, having drifted off in her husband's arms. She thought she had slept for hours it was so dark.

"We're here," Noble said, glad they had reached the croft, a downpour about to unleash on them at any moment.

Leora glanced around and spotted several buildings. The croft looked to have been a thriving farm at one time and she wondered what happened that it was now abandoned and neglected. There were two thatched-roof cottages, both weathered by time and neglect. Patches of untended land surrounded both, and at one time were probably vegetable and herb gardens but now were overgrown with wild foliage. Remnants of fencing that had probably housed livestock lay in disrepair, tools used to once mend them scattered about decayed or rusted with age. There were several barns that horses or other farm animals had inhabited in need of repair, but for now would serve the horses and men well.

Noble stopped in front of the smaller of the two cottages, sending Finley ahead to the larger cottage for the men to share while some of the other warriors went to the barns with the horses.

Leora went to slip off the horse, but Noble's firm hold prevented her from moving.

"You will wait for me to help you off the horse," he ordered.

She did not argue, feeling a raindrop hit her.

Noble hurried off the horse, then reached up to grip her waist and ease her off the horse. One of his warriors quickly appeared to take the reins and lead the horse to shelter after handing a small sack to Noble.

It was as if the dark sky suddenly broke open and released a flood of rain, Noble closing the door against the downpour the best he could since it hung on a lone metal hinge.

The rainstorm brought a chilly wind with it that whipped at the cottage and after seeing Leora deposited on a bench and dropping a small sack on another bench that had survived the decay, he gathered pieces of broken furniture scattered about and started a fire in the small hearth that had seen better days but thankfully still worked well enough to warm the small place.

Leora shivered seeing the vines that had crept through the cracks in the walls and where the wind found passage. She wondered if the place was sturdy enough to hold together or if time and the weather had battered it so badly that it was not strong enough to survive another beating.

"It will serve us well enough for the night," Noble said, seeing the worry on his wife's face along with fatigue and possibly— "Are you hungry?"

He stood and pulled a piece of bread from the sack on the bench.

Leora shook her head, having no appetite, and cringed when a dull pain throbbed in her head. It brought with it a wave of lightheadedness and she reached out to her husband. "Noble."

He was at her side in an instant, crouching down beside her, and his arm going around her waist. "The ride was too much for you."

"But necessary," she said, "or we would be caught in this chilling downpour."

Noble glanced around, better able to see the inside of the cottage now with the fire burning brightly. The bed was broken in pieces, some probably now burning in the hearth. There was no place comfortable enough for his wife to sleep, let alone rest. The earthen floor would hold a chill and they had only one blanket between them.

"I think sleep would be best for me," Leora said and looked around, then laughed softly. "How foolish of me to expect a bed, but, oh, how I wish there was one. I would love to just melt into a soft mattress right now."

"I cannot give you soft, but I can give you something to melt against," Noble said and carried the other surviving bench to set it against the wall near the hearth.

He then helped his wife to her feet and with his arm around her waist, guided her to sit on the bench. He took the bench she had been sitting on and placed it beside her. Making sure the lone blanket was snug around her, he sat and gently eased her into the crook of his arm so she could relax comfortably against him.

She thought of telling him that she could sleep braced against the wall, that she did not need him, but the steady beat of his heart was a soothing melody in her ear and the warmth and strength of his body were far too comfortable to relinquish, and she was far too tired to argue. So, she held her tongue and accepted the comfort her husband offered her.

Noble was surprised his wife did not protest and refuse his offer of what comfort he could provide, but then her fatigue gave her little choice. She was soon asleep, her breathing steady, her body limp against his. She needed rest and he could use some himself. He hoped the rain would end before morning so they could continue on their way, though he planned on stopping at the abbey to give Leora a chance to rest in an actual bed before they reached their destination.

He rested his head against the wall, a vine poking at him, but he ignored it. He had slept in far worse conditions and various positions. This was bearable. Besides, he enjoyed the feel of his wife in his arms, her body tucked against his. He had not expected to feel that way and it was a nice surprise to learn he enjoyed holding his wife.

A yawn escaped him, and he let himself drift off to sleep, knowing morning would come soon enough.

A shiver woke him that wasn't his and for a moment he thought he was in a field of spring flowers on an unusually warm day, the familiar scent invading his senses and feeling a comforting warmth wrapped around him while a slight weight lingered between his legs that had aroused his shaft. He opened his eyes to find his head resting on the top of his wife's head. She was snug in the crook of his arm, her head on his shoulder, her body tight against his and her hand was the weight he felt resting on his shaft. Her intimate yet innocent touch aroused him even more and he gently raised his head to take a needed breath and calm his rising arousal.

She raised her head as he did and her eyes drifted open to meet his and their lips were so close that they nearly touched. He thought of kissing her, wanted to kiss her, and he thought he saw the same desire in her eyes. He was about to do just that when she turned her head away, and suddenly realizing where her hand lay, she yanked it away as if rescuing it from a burning hearth and moved away from him.

"I'm cold," she said, once again doing what started the awkward moment, shivering.

Noble said nothing. He stood and went to the hearth, only embers left, and added more of the broken pieces of furniture, concerned there would not be enough to keep the fire going until morning. He stood when he finished and listened. The wind continued to whip at the cottage and rain continued to pound it, and he saw that in the far corner of the room the rain was dripping in through the worn thatching.

Leora watched her husband. There was a slow stretch to his body as he tended the fire in the hearth. His defined muscles shifted with strength in his arms and legs as if in perfect precision, as if he commanded them. And when he stood, his body seemed to devour the small room, his chest expanding, his shoulders drawing back, and his stance powerful. She should fear him but instead she found him appealing, a definite shock to her senses.

"Are you unwell, Leora?" Noble asked.

He was suddenly in front of her, crouching down, taking her hand in his.

"You look a bit pale. Does your head continue to pain you?" he asked.

Concern. She heard concern in his voice. He cared when she was in pain just as he had cared enough to comfort her when she had suffered a nightmare and not because it was his duty as a husband.

"Leora?"

She realized she hadn't answered him, realized how pleasant her hand felt in the strength of his, realized she missed the warmth and comfort of his arms and his usual scent of pungent pine and burning wood. And she realized that for a moment, only a moment, when she woke and found her lips so close to his that she wanted to kiss him, and she thought she saw in his eyes that he felt the same. And she would have kissed him if common sense hadn't intervened, or was it fear that had forced her to turn away from him?

"Minor pain," she managed to say since it was the truth, pain still lingering in her head.

"You need more rest," he said and sat beside her, taking her in his arms again to tuck her in the crook of his arm so she could rest her head on his shoulder.

It would have been a dangerous prospect if she were not in pain, for he found he desired his wife far more than he ever thought he would. And if not for her wound, he would consummate their vows here and now.

He silently cursed himself for thinking that. This was no place to seal their vows. It would be a proper bed that he coupled with his wife in, and started their lives as husband and wife.

Leora made sure to tuck her hands in at the sides of her waist so that neither would fall where they shouldn't and yet to her shock and curiosity, she was curious to see for herself what lay beneath his plaid and if it would bring her nothing but unpleasantness as some women claimed it did or absolute pleasure as Elsie had claimed with delight. She shook her head. Now was not the time for such foolish thoughts.

"Is something wrong? You shake your head," he said, feeling a tenseness in her body that had not been there previously when he held her.

She spoke the truth. "My mind is cluttered, and I try to clear it."

"What troubles you?"

"Far too much," she said.

"Perhaps I can help clear some of it. Tell me," he urged.

She almost did. It was on the tip of her tongue ready to slip out, to tell him what she thought, how he made her feel, which she did not understand, but she wisely held those words and instead said, "Nay, you cannot for you are the one who clutters my mind the most."

Chapter Six

The forest was left with the aftermath of the thunderstorm, raindrops dripping from the trees' leaves, the ground muddy, and an undeniable freshness in the air. Noble took note of it all while his thoughts lingered on his wife's words from last night as they continued their journey the next morning. That her mind was cluttered with thoughts of him pleased him. It meant she was not just giving him thought but their marriage as well. He would rather she remain in the marriage willingly rather than having no choice but to do so. And he also wondered if the kiss that almost happened between them last night wasn't another reason why he cluttered her mind since it was certainly cluttering his.

His wife tensed in his arms, drawing him out of his musings and he surmised the cause when he saw her eyes widen in fright as she stared at the walls of the abbey in the not too far distance. With her terrible experience at Dundren Abbey, he imagined she never wanted to step foot in another abbey again.

"There is nothing to fear, I am with you," Noble reassured her. "That is Whitehall Abbey, you see. It is run by a group of kind-hearted nuns who are exceptional healers. They offer help and care to those in need and provide healers to Slayer's clan and Clan Skirling when needed, as well as surrounding crofts.

We will rest here tonight and reach Clan Skirling tomorrow."

Leora's fear vanished, her immediate thought on a more urgent matter. If the nuns at the abbey provided healing, when necessary, then could any of them have been summoned to Clan Ravinsher since her sister's arrival and might have met her? She was eager to find out.

She did not share her thoughts with her husband since he would probably warn her against asking questions, and she had no intention of letting anyone stop her.

She did, however, speak the truth to him. "I look forward to a bed rather than the hard ground or a leaky cottage."

Though her body continued to ache her, and her wound continued to pain her, she had slept well in her husband's arms last night and did feel refreshed this morning. She had, however, grown tired of the five-day journey, or had it been longer? She was losing track of time since leaving home. She was relieved their destination was finally close at hand.

"Their beds are meant for a single person, but we will make do," Noble said.

Leora was not ready to share a bed with him, especially after last night. She did not mind being tucked against him as she had been last night and the other nights by the campfire on their travels here. The heat of his body had kept her warm and his presence had kept her nightmares at bay. But something had changed between them last night when she unexpectedly woke and found her lips so close to his and… she almost shook her head but caught herself. She did not want her husband to feel it and question her. While truth was best in starting their marriage, she would not be able to bring herself to tell him that she had an overwhelming urge to kiss him.

She hurried to say, "You can have your own bed and I will have mine," she said.

"That is not the way it will be. We are wed, and all will know we share a bed."

The strength of his voice sounded as if he issued a command.

Leora spoke honestly to him. "I am not ready for that."

He was but Noble chose not to say that. "I have no intentions of consummating our marriage at the abbey, though it will not wait long. I will take no chance that our marriage can be voided, no chance that someone can take you away from me."

"No chance that you fail at your task for Lord Slayer," Leora added and saw annoyance spark in his eyes.

"I accepted this task willingly. Lord Slayer did not have to convince me or command me. He left the decision to me. If I did not accept it, it would have been offered to another warrior. I chose to wed you, to have children with you, to live the rest of my days with you." A smile twitched at the corners of his mouth. "Be grateful it was me who wed you. I heard your sister Elsie was not Cavell's father's first choice for a wife. He wanted you for his son."

"God forbid!" she said and shuddered at the mere thought. "We would have never gotten along. Cavell suits my sister well and I am thrilled that they have fallen in love. Elsie deserves a good man and a good life."

"And she will have it with Cavell, though it would have never come to be if Elsie had not given him a chance."

"More like it would have never come to be if Cavell hadn't given Elsie a chance," Leora corrected, knowing her sister well and how difficult it must have been for her to deal with the mighty and scarred Gallowglass warrior. But circumstances had forced it upon her and she had flourished because of it.

"It would seem they both gave each other a chance," Noble said, a slight raise of his brow letting her know he made his point.

She smiled generously, understanding what he was saying without him actually saying it. "Aye, that they did, but they didn't try to tame each other. They accepted each other for who they are, faults and all."

"A truce then," Noble suggested, and wondered if she believed she had any faults at all or thought only of his, which had him returning her smile. "No trying to tame each other. We remain true to ourselves, be who we truly are, and see what comes of it."

"That seems a reasonable approach that I can agree with," she said, pleased and relieved with the truce.

"We may find we agree more than we disagree," he said.

She laughed. "Miracles do happen."

Noble chuckled as well. "I thought you would say there is always a first time."

Leora laughed again. "There is that, though I think this one is more in need of a miracle."

***

Leora had to admit that Whitehall Abbey greeted with open arms, no stone wall encircling it. Buds had already sprouted, some generously, in the plethora of fields surrounding the stone abbey and several storage sheds dotted the area. Wood fences corralled sheep and cows. Nuns were busy hanging freshly washed bedding on ropes strung between trees. And more nuns were busy tending to other tasks.

One thing that caught Leora's attention was that all the nuns wore smiles, genuine not false smiles. They were content, which meant they enjoyed their life at the abbey. It was a stark contrast to Dundren Abbey and a relief to Leora.

A smile caught Leora when they stopped in front of the abbey, and she saw what hung on the abbey door… a beautifully and abundantly crafted ivy wreath. She wondered if whoever crafted it knew the significance of the ivy or could have it been done on purpose, a nod to the old beliefs that an ivy wreath warded off evil. Whatever the reason, it brought a welcoming smile to a visitor and that was what mattered.

The door opened and a woman stepped out, a generous smile on her lovely face that was sprinkled with wrinkles. She wore the garments of the other nuns, a light gray tunic, with a scapula. It was a long, wide cloth that rested on her shoulders, a section cut open for the head. Like the other nuns, she wore a wimple and veil. Unlike the other nuns a beautifully crafted wooden cross hung from a piece of rope around her neck. Her elegant stance alone let one know she was in charge.

"Noble, it is good to see you again."

"And you, Mother Abbess," he said with a respectful nod. I hope our unexpected arrival and our short stay is not an inconvenience to you."

"Not at all. We welcome all travelers and those in need of care, which we have done for you and your men many times. And we most appreciate the more strenuous chores you and your men do when here," Mother Abess said, then turned to Leora. "That is a minor wound you have on your head and while it appears well cared for, I would suggest another good cleaning. I also have a salve that would help it heal more quickly."

"I would appreciate any help you can give me," Leora said, finding the woman's gentle tone comforting.

"You appeared to have traveled many days. You must be hungry and in need of rest. Food awaits all in the refectory and rooms will be prepared for you. Come and eat first, then we will see to your wound and a place for you to rest," Mother Abess said and led the way into the abbey.

Quiet and a sense of peace welcomed Leora as they walked through the stone abbey. One could see that no price had been spared in building the place. Someone had given generously to the abbey through the years, and she surmised it was Clan Ravinsher that did so. She was about to ask when Mother Abbess turned to enter a room, and she and Noble followed.

The refectory even more so confirmed that a benefactor had been generous. The long hall with its numerous long tables and benches was not only arranged to foster a sense of community but also an intimate meeting place for powerful men to meet secretly and plot battles that would topple enemies and grow their wealth and power. Though she noticed there was no dais where high-ranking members of the abbey might sit, which meant Mother Abbess did not believe in a hierarchy here at the abbey. She believed herself equal to her fellow nuns.

"Please sit, eat, and rest," Mother Abbess said, pointing to a table. "I have a matter I must attend to and will return shortly." With a nod and pleasant smile, she took her leave.

Leora was surprised when they were seated near the large fireplace that burnt low to ward off the chill of the stone walls that often lingered even in late spring and summer. She could hold her tongue no longer, her curiosity poking at her.

"Whitehall Abbey must have a generous benefactor that the refectory is blessed with a fireplace. Most monasteries only have a warming room," she said, something she had learned when at Dundren Abbey. "Could it be the generosity of Clan Ravinsher?" If so, then that might mean Mother Abess knew something about Sky.

"I am not privy to that information, and you will not go asking," Noble ordered. "It does not concern us."

"Why not?" Leora asked with a scrunch of a brow and a slight cringe from the pain it caused, having forgotten about her wound.

Noble took his wife's chin gently in his hand. "I have known some small wounds to be more painful than large ones. Pay heed to it until it heals."

"I do," she insisted.

"Not enough," he argued, continuing to keep hold of her chin and thinking if he was not careful, he could get lost in her lovely green eyes, not to mention her luscious lips.

"It is minor and matters not," she continued to protest, not able to take her eyes off the intensity she spotted in his deep blue eyes.

He gave her chin a slight squeeze. "It does to me."

"Why?" she asked, surprised by the rapid flutters in her stomach.

"Because I do not like to see you in pain, wife," he said and let go of her chin, turning away to watch his men file into the room quietly in respect of the abbey. If he didn't allow himself the distraction, he would have kissed her there and then. His need to kiss her was growing much too rapidly and he knew that soon he would not stop himself.

He hadn't expected to find his passion sparking around his wife. He intended to do his husbandly duty and had hoped to enjoy it, but now... he actually looked forward to bedding his wife, and often. He only hoped she would feel the same way, since he would not force himself upon her if she found her wifely duty unpleasant.

The room soon filled with talk and some laughter, though quieted when Mother Abbess returned, her hands tucked beneath her scapula and a pleasant smile on her face. Every warrior gave her a nod of respect as she walked past them.

Noble showed her respect as well, standing as she approached their table.

"Word was sent to Lord Slayer's warrior, Ross, as I was instructed to do if you stopped here. He will arrive shortly and will speak with you privately. You can use my solar to talk if you'd like," Mother Abbess said.

"I accept and appreciate the offer," Noble said with a nod.

Mother Abbess joined them and Noble kept a conversation going about the abbey, trying to avoid his wife asking questions that did not concern her, when Ross entered the refectory.

Noble greeted the man with a grin. "Your fast arrival tells me that you were already on your way."

Leora cast a quick glance over the man. He had decent features; a thick neck and thick waist as well, but firm as were his arms and legs. His rigid stance let one know he was not a man to trifle with, as did his stern look.

"Your men, you sent ahead, reached me, and informed me of your intentions of stopping at the abbey so the nuns could tend to your wife's wound. Tell me of this attack, though first tell me how she fares?" Ross asked.

Leora often wondered why men spoke about women as if they were not present when it was obvious to Ross that she was sitting right there beside her husband, and he could direct the question to her. She had not tolerated being ignored or disregarded in her home when her da's friends visited and she would not tolerate it now. Her mum had taught her an easy way to have men respond to her without them even giving thought to it. Praise and a smile worked wonders on a man.

"How thoughtful of you to ask," Leora said with a generous smile, startling the large warrior and forcing him to look at her. "As you can see for yourself, I am doing well."

Ross was one man Noble did not think would fall victim to his wife's beauty. He rarely paid women attention, seeking out willing women for a coin or two when necessary. His duty to Slayer, they having been friends since they were young, was a priority that came before anything else. But he was wrong.

Ross stared at her, his mouth slightly agape,

Leora took advantage of the moment and continued smiling. "By any chance have you met my sister Sky, the woman Lord Slayer rescued from Dundren Abbey?" Her husband shot her an annoyed look, which she promptly ignored. "I am eager to see how she is doing and to get a message to her."

It took a few moments for Ross to regain his senses, shaking his head as if clearing away a fog, and turned to Noble. "There is little for me to say, Lord Slayer decides all that goes on with Sky."

Leora hurried off the bench, and keeping her smile sweet, she rested a gentle hand on Ross's arm. "I am her sister. I have been worried about her. Please tell me how she fares."

Ross was shocked that she not only touched him but spoke directly to him, and he appeared to panic not knowing what to do. He turned a pleading look at Noble to help him.

Noble felt for the flustered man, but he was more annoyed that his wife would lay her hand on him, a man who was not her husband. "Take your hand off him, wife. Ross can tell you nothing. You will leave him be," Noble ordered and saw Ross look relieved, though not for long.

Leora removed her hand, so anxious to learn anything she could about her sister that she had forgotten it was not proper to touch a man who was not your husband. "Please, can you at least tell me if my sister is being treated well."

"She is," Ross answered without thinking and shook his head, then cast another pleading look to Noble.

His wife would have Ross telling her things he shouldn't if he didn't stop her, and Slayer would not be happy about that. He took hold of her arm and tugged her away from Ross. "Go with Mother Abbess so she can see to your wound."

Her husband's firm command warned Leora that she had gone far enough. But she had one last thing to say, and she did so with a brilliant smile that completely mesmerized Ross. "Please tell my sister that I will visit with her soon."

That snapped Ross out of his daze, and he frowned at Noble. "She must wait to be summoned."

"We look forward to the summons whenever Lord Slayer issues it," Noble said to Ross's relief, not so his wife. Her smile faltered though she caught it quick enough.

Noble was not fool enough to think his wife intended to wait to see her sister and she confirmed his thought as he heard her say to Mother Abbess as they passed by him, "How far is Clan Skirling from Clan Ravinsher by horse or foot?"

Chapter Seven

Mother Abbess's solar was much like the other parts of the abbey, clean and sparse. A table and a few chairs sat in the center of the room and a beautifully crafted tapestry of a nun praying over a dying warrior hung on one wall. Tall iron candelabras held numerous candles all lit, while a fire crackled in the small fireplace that Noble recalled Slayer insisted be installed for Mother Abbess.

Ross filled two tankards from the jug of ale on the table and sat, pushing one of the tankards across the table opposite him, a signal that Noble should join him, and he did.

"Lord Slayer guards Sky closely, and she fares well but that is all I am at liberty to say, so we will discuss your wife's sister no more," Ross said as if he feared having said too much already.

"One question since my wife will nag me endlessly if I do not return with an answer," Noble said.

Ross leaned forward, resting his arms on the table and looked at Noble bewildered. "How do you handle such a beautiful woman with a smile that just wants you to agree with anything she asks?"

Noble laughed. "I will let you know when I figure it out, until then I do my best to keep my wits about me."

"You poor bloke. Give me an ugly woman anytime." Ross took a generous swig of ale. "One more question about Sky, then no more."

"Do you think Slayer will allow my wife to visit her sister soon?"

"I doubt it. Both women are safer remaining home, where they are, making it easier to protect them, and I assume you agree with me."

"I do but it depends on where I call home as to how safe I can keep my wife," Noble said.

"Slayer expected you would question that since it concerned your wife, but you would not question the task he set for you at Clan Skirling since he knows he can depend on you without question."

"He can and I will see the task done."

"And Lord Slayer will honor his word. Clan Skirling is yours to lead. You are the new chieftain of Clan Skirling. With Lord Slayer claiming you the new chieftain, there should be no problem with you taking command since none will want to go against the Gallowglass. The clan is yours to command. It is not a large clan, but I am sure you will see it grow and Lord Slayer is not adverse to sharing some of his land with you when needed. He also grants your warriors the choice of remaining with you or returning to Clan Ravinsher if they prefer not to settle at Clan Skirling. Though, he believes all your warriors will remain with you."

"I tend to agree with him, though that will be their decision to make," Noble said, joy and relief running through him. He had wanted this for some time, a clan to call his own, and it was thanks to this marriage that he was getting it sooner than he had expected. He owed Slayer for the opportunity, but he owed Leora much more since she, unlike him, had not been given a choice.

"Lord Slayer also wants you to know that if by any misfortune your wife falls victim to from whoever seeks her death, Clan Skirling still remains yours."

His remark struck Noble like a hefty blow. He did not want to lose Leora. He favored her and surprisingly cared for her. He wanted a chance to establish a good marriage with her, a good future, a good life. A clan of his own, a wife, and bairns had been only dreams a few years ago—no more. They were in his grasp, and he would not lose them.

"Leora will not fall victim to anyone. I will keep her safe," Noble said as if declaring it already so.

"Slayer knew that would be your response. But he warns of the two fractions that seek your wife and possibly Sky."

"I am aware that one person wants her dead and another wants her returned to the Lowlands where it is believed an inheritance awaits her. It is natural to assume that the one who seeks her death is next in line for the inheritance."

"Probably a sizeable inheritance with the amount of mercenaries being paid to find and kill her," Ross suggested. "You might want to claim it for yourself since it truly belongs to you now that Leora is your wife. That is if your wife proves to be the woman they search for."

Noble shook his head. "My home is here in the Highlands now and forever."

"Aye, Highland born for life," Ross agreed and refilled his tankard. "Slayer has sent more warriors to see what else can be found out about both persons hunting for your wife and possibly Sky, so this matter can be settled, and the threat resolved. He will keep you apprised of all he learns and if you should learn anything—"

"I will inform Slayer immediately," Noble said.

"Something he does not question… your loyalty," Ross said, raising his tankard and after taking a gulp continued. "Now tell me truthfully, since I believe it is no more than a rumor that you failed to track down your wife." The scowl on Noble's face had Ross laughing. "So, you did fail to track her down. How did she ever best you?"

Noble shook his head. "It is something I have yet to find out."

***

Leora was surprised when Mother Abbess tended to her wound rather than one of the nuns, a young novice standing nearby watching and learning from her every move and waiting patiently if the Abbess should need help.

The Abbess had a soothing touch that not only relaxed Leora but comforted her as well. It took no time to see the wound cleansed and a salve applied.

"Novice Angelica will pack this small crock of slave for you to take with you. Apply it for the next few days and the wound will heal nicely and not leave a glaring scar. I will visit with you soon at Clan Skirling to see how you fare."

"I look forward to your visit, Mother Abbess," Leora said, grateful for it since the woman's presence brought her comfort.

"I thought we might take a walk so I can show you our planting fields, since your husband is still occupied," Mother Abbess suggested, handing the small crock to the novice.

"I would enjoy that," Leora said, and watched the young novice while Mother Abbess washed her hands in a bucket filled with clean water.

Novice Angelica was attractive or could be if she did not wear such an intense expression as she placed the small crock in a pouch. Leora wondered about her, about why any woman would commit her life to an abbey. Had she done so of her own free will? Or had she no choice, her family having sent her here? Or did she have no other place to go and sought the sanctuary of the abbey? Whatever reason the young woman appeared truly interested in learning from Mother Abbess.

Leora was surprised when the sun greeted them once outside the abbey, clouds having followed them there earlier and worried that another rainstorm might hit.

"This is our medicinal garden," Mother Abbess said, walking to a large garden divided in two sections that was enclosed with a wooden fence. "Novice Angelica tends the garden well. She is a quick learner and will make an exceptional healer. And we are grateful that the good Lord has blessed us with a variety of plants, some local, while some merchants and travelers have shared their finds from foreign places with us, which is the reason for the divided garden. Even though the new plants' healing properties were explained to us, we work with them first to make sure they work as explained."

"What is that small garden over there so far removed from all planting fields?" Leora asked curiously, pointing to a fenced-in patch of land.

"Those plants are deadly," Mother Abbess said.

"Then why have them?"

"Because they can help in certain situations but must be handled with care and knowledge," Mother Abbess explained. "Now come and see the other fields."

"Nettles," Leora said, seeing a huge patch of them. "You can find them in abundance in the Highlands."

"True, but we use a fair amount of nettles, the sisters favoring nettle broth, and it is easier for us to keep a patch of it close by."

After viewing several more fields with a variety of plants, Leora stopped walking and turned to Mother Abbess. "Tell me if I am wrong but you show me these fields for a reason. Does it have anything to do with Clan Skirling?"

"You are astute," Mother Abbess said with a soft smile.

"More logical," Leora said. "There was truly no reason to show me the fields unless you believed it would be of use to me. Does Clan Skirling require work?"

"I am afraid so. The previous chieftain cared more about himself than his clan. He provided little in the way of leadership, and he neglected his clan's needs. The two men now who fight over the chieftain title are much the same. They want the clan for what it can do for them, and the people know it. But they fear Lord Slayer interfering, for they worry they will suffer far worse under his command than the two fools that now vie for control."

"Do the people fear my husband?" Leora asked, thinking it would not prove helpful.

"They more fear his reputation—the fiercest Gallowglass warrior—which to them means Noble would show no mercy that he would rule with a brutal hand as they believe Lord Slayer does."

That news had Leora's stomach roiling with worry for Sky. "Until I can see for myself, I am concerned about my sister being in Lord Slayer's care. Do you know if she is safe with him?"

Mother Abbess's hand went to the wood cross resting against her chest, and she patted it gently before her hand fell away. "When it comes to your sister's safety, she could not be in any more capable hands than Lord Slayer. No one will get near her with him protecting her."

"You tell me what everyone assures me and yet I feel I am not being told the whole of it," Leora said, annoyed she received the same response time and again, telling her little and leaving her wondering what truly was happening to her sister.

"Lord Slayer is… can be a harsh man at times. His brother Warrand was trained from a young age to eventually lead Clan Ravinsher, Slayer was trained since he was young to be a relentless warrior, to never accept defeat, so that he could protect his brother and clan. Now with his father and brother's deaths, it not only falls on him to lead the clan but to protect it as well while continuing to command the Gallowglass in this area."

"It sounds like he would not even have time for my sister," Leora said, feeling a bit relieved yet concerned Sky would find herself alone with no one befriending her. Though knowing her sister, all Sky would need were the animals in the area. She could sit for hours with the forest animals keeping her company or have the dogs and cats following her around. She once told Leora she was never lonely as long as she had animals around her.

"That is quite likely and since I have not been summoned to Clan Ravinsher since his return with your sister, I would assume she is well."

"You tend to the ill at Clan Ravinsher?" Leora asked, a possibility forming in her mind.

"Aye, all at the abbey do, and we are midwives to Clan Ravinsher as well as Clan Skirling."

"I have attended a few births, if you should ever need help," Leora offered, though she hadn't truly assisted in a birth. However, she had paid attention, learning all she could, having been determined to know what one day she herself would experience.

Mother Abbess smiled and nodded. "The women in Clan Skirling will be pleased to learn that."

"My husband is going to be the new chieftain of Clan Skirling, isn't he?" Leora asked, having learned from conversing with Mother Abbess that she knew more than she said and provided more information than was spoken, if one knew how to understand her responses.

"Wagging tongues seem to believe so and where rumors prevail you will always find a smidgen of truth," Mother Abbess said. "If so, I believe Clan Skirling will be pleased with their new mistress. They will find you knowledgeable, caring, and a woman of great strength."

"I appreciate your confidence in me, Mother Abbess, and any guidance you can offer me would be most welcome," Leora said. She already missed talking with her sisters, so it was nice to know she would have a woman to talk with now and again.

Still, though, Mother Abbess was not versed in the ways of a wife or mother having no experience with either, but the woman was well versed in patience and that was something Leora lacked… at times.

"LEORA!"

Leora jumped at her name being shouted and turned to see her husband rushing toward her and greeted him with a brimming smile.

"Never, ever, go anywhere without speaking to me first," Noble ordered, his heart having begun to pound in his chest after no one was able to tell him where his wife had gone and thinking the worst of her disappearance, irrational as that was since more than enough warriors surrounded the area.

"It is my fault, Noble," Mother Abbes said.

"Nonsense," Leora said before Mother Abbess could say anymore and kept her smile strong when she turned her eyes on her husband. "I am your wife, not a prisoner. I do not need to keep you abreast of my every move."

Noble stepped closer to her. "Aye, you do, wife, if I command it. And until this threat on your life is settled, you will keep me abreast of your every move."

"You are right about the threat, but I am confident in your ability to keep me safe."

She pleased and annoyed him all at once. He was pleased she had confidence in him but annoyed she avoided acknowledging that she would obey his command.

"One of the ways I can keep you safe is by knowing where you are at all times."

"Where else would I be but here at the abbey?" She waved her hand, turning as she did, acknowledging not only his warriors but Ross's as well. "Surrounded by endless warriors."

"Just as you were when the arrow struck you," he reminded.

"And you do not have warriors in the distant woods making sure that doesn't happen again?" she asked, having noticed that several of his warriors were not with them or the prisoners as well.

"That makes no difference, wife," he said.

"It does make a difference, husband," she argued. "You demand I keep you abreast of where I go, but if you do the same, keep me abreast of where you station your sentinels, then I know better where I can safely go and where to avoid. Working together would make it easier on us both."

"You are not in command here," he said, annoyed that he was unable to argue against her sensible suggestion.

Leora shook her head. "Nor would I want to be, but I also do not want to be excluded when it comes to my safety. I am no fool. I prefer to make it easier for you to protect me rather than more difficult, husband."

"We will discuss this further later," Noble ordered.

"I would appreciate that," Leora said with a pleasant smile. "Now, if you do not mind, I think I will go rest a bit."

Noble reached out to quickly take hold of her arm. "Are you not feeling well?"

The concerned look in his eyes and his worried touch made it obvious to Leora that he truly cared how she was feeling, and since he had demonstrated the same on other occasions, she was beginning to believe that he did truly care about her, and she felt a flutter in her heart.

"Nay, I feel well enough. I am simply tired from the journey and wise enough to know rest would serve me well," she explained.

"I will show you to yours and your husband's room," Mother Abbess said.

"Is it the room I used when last here?" Noble asked, and Mother Abbess nodded. "I will take my wife there."

"It is not necessary," Leora argued, preferring Mother Abbess to escort her there and to be left alone for a while to think. "You must have more important things to see to."

"I will see to you first," he said, leaving no room for it to be any other way.

A hefty flutter almost had Leora gripping her stomach. That he saw to her before anything or anyone else made it seem that she was more important to him than anything else, and crazy as it seemed, it touched her heart, not to mention that it caused another flutter.

He took her hand as they walked, and she enjoyed the feel of his warmth and the firmness of his grip, and she returned it with a snug grip of her own.

"Clan Skirling will be our home," Noble said, wanting her to hear it from him before it became known. "Ross informed me that Lord Slayer has given me the clan and though small, he encourages it to grow."

"I am pleased for you—"

"For us," he corrected.

"How do we truly commit to each other, Noble, when we barely know each other?" she asked, still not sure if this marriage was right for her. But what difference did it make? It was done and if she did not accept the marriage, what then? Did she return home and search for a husband of her choice? Did she remain living with Elsie and her husband and be a doting aunt to their children? It was not something she saw herself doing after having been more chieftain of the clan than her da.

"We will come to know each other well," he said, as if he was certain of it.

She turned a soft smile on him. "And what if we find we cannot tolerate each other?"

Her smile caused him to smile. "We have done well enough so far."

Her smile grew. "You would say that since you are in command."

He chuckled. "And you rarely obey, so already we are learning about each other."

"But how will we get along if you always command and I always disobey?"

"You will learn that I am wiser and, therefore, you will obey me."

Leora burst out laughing. "I do love your sense of humor."

"I was not being humorous, wife," Noble said seriously.

Leora could not stop laughing.

"It is not funny," Noble said, as if commanding it so.

"Oh, but it is if you genuinely believe that," she said through her laughter.

"Good wives learn," he said, trying to make her understand.

"Good wives take charge," she countered, trying to stem her laughter.

Noble brought them to an abrupt stop and swung his wife around to plant her snug against him, halting her laughter. "You will obey my commands."

"On occasion I may," she said, his hard muscles reminding her of his strength. "And on occasion you may find it wise to pay heed to my word."

"You can be a difficult at times, wife."

"And you can be difficult, most times, husband," she said, the sparks of annoyance in his eyes fading.

"We both have much to learn about each other," he said and eased them to continue to walk.

Leora let him have the last word, too tired to continue to argue and wanting time to think over her situation.

Once in the room provided for them, Leora sat on the bed, that she was sure would not fit them both, removed her shoes, and stretched out. Before she could reach for the blanket to pull over her, Noble had it in his hand and was tucking it around her.

When he was done, he leaned down over her, his face not far from hers. "We will learn to get along, wife, for as I have reminded you before... you will stay my wife now and forever."

Then he did something that Leora never expected but had thought about... he kissed her.

Chapter Eight

Leora felt a delicate press of his lips against hers and then there was nothing. It was so brief that it was over before it barely had begun and before she barely felt anything. She was disappointed unless, of course, her husband was not good at kissing. Elsie had told her that she tingled inside every time Cavell kissed her. She had felt no such tingle.

"Rest, and I will see you later," Noble said and walked to the door.

"Is that all there is to a kiss?" Leora asked before he reached the door.

Her remark brought Noble to an abrupt stop, and he turned. His wife lay on her side, her elbow braced on the mattress, and her head pillowed in her hand.

"I expected a kiss to be more remarkable. My sister told me that Cavell's kisses send tingles through her."

Noble rushed at her so fast that Leora dropped back on the bed, but only for a moment. Her husband's arm slipped beneath her waist to yank her up toward him and his other arm slipped beneath her head, his hand firmly cupping the back of it as he brought his face down and her face up to meet his lips, and his kiss was anything but gentle.

It scorched, sending a fiery heat through her, its fierce intensity feeling as though he had lit her on fire, it spread through her so fast and with such fury. The flames felt like they licked at every part of her body, the heat increasing as the kiss continued to intensify, sending a strange sensation racing through her that, to her surprise, she found pleasurable. She would have gasped with shock if she could have when his tongue forced its way into her mouth and her own tongue instinctively responded.

She was about to wrap her arms around him, the ache to touch him, draw him close overwhelming, when he suddenly released her, and she fell back down on the bed. She was too breathless to speak. All she could do was watch him walk out the door and slam it shut.

Noble took a few steps away from the door to their room, turned, and braced both hands against the stone wall, letting his head drop down between them. He fought to control the passion that had fired so fast and furiously when he kissed her that it had turned his manhood rock hard in an instant and left him aching painfully.

His wife had fired his anger when she had asked if that was all there was to a kiss. He had not intended to kiss her. He did not know what made him brush his lips over hers. It seemed to be instinctive. But she really lit his fury when she all but compared his kiss to how Cavell kissed his wife. Honor forced him to respond and give her a kiss that she would not forget. Unfortunately, it was a kiss that he would not forget any time soon. Never had a kiss fired his passion so quickly, turned his manhood hard so quickly, made him want to sink his shaft into her so quickly.

He slapped his hand against the stone wall. "Stop thinking about it."

He pushed himself away from the wall and for a moment, a sheer moment, he thought of returning to her and consummating their vows. It was inevitable that they would do so, why not now?

"Not the right time," he mumbled to himself and hurried off before he changed his mind, though he worried he would have to find a private place to relieve himself if his shaft did not shrink soon. That annoyed him even more and he continued to mumble as he quickened his steps and rushed away.

***

Leora could not take her eyes off the door. She was not sure if she worried that he would return or worried that he wouldn't return. The kiss had left her befuddled and her body aching strangely.

Passion.

Elsie had strongly expressed how much she loved coupling with her husband and how the passion between them was remarkable and memorable. She had said she felt lucky since she had heard some women complain about a wife's intimate duty. Elsie had no such complaints. It was a benefit of marriage she quite enjoyed. Could Leora feel the same? Would she find the benefits to her liking? From Noble's kiss, the second one, she would think her wifely duties might not be as bad as she had thought they might be.

Leora sighed as she adjusted the blanket over her. She was glad she had talked with her sister about the intimacy of marriage, though she would have preferred more detail about the act itself. Elsie mostly spoke about how wonderful it was but gave little detail. With it being such a private act, Leora had not wanted to intrude into the deeply personal side of it. Now, however, she wished she had.

She yawned, the tiredness she had felt creeping up on her once again. She had intended this time alone to be one of contemplation. Time for her to think over her situation, gather some thoughts as to how best to help Sky and think over her marriage, but the kiss had changed everything. Now all she could think about was the kiss. She yawned again and sleep soon claimed her.

***

Leora was hungry the next morning, having missed supper and feeling far better than she had in days. She had been shocked to wake and discover that she had slept until dawn. She had no idea if her husband had joined her in bed or not, though since she had not woken once during the night, she assumed her husband had not returned to their room. He also did not join her at breakfast, leaving her to sit with Mother Abbess while he sat talking with Ross and Finley. She wondered if he purposely avoided her and if so, why?

The thought that she had done something wrong had entered her head, but she had quickly dismissed it. After all, what did she know about kissing? She had never been kissed, therefore, she could not be expected to know how to respond, though instinct had taken hold. She would not be averse to having her husband kiss her again so she could learn more and become

102

proficient at it. As soon as she had a chance, she would speak with her husband about it.

Her chance came not too long after she bid Mother Abbess goodbye and they were on their way, her husband not objecting to her riding her horse.

Her husband rode up alongside her. "You slept well?"

"Aye, I did. Why did you not join me as you said you would?" she asked.

"I looked in on you several times and you slept so soundly I did not want to disturb you."

He spoke the truth though he did not share his concern that if he did join her, he worried neither of them would get any sleep.

"That was thoughtful of you, husband," she said, smiling.

The gray clouds parted just enough for the sun to peek through for a moment and Noble swore beneath his breath that it was his wife's stunning smile that forced the clouds to give way so the sun could return her smile, if only briefly. He also caught smiles on some of his warriors' faces that looked his wife's way, though the smiles quickly vanished when their eyes met his.

"I wanted to speak to you about our kiss," she said as if it was a natural conversation for them to have.

"Not here, not now," Noble ordered, noticing the heads of the warriors closest to them turning slightly to listen.

"But—"

"That is a private matter to be discussed in private, wife," Noble said, his eyes darting to the warriors around them.

Leora was ready to protest, impatient to discuss the matter, but his quick glance at the surrounding warriors made her realize he was right. Though she could not hold her tongue completely.

"As you say, husband, though I will say—" Her husband shot her a look that was meant to silence her, but she continued. "I look forward to sharing more kisses with you."

That caught Noble off guard and he was never caught off guard, but bloody hell if his wife hadn't done so, and that she spoke so others could hear that she enjoyed his kiss swelled his chest with pride. He wanted to dismiss the warriors surrounding them to ride ahead so they could speak in private but that would leave his wife vulnerable and that he would not do.

"Mother Abbess spoke of Clan Skirling and how it is in dire need of good leadership and help," she said.

"Aye, she is right from what I have heard," Noble said and realized his wife had taken command of the situation, moving the conversation forward away from their kiss. Something he should have done.

"I believe I could be of much help to you with clan matters. I helped my da with the running of our clan and did much on my own when my da took ill," she said.

"Your wifely duties will keep you busy. I am sure the running of the keep alone will take much of your time."

"I am not well versed with running a keep, nor do I stitch, and I know nothing about overseeing the keep's cook. Hopefully, whoever sees to that now is good at the task and can continue to see to it. However, Elsie taught me the importance of having someone in charge of managing the fields, the animals, and outer crofts so that the clan produces what it needs and more to sell at markets and to merchants. I am good at planning, my da having taught me its importance and Elsie as well. So, you can see it would be foolish of you not to take advantage of my knowledge."

"We shall see, wife," he said, impressed with her skills and thinking they may very well prove helpful since he nor his warriors knew anything about planting fields or caring for farm animals.

"You cannot assume that the people who presently see to certain tasks are capable of the chore. It would be wise to learn the skills of the clan members so they can be appointed to the tasks that will best serve them and the clan."

He continued to listen to her talk. She was far more knowledgeable about clan matters that were usually not a concern of women. That she was well versed in running a clan was becoming more obvious and he wondered about it. Such skills could be taught by parents and peers but the ability to acquire knowledge as easily as his wife seemed to do could also be inherited from a parent. He believed that he himself had inherited his grandfather's tracking abilities and his patience, though his grandfather had insisted that a man could not be an exceptional tracker if he lacked patience. It made him wonder about his wife's true parents. Could one or the other have had the ability to gain knowledge easily?

"So, I thought after that is all settled, we go our separate ways."

Her remark brought Noble out of his musings. "What was that you said?"

"So, I was right in thinking you were not listening," Leora said. "I thought that remark might catch your attention."

"My thoughts got away from me, but I do see that your vast knowledge will definitely prove useful to the clan since it will be your home for the remainder of your life," he said, once again letting her know there was no escaping their marriage.

"As much as I would prefer to argue with you about that, lately I wonder if there is any point to it," she said, sounding a bit discouraged and a bit surprised she was admitting it to him. "If not marriage to you, then it would eventually be marriage to another."

Noble gave voice to something that he had given thought to. "What if it proves true that you are a child of a Lowlander with an inheritance waiting for you? Would you not want to go and claim it?"

"My home and heart are here in the Highlands. Here is where I will stay and here is where, someday, I will be buried."

Noble was glad to hear that, but he also knew that if his wife proved to be anyone of importance in the Lowlands, then the choice might not be hers to leave the Highlands. But it would be his since he was her husband, and he would do whatever was necessary to keep her here in the Highlands.

***

Leora did not have to share with her husband what she thought when they arrived at Clan Skirling. Though it would not be obvious to all, she could detect in the rapid way his eyes glanced over the village and the people that he was just as shocked as she was. Cottages were in dire need of repair, food storage sheds appeared to be falling apart, garments were so worn they were beyond repair. And worse... there weren't sufficient fields to feed the clan and planting had had yet to begin.

"This is a battle of a different kind," Leora said softly so no one could hear since people stopped and stared at them, but not a soul offered a single greeting.

A battle not familiar to him, Noble thought. He could easily handle a surge of warriors coming at him, weapons drawn, and effortlessly subdued them. These people had already been conquered. It was on him to see them rise from defeat.

Leora was not surprised to see that the keep was a good size and in good shape and well-maintained. She waited for her husband to help her off her horse. It was important for the clan to see he was in charge and that his wife respected him.

Noble set his wife on the ground beside him and turned to Finley. "Send a hunting party to hunt and return with sufficient food to feed the clan. Have six warriors follow me into the keep, and you come as well. There is much work to be done here and we start today."

Finley turned to speak to several warriors and Noble turned to his wife.

"You will remain beside me and hold your tongue while I deal with the two men attempting to claim the title of chieftain."

"What—"

His fingers pressed firmly against her lips to silence her. "You will hold your tongue and remain beside me, for I don't know what awaits us. Am I clear, wife?"

"As you say, husband."

His eyes shot wide and if Leora didn't spot a teasing glint in them, she would have thought he was surprised.

"An obedient response... miracles do happen," Noble said with a smug grin.

"Only when I grant them," she said with a brilliant smile and with a slight lift of her garment, walked up the keep steps like a regal queen.

Noble hurried after her, shaking his head and wondered why she bent down when she reached the top step and heard her say, "You poor, little thing you."

Leora turned to her husband when he reached her side. "A starving pup. He can barely hold his head up."

His wife gently cradled a small, black pup, except for one paw that was brown, in her hands and she was right, the pup looked to be starving.

"I must get him fed," Leora said, thinking of her sister Sky and how she would have seen to the tiny pup's care. She recalled how Sky tended to the young pups and kittens in need. "Milk. I must get the pup milk."

"We will get the pup milk once inside," Noble said and placed his hand low at her back to usher her through the door after opening it.

Shouts and fists pounding on a table greeted Noble and Leora as they entered the Great Hall, a fair-sized room. Two men stood at the far end in front of the dais, yelling in each other's face, each one slamming their fists on the table in between shouts.

"The clan rightfully belongs to me since Argus claimed me chieftain before he died," the gray-haired man yelled.

"Bloody hell Argus did," the shorter man shouted. "You weren't even here when he died. I am rightful heir to Clan Skirling being a distant and only relative to Argus."

Leora cared not about the two arguing men, her only concern was for the weak pup. She called out to a nearby servant lass. "Fetch me a bowl of milk."

"Begone with you woman, you have no right to give orders here," the gray-haired man shouted without even turning to look at Leora.

Noble's angry voice boomed throughout the Great Hall. "My wife has every right to issue orders here since I am Chieftain of Clan Skirling!"

Chapter Nine

Both men turned with fiery glares in their eyes and hands on the hilts of their daggers ready to challenge the claim. The shorter man's hand instantly fell away from his dagger upon seeing Noble, not so the gray-haired man, his hand gripped the hilt of his dagger even tighter, and his eyes narrowed suspiciously.

Leora tilted her head toward her husband and spoke low. "I will sit by the hearth with the pup while you deal with these two fools."

Noble almost smiled, that his wife made a point of letting him know what she thought of the two men. He was not surprised they were of like minds and again his wife's astute nature impressed him.

Noble's strong voice continued to boom in the Great Hall. "Lord Slayer has appointed me the new Chieftain of Clan Skirling." He snapped his hand at the servant lass. "Do as my wife says and fetch her a bowl of milk for the pup."

The servant lass hurried off before someone could say otherwise.

"Lord Slayer has no such right to appoint Clan Skirling's chieftain, and you have no right to dictate here," the gray-haired man argued. "Argus passed the title to me on his deathbed. Clan Skirling is mine."

"You are a liar, Haig," the shorter man accused. "The people talk about how you were not even here when Chieftain Argus took his last breath."

"They lie, Cecil," Haig said, brandishing his fist in the man's face. "They are a lazy lot and know I will rule with a firm hand so they do not want me as chieftain, but they will learn the title and clan are mine."

"The title has already been claimed. You both will take your leave of Clan Skirling… NOW!" Noble ordered as he approached both men.

Haig stepped forward. "I will not surrender what was promised to me."

"Aye, you will," Noble said calmly and with such confidence that any sensible man would bow to his command.

Cecil was wise enough to step back, not Haig, he held firm.

"YOU!" Haig shouted at the servant lass when she returned and she startled, some of the milk spilling over the wood bowl she carried in her hands. "Tell them I was here when Chieftain Argus died or suffer for your lies."

The young lass paled, her hands began to tremble, and her mouth opened to speak but no words came out.

"Speak the truth, lass. You will not suffer for it that I promise you," Noble said.

The lass spoke hastily. "Haig arrived the day Chieftain Argus was buried, sir."

"You lie!" Haig said and went to go after the lass.

Noble stopped him, stepping directly in his path, Haig almost colliding with him.

111

The lass hurried to Leora, and she took the milk from her and ordered the trembling lass to sit.

"I will not be denied what is mine," Haig protested.

Noble realized then that this was the mess Lord Slayer intended for him to see to if he was to claim his title of Chieftain of Clan Skirling.

"There is an easy solution," Noble said, and all eyes turned on him questioningly. "We go outside and draw our weapons. The victor will be the new Chieftain of Clan Skirling."

"I will not fight a Gallowglass warrior," Cecil wisely said and shook his head at Haig. "And you would be wise to do the same."

"I do not fear the Gallowglass," Haig boasted.

"Then you are more of a fool than I thought you were." Cecil bobbed his head at Noble. "I wish you well, Chieftain Noble."

"You surrender too easily," Haig said with disdain. "You are not fit to lead any clan."

"I do not surrender. I bow to a warrior I would rather call friend than enemy," Cecil snapped back. "I bid you much good fortune, Chieftain Noble."

"That is honorable of you, and you have my friendship, Cecil, if you should ever need it," Noble offered. "Lass," he called out to the servant. "See that Cecil is provided with food for his journey."

"Aye, sir," the lass said, standing reluctantly.

"Is something wrong, lass?" Nobel asked.

"Nay, nay, sir, I will fetch the food," the servant said.

"What is your name, lass?" Noble asked.

"Calla," the lass said, her fingers twisting nervously at her apron.

"I expect the truth from my servants, Calla," Noble cautioned.

"Forgive me, sir, but I fear there will be little food left for you and your wife and no food to feed an already starving clan if food is provided for the gentleman," Calla said, her thin frame proof of her words.

"Worry not, Calla. My warriors hunt now and will provide a feast tonight for the clan," Noble said.

Calla stared at him, shocked, before saying, "Truly?"

"Aye," Noble confirmed. "The clan will eat well today."

"Bless you, sir, bless you," Calla said close to tears.

"Don't be so quick to feel joy, for when I win the title of Chieftain of Clan Skirling, you will suffer for your lack of respect," Haig warned.

Leora's hardy laughter had everyone looking at her. "You are a fool. Who do you think Lord Slayer would entrust a clan to… a simple warrior? You have no idea who you fight. I would offer prayers for my husband's safety, but he has no need of them, but you do." She continued to laugh, though softly, as she returned to feeding the pup, who licked the milk off her finger, too weak to lap it from the bowl.

Noble's men snickered, trying to contain their laughter. Finley had to turn away, looking ready to erupt with laughter.

"Watch your tongue with me, woman, or I—"

Noble moved fast, his hand clamping so tightly around Haig's throat that he struggled to breathe. "Threaten my wife again and I will cut your tongue out of your mouth."

Haig stumbled and coughed to regain his breath when Noble released him with a hard shove.

Noble pointed at the man. "Outside so we can be done with this. There is much work to get started in the clan, feeding the people the first of it."

A smile broke out on Calla's pretty face, and she raced from the room.

Noble had no doubt that while she gathered food for Cecil, she would also spread word in the kitchen that would quickly spread throughout the clan that they would all eat well today.

Haig pulled his sword from its sheath. "I am ready to claim this clan."

Noble felt an uncomfortable nag in his gut. Something was wrong. He cast a glance around the room. His warriors still chuckled over his wife's comment while talking amongst themselves while the few men that had been sitting at one of the tables when they first entered the room kept watch on them. Cecil waited by one of the tables for the food Calla was fetching for him. Noble hurried to look at Haig, the man headed toward the door, though not in a direct path, a path that took him too close to Leora.

"MOVE, WIFE!" Noble bellowed, drawing his sword and knowing his warriors would immediately reach for their weapons.

Leora reacted instinctively at her husband's blaring command. She hugged the pup to her chest and fell back off the bench, the bowl of milk splashing in her face as it toppled with her.

Haig's blade was about to hit the table when Noble's blade went through his back and out through his stomach. The sword fell from Haig's hand and when Noble yanked his sword out of Haig, the man fell to the floor. A quick glance showed that Noble's men had easily subdued Haig's few warriors.

Noble hurried around the table to see to his wife. She lay on her back, the pup licking at the milk spilled on her face. He reached down and eased her to her feet, the pup tight against her chest as he continued to lick the milk.

"Are you hurt?" Noble asked concerned, wondering how she could be even more appealing with milk dripping from her face or perhaps it was the way she put the pup's needs before her own.

"Nay, I am fine," she said.

"You did good, wife," Noble praised.

"Matters not," Haig said with a struggle.

Noble rested his hand on his wife's back as he eased her around the table for them both to glance down at Haig.

"She will die," Haig said and coughed, blood gurgling from his mouth.

Leora said the obvious. "You are the one who dies."

"Regret my failure," he hurried to say. "Cannot inherit… not worthy."

"I want no inheritance," Leora said, angry at the trouble it was causing and fearful for her future."

"Your claim to Clan Skirling was nothing more than a ruse," Noble said. "You somehow learned Leora would eventually show up here, so you came here to wait and what better way than to lay claim to the title."

Haig continued to struggle to speak, fighting against death that was creeping ever closer.

"She—" Haig coughed, blood spewing from his mouth. "Never inherit. He will make sure of—" His head lolled to the side, death finally the victor.

Noble's men were already clearing the Great Hall of the bodies of the fallen warriors, and he gently eased his wife aside so the men could see to Haig as well.

Cecil approached Noble cautiously. "I knew nothing about this, Chieftain Noble."

"What do you know about Haig?" Noble asked, seeing the man's hands tremble and noting how he made certain to address him with respect.

"I only met him when I arrived here, and only after hearing the servant lass say that he arrived the day Argus was buried did I know we arrived on the same day since he adamantly disputed otherwise. When I received word that Argus was close to death, I journeyed here since I am his only relative. I was shocked when Haig claimed he was the rightful heir to Clan Skirling. I had not heard of him before then." Cecil shook his head. "I cannot believe this was all a ruse, Haig's only intention—to kill your wife. You must believe me, Chieftain Noble. I had no idea of Haig's intention."

"You are welcome to remain the night if you wish, Cecil," Noble offered, believing the man no threat, though that did not mean he would not send a couple of warriors to follow discreetly behind him when he took his leave and make sure that he was no threat.

"I appreciate the offer, but I prefer to take my leave immediately. My brother will be pleased at my return since I help him manage the clan. Clan Skirling was once a thriving clan and I thought I could appoint someone to take charge of it so that my brother and I could benefit from it. I was shocked to see how much it had fallen into disrepair since my last visit many years ago. You have far more resources in the area to revive the clan than I do, and I would not dare go against Lord Slayer's command."

"Then friends we are, Cecil," Noble said.

"A friendship I will cherish, Chieftain Noble."

Cecil left with a sack of food and the few men who had come with him.

Noble turned to his wife and could not help but smile. Most of the milk was gone from her face, licked off, and the pup slept curled contentedly in her arm.

"What will you name him?" Noble asked, running a gentle finger over the pup's black fur.

"If I may, sir?" Calla said, requesting permission to speak.

"Say what you will," Noble said.

"We named the pup Chief since he had a regal stand before he grew weak from lack of food. He was too young to hunt and with food so sparse—" She shook her head. "It got to the point where the animals were fighting for food amongst themselves. The two men's arrival only worsened the already dire situation."

"You need not worry about that any longer, Calla," Noble said. "There will be food aplenty for all from now on."

Tears filled the lass's eyes. "Bless you, Chieftain Noble. Bless you. The clan is most grateful."

"Is a hot brew possible, Calla?" Leora asked. "I could use a nice brew after all that has happened."

"Aye, mistress. I can brew chamomile for you," Calla said eagerly.

"That would be perfect and ale for my husband, if possible," Leora said, receiving an appreciative nod from her husband for thinking of him as well.

"Of ale we have plenty and wine as well, Chieftain Argus having kept it for himself," Calla said and with a respectful bob of her head hurried from the room.

Noble led his wife to the table to sit and joined her while she placed the sleeping pup on her cloak that she had draped over the bench and tucked it around him.

"The pup will grow strong with such good care," Noble said and felt a twinge of envy. Why should it matter that she paid such attention to the pup? He, himself, needed no such attention from her, or did he?

"Sky said food was essential for animals to grow strong, but that good care and love is what truly sustained them." She turned her glance away from the sleeping pup to fall on Noble. "You said that Lord Slayer had hounds that obey only him. They must care for him if their obedience is only to him, and he must care for them somewhat."

"I have known Slayer several years and in all that time I have never seen him show any affection of any kind to anyone. But he is a leader of a large troop of elite mercenaries, showing affection would not serve him well. Strength, superiority, fearlessness would be necessities to him." He reached across the table and took hold of her hand. "I know you are eager to see your sister, but she is safe where she is. Slayer will let nothing happen to her. However, with Haig waiting here to take your life and the attempts on your life when traveling here make it seem that there is more interest in you than Sky. Any visit with your sister must wait."

"As you probably already surmised, I do not like hearing that, yet I am not foolish enough to realize the wisdom of it," Leora admitted, but it would not stop her from finding other ways to be in touch with Sky.

Noble gave her hand a gentle squeeze. "I am glad to have wed such a wise woman."

Leora's smile started out soft then spread. "On that we agree."

He shook his head and chuckled. "You are not what I expected."

"I know… I am so much more."

Noble continued to shake his head and chuckle, thinking that he favored his wife more and more each day and that life would definitely not be boring with her.

Calla returned and after placing a tankard in front of Leora and filling the tankard she had placed in front of Noble from the jug of ale she had set on the table, she smiled. "May I, sir?"

"You seem to have a penchant for saying what you will, Calla, so again, have your say."

Calla looked contrite, though produced a slight smile. "Thank you, sir, and pardon me for saying, but it is so heartwarming and wonderful to have a chieftain and mistress who love each other as much as you both do to finally be leading Clan Skirling. And all will be delighted to finally hear the laughter of a gaggle of children in the keep once again and to know Clan Skirling will finally thrive."

Chapter Ten

"We do well in hiding our situation with Calla believing us in love," Leora said, the lass's remark having shocked her. She barely knew Noble so how could she love him?

I barely knew your da when I realized I loved him.

Her mum's words rang clear in Leora's head. She recalled how Sky thought it was lovely. Elsie wondered if it was that way with everyone, while Leora had thought it impossible. Love was not found that fast. Her mum had laughed and commented on how she might just find out since we, by no means, control love.

Noble found his wife easier to read as time went on. While she said one thing, her lovely green eyes often told him another. That's what her eyes did now. Calla's unexpected remark had left her wondering. It had left him wondering as well. He knew little of love, but he would not mind exploring the possibilities of it with his wife. It would be nice for them not just to accept their marriage and learn to live with each other but rather love each other and be thankful they were brought together.

He almost shook his head at the thought. He had not even considered love when Slayer had presented the marriage proposal to him. He thought it was nothing more than a means to fulfilling his dream. Whether he would get along with the woman who would be his wife did not matter to him. What had changed that?

Leora.

He had been warned she could be a handful but there was a courage to her that he admired and that the only reason she had agreed to leave her home and go with him was the love she had for her sister Sky, which proved she was selfless and would do whatever was necessary to protect her family.

He leaned over the table, a bit closer to her. "Are you afraid to let yourself love me, Leora?"

With a slight tilt of her head and a soft laugh, she said what her mum had advised, "Love controls us. We don't control it. We couldn't stop ourselves from falling in love if we wanted to."

"So, if you did fall in love with me, you would not deny it to yourself or me?"

"One cannot deny love. I would embrace it, keep it close in my heart, and cherish my love for you every day, though—" She grinned. "It would take a miracle for that to happen."

Noble scrunched his brow. "What was it you said to me once?" He turned a matching grin on her and not waiting for a response, said, "Miracles do happen."

***

Leora was still thinking about what Noble had said to her as the day began to wane. She had not seen him since then, Finley having arrived in the Great Hall and the two men going off to talk. She had never wasted time thinking about love. What was the point?

122

Marriages were arranged for women, and a woman only hoped the husband chosen for her would be suitable or at least tolerable. So, why concern herself with love? It would make no difference when it came to selecting a husband and only leave a woman longing for something she would never have.

She had to admit, though, that having seen Elsie and Cavell so much in love had her thinking about how nice it would be to have someone feel as if you are the most important person in the world to him, that life would be meaningless without each other.

Could she possibly ever feel that way about Noble? She did not dislike him and maybe she cared a bit for him since he protected her, though she had thoroughly enjoyed his kiss, but did that equate with love?

She shook her head for the umpteenth time since she had last seen her husband, her thoughts drifting to him far too often, and reminded herself that Sky came first. Once she was sure her sister was safe, she could tackle her own situation.

Not one to sit long, Leora had gotten herself busy with seeing to what needed to be done in the keep. She had learned that Chieftain Argus had failed to place someone in charge of the keep's servants, so the staff had worked together to see to the running of the keep. From what Leora could tell, they had done a good job. They were already busy scrubbing, cleaning, and changing the bedlinens in the chieftain's bedchamber. She was even more pleased that the servants were doing the same to the bedchamber the old chieftain's wife once occupied.

What upset her the most was how thin the servants were, just like many of the people she and Noble had seen upon entering the village. She headed to the kitchen after checking on the pup. He continued to sleep, cuddled in the bed she had fashioned for him from a blanket and placed near the hearth in the Great Hall for warmth.

Leora could not help but smile, thinking how proud and pleased Sky would be that she was tending to the pup. She hoped with all her heart that whatever was happening to Sky that she had animals around her, for at least then she would know some comfort. She left the Great Hall and headed to the kitchen, entering a narrow passageway just beyond the Great Hall that connected the two but was barely lit. She heard voices as she got nearer to the end, and she stopped to listen.

"What if he feeds us now to win our trust, then leaves us to starve?" a young male voice asked.

"We can only pray that he will treat us well," a female said.

"He is Gallowglass. They are vicious warriors," the young male said.

"Then he will surely see that his clan is protected," the female said. "Besides, what choice do we have? He is our new chieftain. Pray he will be a good one."

Leora stomped her feet, so it sounded as if someone approached, and silence quickly followed. She entered the room with a pleasant smile.

"Welcome, mistress, welcome," a woman, her long, gray hair drawn back in a braid, said. "I am Emma, the cook, and I speak for us all," —she turned and looked at the others who nodded vigorously—

"when I say we are most grateful and blessed to have Chieftain Noble ruling the clan and his lovely wife beside him. We are even more grateful that he has already kept his word to the clan and sees that we have food." She pointed to several skinned animals on the tables waiting to be cooked. "Chieftain Noble has ordered that you and all in the clan get fed before he and his men do. But we all agree that the food will be shared by all, so that our chieftain and his warriors stay strong and can protect us."

The others nodded their heads vigorously, worry showing in their wide eyes.

"That is very thoughtful of all of you but worry not, for my husband will supply you with more than enough food from now on," Leora said, to encourage trust in her husband, for she knew Noble would not fail them. "I will leave you to prepare a much-needed feast."

Emma's hands twisted at her apron as she said, "It will not be as tasty as it should be since too many of us have been too weak to sufficiently forage in the woods for wild onion, nettle, and meld weed."

"I will see about getting you help with that, Emma, and whatever you serve tonight, I am sure will be delicious."

Tears filled Emma's eyes and she bobbed her head. "You are most generous, mistress."

"And every one of you," —Leora looked from one to another— "are most courageous for surviving a cruel chieftain."

They appeared stunned by her words and with her smile strong, she turned to leave, then thought of something. Servants were privy to much of what went on in the keep: visitors, conversations, even whispers that were not meant for their ears.

She turned back. "A quick question. Did anyone of you hear anything about the sister-in-law that Lord Slayer rescued from Dundren Abbey?"

They all exchanged quick glances, then lowered their heads.

Leora knew what that meant. Sky's affliction had become known and that frightened her, for it could mean Sky wasn't safe.

Leora said what she knew they all were thinking. "I was just wondering since I heard that she is possessed."

That loosened tongues fast.

"Lord Slayer will see the demon cast from her," the only male there said.

"I heard he lets no one near her," a lass said.

"Wendell told me that Lord Slayer's warriors keep their distance from her," a red-haired lass said.

"Your name, lass?" Leora asked, fighting to keep calm when she wanted to rush questions at the lass. That would do her no good nor would telling them that Sky was her sister, at least for now. She needed them to speak freely and honestly about Sky, even if it did hurt her to hear it.

"Adele, mistress," she said with a bob of her head.

"And who is Wendell, Adele?" Leora asked, sounding nothing more than curious.

"A young man from Clan Ravinsher who fancies me and visits when he can," Adele said, a blush staining her cheeks.

"How nice for you," Leora said, already planning ways to meet him the next time he visited. "I appreciate all you shared with me." And with a nod, took her leave.

Leora returned to the Great Hall with much on her mind, her sister topping the list. She felt hopeful with what she might be able to learn from Wendell but worried how safe her sister truly was. She would love to get a message to her, and she was already conjuring plans in ways she might succeed with that. Then there was her husband, who realized before she did that the most important task at hand was to see the clan regain their strength, only then could it flourish, much like the pup who continued to sleep in the make-shift bed, and then, of course, repairs to the village had to be done before winter. It would be a busy time and she worried there would be no time for Sky's plight or to solve her own dilemma. But she was not about to fail her sister or let her dilemma go unsolved.

She chose to do what she normally did when her thoughts grew heavy. She would go for a walk, explore, and become familiar with the village and its people. Her husband had made no mention of her remaining in the keep, so he should not object, but she would remain cautious of her surroundings since she did not know who she could truly trust here.

Gray clouds hung low, promising rain, and there was a cool, spring breeze though summer was only days away. Leora had spotted the decay when she and Noble had entered the village, but it was more pronounced seeing it up close. Several thatched rooftops sagged while others suffered gaping holes. The stone walls of the structures that stored food were empty and crumbling.

Still, the villagers went about their daily tasks, their faces thin from lack of food yet their determination to survive strong. Many wore expressions of weariness with a touch of hope and skepticism for their new chieftain, and Leora could not blame them. Noble would have to prove his worthiness for the clan to accept and respect him.

The scent of woodsmoke was heavy in the air as she continued her walk, but no scent of freshly baked bread joined it as was the way in most clan villages. The people watched anxiously as Noble's warriors constructed spits for the fires that would wait for the meat to be placed on them, cooked, and distributed as Noble had promised, and she had no doubt he would see it done.

She continued walking, her nose catching the tang of iron from the blacksmith's forge, a scent that she had not noticed when first entering the village and she saw why. Noble's warriors had gotten the forge working and were busy working it, the old blacksmith sitting and watching them with appreciation.

Leora jumped when a screech ripped through the air, then smiled when several children suddenly rounded a cottage laughing, a defiant contrast to their melancholy surroundings. Women sat together, busy mending garments, while others tended to small gardens.

Noble had given the clan something precious with the gift of food, something they hadn't had in a long time… a spark of hope, a belief that Clan Skirling would thrive once again.

Heads suddenly began to turn, and women stood, their mending falling off their laps onto the ground. Children halted their play and stared at the warriors entering the village with skinned game and an abundance of fish hanging from branches stripped of their bark.

Leora could see the people were eager to run to the warriors and grab what they could to cook and feed their families, but Noble led his warriors and no one dared to approach him. The warriors got the game on the spits quickly while the fish were cleaned and made ready to cook.

"Listen well!" Noble called out and the people began to gather around him.

"You will go hungry no more. I will see that there is plenty of food for the clan. The fields will be sowed with enough seed to produce a good harvest, repairs will be made to cottages and storage sheds, you will forage in the forest for plants to add to your gardens, and I will see that the nuns from Whitehall Abbey visit here soon to tend your ills. We will grow together as a clan and forge a bond that no one can break."

One brave man called out, "How do we know you will keep your word?"

Leora could not hold her tongue. "My husband is an honorable man; his word is his honor. He will do as he says of that you have no worries. And he proves it to you with this food that will fill your starving bellies today. But you owe him as well, to join with him and do all you can to make Clan Skirling strong once again."

That she so hastily came to his defense surprised Noble and that she also spoke with a firmness that held everyone's attention. Only a moment after she finished, the crowd erupted in a loud cheer and men and women stepped forward to help Noble's warriors, all eager to feast.

Seeing that her husband approached her, Leora walked toward him. "You gave me no order to remain in the keep."

His hand went to rest on her lower back, guiding her through the people busy helping his warriors with the food. His touch was light, but somehow it felt intimate, and it sent an odd tingle through her.

"I do not wish to confine you, wife, but caution is needed," he said as they moved away from the crowd.

"I agree, and I will not take any unnecessary chances. With so many of your warriors around I believe the village is safe enough for me." The slightest scrunch of his brow told Leora that he didn't agree.

"I would like to believe that, but the people here are unfamiliar to us, and with Haig having worked his way in here, what is to say someone else hasn't as well? My warriors know to keep watch over you and I believe you are wise rather than foolish," —his scrunched brow deepened, though a bit of a smile surfaced— "at least most of the time... not to take any chances you shouldn't."

"Are you saying you trust me, husband?" she asked with a wickedly teasing smile.

"Is there any reason I shouldn't?" His hand settled a bit stronger against her lower back, her mischievous smile doing wicked things to his insides, not to mention his manhood.

"None at all, I strive only to please you," she said with a teasing twinkle in her eyes while her thoughts lingered on how he touched her with a comfortable intimacy that sent a flourish of flurries through her. It made her wonder about her wifely duties. Was it possible that she would enjoy intimacy with her husband? She had certainly enjoyed his kiss.

Noble leaned his head down to whisper, "And you will please me later tonight, wife."

That halted her steps abruptly, she did not know if she was ready for intimacy with her husband or even if she truly wanted to remain in the marriage or so she told herself.

She spoke her piece to him. "Sealing our vows commits me to the marriage and I do not know if I am ready for that."

"I do not need to remind you how I feel about that. I have said it often enough for you to know we will remain husband and wife. I have come to know that you are a woman who sees reason in things. Our union is a sensible one, once you realize that I believe you will see the wisdom of it and question it no more."

That his wife remained silent as they walked to the keep had Noble assuming she was thinking about what he had said and possibly realizing the wisdom of their union and finally accepting it. Unless, of course, she remained...

"Do not remain stubborn about this, wife, or it could prove dangerous for you," he said.

"Are you threatening me?" she asked, anger sparking in her voice.

Noble scowled and was surprised that her chin went up defiantly when usually people backed away from him. "If I threatened you, wife, you would know it. It is the threat of someone taking you from me if our marriage vows fail to be consummated and sweeping you away to the Lowlands. Do you want that?"

"Nay," she said, feeling trapped and annoyed that the decision had not been hers to make.

Noble brought them to a halt by the keep's steps and kept his voice low though no one was nearby. "It is imperative that we consummate our vows, but I will not force you. I prefer you to commit willingly to our marriage before it is too late, and I can do nothing to stop someone else from deciding your fate."

***

Noble lay in bed thinking about what he had said to his wife regarding being unable to stop someone from deciding her fate. His words rang hollow in his ears, for he would never allow that to happen. He wanted her to understand it was a possibility that could easily be avoided. He had left her at the keep and returned to see to the many issues that needed his attention. When he finally returned to the keep for supper, he learned his wife had retired to her bedchamber early.

It was not the way he expected the night to go, not that he expected to couple with her tonight. He had thought they would at least share a bed, grow more comfortable with each other. Separate bedchambers would only serve to widen any gap existing between them. He let it be since he figured she was tired from the journey, but it did not sit well with him.

He lay there unable to sleep, his mind refusing to let go of it. Their first night in their new home should not be spent in separate bedchambers. Servants would talk, not that he cared if they did,   it was just another thing about their situation that annoyed him.

He should let it go, he had enough to concern himself with and yet his wife had taken priority, forever being on his mind and he had not expected that. It was because of her that his dreams of becoming chieftain of his own clan had come to fruition, and yet... he found he favored his wife. A lucky surprise since the warning that she could be a handful had had him thinking that he would need to be forceful when handling her.

He chuckled. She could be a handful at times, but not as he had suspected. He enjoyed sparing with her, loved her beautiful and sometimes playful smiles, loved her innocent touches, and loved touching her, and looked forward to touching her more intimately.

He shook his head, sounding as if he was besotted with his wife. That would not do. He was a Gallowglass warrior, a fierce one at that. He could not allow a woman to rule his thoughts. He was in command, he ruled.

He swung the blanket off himself and went to the door naked. He would get his wife, carry her if necessary, and return her to his bedchamber where she would sleep.

He swung open the door to find his wife standing there in her nightdress, barefoot, her hand raised as if about to rap on the door and the pup tucked in a blanket that she cradled in her arm.

Her eyes ran over him from head to toe and her cheeks flushed red as he grabbed her arm and pulled her into his bedchamber.

Chapter Eleven

With her cheeks flaming and words failing Leora, all she could say was, "You're naked."

"That's how I sleep," Noble said.

"I don't," she said, fighting to keep her eyes on his face since curiosity had her wanting to explore her husband's naked body.

"That can be rectified," he said, not only eager to see his wife naked but to feel her naked against him.

"I won't sleep naked," she said as if declaring it so and grabbed hold of her nightdress at her throat as if he might rip it off her.

He didn't debate it with her since he would have his way and have her sleeping naked beside him every night… willingly.

"What are you doing here, Leora?" he asked, curious as to what brought her to his bedchamber, though not admitting he planned on going to her bedchamber.

She held his gaze for a moment, getting lost in the depths of his dark blue eyes and oddly enough finding comfort there, and she spoke honestly. "I'm not sure what brought me here. I have gone over what you said and have given thought to my own misgivings about our marriage. I wonder if it is more my stubbornness than anything else that keeps me from accepting the inevitable... that I am your wife and will remain so. So, why do I question it so much?"

He released her arm, his hand going to her hair, unable to ignore the urge to tuck a few stray strands behind her ear and enjoying how silky soft it felt and how much he liked her hair free of its usual haphazard constraint.

"You are who you are, Leora. It is your nature to question and make sense of things before proceeding headlong into something. Perhaps you inherited such a sensible nature from one of your true parents."

"I have given thought to them, wondering about the danger that forced my mum to give me away. Was my da not a good man? Did she fear what he might do to me? Or had they both decided it was best I be given away? I admit it troubles me and I would not mind finding out the truth."

"Put the pup by the hearth to sleep and come to bed and we will talk," Noble said, wanting to do more than talk, but realizing his wife needed his ear and not his manhood tonight.

Leora did not hesitate. She placed the pup near the low burning hearth and when she turned, her husband had already gotten into bed and held the blanket back for her to join him. Once she did, she knew it was a step that took her closer to permanently sealing her marriage. If she were honest with herself, she would admit that she had accepted their marriage the day she left her home with him. Elsie hadn't only sent her to find out about their sister Sky, but to give her time with

Noble to realize the marriage was inevitable and to make the most of it.

She went and got into bed with her husband, though kept herself from lying too close to him and tucked the blanket under her chin as if it could shield her.

Noble moved a bit closer, resting on his side, his elbow braced on the mattress, and his head resting on his hand. "I will do all I can to find out the truth about your true parents, Leora."

She turned to him with a smile. "I know you will, as will I."

"And I will do all I can to see that we have a good marriage."

Leora recalled Cavell's remark to her about how Noble would make a good husband if she would let him.

"Then I must do the same," she said.

"Willingly or reluctantly, wife?" he asked.

The seriousness in his eyes belied the slight smile on his face.

"A bit of both," she admitted.

"That is what I favor most about you, wife, your honesty. It is what makes you so trustworthy, also your smile. I do love your smile. It's contagious, forcing people around you to smile as well, even I smile, which is not something I did often until you came along."

"Why? I cannot imagine living without smiling every day. What kept you from smiling?" she asked and when he fell back flat on the bed, she turned on her side to gaze at him, releasing the blanket tucked beneath her chin. It fell to her waist which was where the blanket fell on her husband.

His naked chest and arms were impressive, such muscle earned from the endless swing of a sword or axe. She itched to reach out and run her hand over his chest, but it would not be at all proper to touch her husband so blatantly.

"My family," he said, staring overhead. "There was no room for smiles when my family argued endlessly. Someone was always yelling at someone, then arguments would ensue, and soon more people were arguing until finally no one was talking to each other. My mum and da fought so much I began to believe they hated each other and wondered how they ever had four children together."

"Perhaps they do not think of it as arguing, perhaps being boisterous is simply their way of speaking, connecting with each other. A friend of my da's who would visit occasionally spoke in a loud, angry tone. I asked him one day why he was so loud and angry."

"Of course, you did," Noble said with a soft chuckle.

"How else was I to find out?" Leora said. "Besides, I was only ten years and tired of sticking bits of cloth in my ears when he visited. Anyway, I remember he looked at me with such a shocked expression that I thought I had said something terribly improper. I was surprised when he told me, while sounding as if he scolded me, that he did not speak loudly and he was not angry."

"He must have been a relative of mine," Noble said, unable to stop himself from laughing.

She poked him in the arm playfully. "The point is he did not realize how others heard him. To him, he spoke like everyone else. It could simply be your parents' way."

He cringed at the suggestion. "But not my way and you would need more than a few bits of cloth not to hear my family when they are together. Thankfully, you will not have to suffer a visit from them. They live a distance away and I have not seen them in years, and that is fine with me."

Leora found her husband less a stranger as she learned more about him, especially hearing about his family. She had only known him as a fierce Gallowglass warrior, leaving her with a bit of fear of him and rightfully so after seeing him fight. He killed fast and without regret, but then the Gallowglass was not known for mercy. However, talking with him, hearing about his family, made him appear more like most people, not some elite mercenary. That led her to believe that the man she was discovering beneath the façade of the fierce warrior was a man she could possibly love.

Leora yawned, unable to stop it.

Noble turned to his side. "You're tired and rightfully so. It was a journey fraught with unexpected perils and wounds. You need to sleep."

Leora was enjoying their talk and didn't want it to end, not yet, but she could feel the tiredness in her body and sleep creeping ever closer.

"I am glad I came to your bedchamber and we talked. I feel I know you a bit better now."

"And we will learn more and come to know each other well and share a good life together," he said, letting her know it was possible if they took the time to make it so.

He hadn't planned on kissing her, just the opposite. He planned on avoiding it, but he could not resist with her lips so close to his. Their plump softness made them ache to be kissed. He brought his lips to hers and kissed her gently. But it wasn't enough, so he kissed her again, thinking that would do, but, of course, it didn't. His hand went and gripped the side of her face, holding it as he turned their kiss more intimate.

Leora had wanted him to kiss her, had hoped he would, and she wondered if that was what had truly brought her to his bedchamber. Strange yet pleasurable feelings had been racing through her all day, especially when her husband had innocently touched her by taking her hand or touching her arm or wrapping his arm around her or pressing his hand to her back. She did not quite understand it, but she wanted to learn more about it.

But now that she was here, sensations building in her that she ached to explore, she wondered—was this wise of her? Was she selfish in not seeing Sky safe before she found any pleasure for herself?

The thought had her ending the kiss, easing her mouth off his when she wanted desperately to continue kissing him. "I should return to my bedchamber."

"Nay, wife, this is *our* bedchamber and here is where you will stay from this night on," Noble said with a firmness that left no room that it would be any other way. He saw confusion in her eyes. "We will continue this another time. You need to sleep."

Confusion remained in her eyes, but relief reared its head as she nodded.

She turned away from him hugging the side of the bed and he wanted to pull her into his arms and sleep wrapped around her. But something had disturbed their kiss and he planned to find out what it was so that it never happened again, since the next time he kissed his wife, he planned on sealing their vows.

***

With full bellies from last night and even more so with this morning's meal and a renewed hope in their hearts, people wore smiles as they eagerly helped Noble's warriors with the many chores needed to restore the village to its prime. Praise, from young and old alike, for their new chieftain was heard everywhere as busy hands worked.

"The missive was sent to Lord Slayer this morning?" Noble asked Finley, though conformation wasn't necessary since he never failed to obey an order, but Noble also never failed to make sure a task got done.

"Aye, we should hear soon from Lord Slayer," Finley said. "Warriors vigilantly roam the surrounding woods, and two trackers are marking areas to alert us if anyone passes through there."

His men were well aware of what he expected of them and often did so without any command from him.

They had learned well, and it was one of the reasons they had been victorious in so many battles.

"The men look forward to establishing a home here. They will work hard to get the necessary work done before winter sets in," Finley said as they walked through the village.

Noble cast a wide glance around, pleased that two thatched roofs were nearly repaired and a third getting started, and cottages too decayed to occupy were being torn down to make way for new ones.

"It is good we have the whole summer to see the work completed and the fields ripe with growth," Noble said and spotted his wife talking with two women, one round with child, whose smiles brightened their pretty faces.

"Your wife's smile is magical. One cannot help but smile when she smiles, though it might be her beauty that makes one smile."

Noble turned a stern look at him.

"You can always count on me to speak the truth," Finley said. "Besides, I simply voice what you already know."

Finley was right. His wife's beauty immediately caught the eye, but just in the last week they spent together he had come to realize that her beauty might catch the eye, but it was her genuine nature that truly attracted people to her. Little by little she revealed more about herself to him, and he found himself doing the same with her. He found comfort in talking with her about things he had never revealed to anyone and yet it seemed natural to do so with her. He had been amazed that he had spoken about his family to her. He never spoke about them to anyone and yet it came easily with her and surprisingly it gave him a sense of relief to do so. It was like ridding himself of a burden he had unnecessarily carried.

He suddenly had the urge to talk with her, but he did not want to interrupt her discussion with the two women. It was important she got to know the clan members, her new family, and they her.

Finley continued talking, letting him know what had been done since they had talked earlier this morning, deciding on the tasks that would be accomplished today. He listened while casting a keen eye around the village. In time, he would get to know everyone here, their strengths, their weaknesses, and their skills and know how they would most benefit the clan. He saw even now how some men worked better at some tasks than others and was pleased to see the strong camaraderie among the people. They had wisely banded together to survive a difficult situation, which had helped them do just that.

His glance continued to shift and survey, and he saw that Atworth, the prisoner who claimed to be skilled at fashioning weapons was presently busy demonstrating his skill of arrow making with a few of Noble's warriors who shared the same skill. The other prisoners had been put to work repairing one of the stone storage sheds under the closely guarded watch of two warriors who worked alongside them.

Noble caught the quick movement out of the corner of his eye and shifted his glance to see one of his trackers, Bew, hurrying toward him. Something was wrong. He could see it on Bew's narrow face. Instinct had him shifting his glance once again, and he caught the quick movement.

Noble rushed toward his wife as he shouted, "LEORA, DROP!"

Leora hesitated briefly, her protective instincts asserting itself on the two women she was speaking to and giving them a shove that had them tumbling before she dropped to the ground, though not before feeling a sharp pain strike the top of her right shoulder.

Only moments later Noble's arm was around his wife's waist, helping her to her feet, more concerned with her than with the culprit who had thrown the sizeable stone and who his warriors had already caught and held firm.

"Glenna!" a young man called out frantically as he ran toward the two fallen women who were helping each other to get to their feet.

"I am all right, Rob, thanks to Mistress Leora, without thought to her own safety she pushed me aside or the stone would have hit me," the woman round with child said as her husband took her in his arms.

"We are grateful, most grateful, mistress," Rob said, hugging his wife tight.

Leora ignored the pain in her shoulder, but kept her hand gripped to her husband's arm so he would not let go of her, though with the strength in which he held her, she didn't believe he had any intentions of doing so and that was fine with her.

"I would never let another suffer injury that was meant for me," Leora said, then looked to her husband. "My husband knows me well enough to know that."

There was no point in arguing with her when she was right. When he yelled at her, he knew she would not leave the two women vulnerable, which did not allow for the stone to completely miss her, though it did allow for it to only graze her shoulder than to suffer a strike to her head that could have left her with a severe wound.

"My wife is right, though she will refuse to admit that her shoulder pains her from the stone striking her there," Noble said, the stern look he settled on her challenging her to deny it.

"Oh, mistress, please let us see to your care," the other woman, who was now steady on her feet said.

"Aye, mistress, Brenda is learning the healing ways from the nuns at Whitehall Abbey. She can help you and I can assist her," Glenna said.

"That is very kind of you both, but it is nothing more than a sore shoulder. It will heal fast enough," Leora said. "Brenda should see to you, Glenna. You are close to delivering your bairn and a fall cannot be good for you."

Her words had Glenna's husband nodding. "Mistress Leora is right. You need to let Brenda look after you."

"Your husband is right, Glenna," Noble said. "Rob, go along with your wife and Brenda and see for yourself that all is well."

"I am most grateful, sir," Rob said with a bob of his head. "Most grateful and pleased to call you our new chieftain."

The three turned toward Brenda's cottage and while Noble wanted to make sure his wife suffered nothing more than a sore shoulder, he spotted Bew waiting impatiently nearby, and so did his wife.

"Your tracker is impatient to speak with you. It must be important news. You also have the fool who threw the stone to confront."

"Both can wait. It is more important I know the truth about your injury."

"It pains me some. Now let's talk with your tracker and then with the stone thrower," Leora said, fighting to hide the cringe that surfaced far too quickly when she turned. The chunk of stone had hit harder than she had realized.

Noble leaned his head down toward her face. "I can feel you tense with pain."

Leora sighed, frustrated. "Truthfully, my shoulder pains me, but it will pain me more if I do not hear what your tracker has to say especially since it might pertain to me and to know why the man would take such a foolish chance to wound me when he was aware he would suffer greatly for it, and will other prisoners follow suit? Did we bring danger into the clan?"

It continued to amaze him that her mind worked much like his, more like a warrior bent on victory than a woman set upon and injured.

Leora continued talking. "It is something that must be determined immediately so that no one suffers that which is meant for me."

"You have already suffered more than I—"

"Minor wounds," she said, interrupting him. "You have done exactly what my da wanted of you when he arranged our marriage. You have protected me and saved me from far worse injuries and possibly death.

My da would be pleased," —she hesitated before continuing— "and so am I."

A slight smile tempted the corners of his mouth as he lowered his voice to ask, "Are you saying you are pleased that I am your husband?"

"At the moment," she said and smiled.

Bloody hell, if her smile didn't jab at his heart, not to mention the punch to his gut, but it was her quick responses that always seemed to challenge him that he truly enjoyed.

"Now we must not waste any more time. We need to speak to your tracker then to the stone-thrower."

His arm, firm around her waist, stopped her from taking another step.

"What now?" she asked, impatiently.

"You will tell me if you are in too much pain?"

"That sounds like a command."

"Does it need to be?" Noble asked.

"Nay, husband, since we have no time to argue over it," she said, and her smile brightened. "And you knew that when you commanded it. You are far too predictable, husband."

Noble did not hide his smile and didn't respond. She did not realize he was learning more about her each time he presented himself as predictable. He waved Bew over.

"What's wrong?" Noble asked.

"Lance and I were tracking a sizeable troop but lost them in the thick of the forest and now I cannot find Lance, cannot find so much as a sign of him. It is as if he has disappeared."

Chapter Twelve

Noble knew his wife's thoughts were churning and no doubt matching his own as he called out for Finley, who was not far from them.

"Go get food, Bew, and rest while you can," Noble ordered the young man. "We will go find Lance."

"Aye, sir, I will wait on your summons," Bew said with a nod and took his leave.

Leora saw that the young tracker had no doubt that Noble would issue such an order and she surmised that Noble was not a warrior who left any of his men behind.

"Lance is missing. Prepare a troop who will join me in tracking him," Noble ordered Finley. "And another troop who will follow discreetly since Bew has found tracks of a sizeable troop passing nearby but lost them."

"Could it be Lord Slayer's troop Bew lost?" Finley asked.

Noble shook his head. "Lord Slayer would have sent word if a sizeable troop of Gallowglass was in the area. You will remain here and make sure the men are ready in case of an attack. And you will need to alert the clan and organize a defense plan to be prepared in case of an attack."

"I can work with Finley on that," Leora offered. "I had spoken about such a plan with my da, and we were planning to implement one."

Noble thought to refuse her, then thought better of it. If she worked with Finley, he could keep a close watch on her.

He turned to Finley. "Work with my wife and see if she has more to offer that may help us."

If Finley was surprised, he didn't show it. He simply said, "Aye, sir."

After Finley hurried off, Noble said, "Share what you feel will help but also listen to what Finley has to say and learn, for he knows well what is needed to protect a clan."

"I intend to do just that since who better to know how to protect a clan against attacks than the warriors who attack the clans," Leora said and took hold of his hand for them to walk. "Now tell me, do you think it is nothing more than a coincidence that tracks of a troop are found in the forest and another attempt is made on my life?" She smiled. "That sudden flare in your eyes tell me you questioned the same yourself."

"It is uncanny how much we think alike," Noble said.

"Not really, we are both wise enough to question things. Rarely do people question things. It is easier to accept something we are told or see instead of pondering it to make sure the truth isn't hidden somewhere beneath."

"And do you think this man we go to question will reveal any truths?" Noble asked.

"I believe you will make certain he has no choice but to do so."

***

"You will not stop him. He will see her dead and all who stand in his way," the man called out as Noble and Leora approached him. "And the one who claims her life will reap the reward."

"And how will you reap the reward when you are dead?" Noble asked, stopping enough distance from the man that he could not prove a threat to Leora. Not that he could make another attempt on her life secured as he was with his arms tied behind his back and surrounded by four warriors, but Noble did not intend on taking any chances.

The man raised his chin with pride. "My family would benefit. They would no longer go hungry. They would have all they need."

"You believe this?" Noble asked as if the man was a fool.

The man stared at him, befuddled. "He gave his word."

"And you trusted a man you do not know well?" Noble asked.

"Kinnel knows the man making the offer. If he does not keep his word there is not a mercenary that would ride with him again and plenty who would want him dead," the fellow argued.

Noble could tell those were not the man's words. They were the words used to convince desperate men to ride with him, the man called Kinnel. "But as you say, if there is much coin offered, Kinnel can collect the reward, keep it for himself, disappear, and live his life without worry. Your family would never know the sacrifice you made for them."

"Others would speak up," the man insisted but not with confidence.

"Not if coins were offered to them," Noble said.

The man's eyes shifted nervously.

"One way or another you sealed your fate," Noble said. "Tell me all you know, and I will make your death a quick one. Stay silent and I will see you suffer endlessly."

"I have a family who needs me," the man said as if it would make a difference. "They must be suffering greatly."

"Then why leave your family in such dire circumstances?" Leora asked. "A man who loves his family would not abandon them when they already suffer. He would do all he could to feed them and see them safe. The forest teems with life. A good husband and father would hunt, fish, and teach his children to do the same but he would never leave them when they needed him the most. You lie."

"My wife says what I thought myself, but there is more that troubles me about your tale and quite a tale it is. We discovered a troop of men in the area, and I imagine they search for you. I believe you chose to remain a captive so you would get another chance at killing my wife, escape, and collect the reward. But there is only one reason the troop searches for you... you are the man who leads them... you are Kinnel."

"That is brilliant, husband, I did not think of that," Leora said with admiration and pride.

"It takes a mercenary to know one," the man said,

Once again, Leora spoke proudly. "My husband is no common mercenary. He is a fierce Gallowglass warrior who leads an elite troop of skilled warriors."

The warriors, who surrounded Kinnel and those nearby who heard, lifted their chins and expanded their chests with pride.

"Let me live and I will tell you all I know," Kinnel said.

Noble's expression darkened and his words sounded like a declaration. "You will tell me all you know either way."

"So, either way I am a dead man?" Kinnel asked, a nervous sweat breaking out along his brow.

Noble's eyes settled directly on Kinnel's eyes. "You intended to kill my wife and still would if given the chance. What do you think your fate will be?"

Finley approached in haste. "Our men return with a message from Lord Slayer."

"Tie him to a post," Noble ordered. "I will deal with him later."

"Do not think to send me to the keep," Leora said when he turned and looked at her. "And do not try to stop me from asking if your men saw my sister."

"Your shoulder?" he asked.

"No pain will stop me from inquiring about Sky," she said adamantly.

Noble did not hide his annoyance. "You admit you're in pain."

"How could I not be when a chunk of stone hit me but my worry for my sister is far greater than the pain in my shoulder. Besides, it is not bleeding, and time is the only thing that will ease the pain. Have you not fought through pain yourself?"

"Aye, but that is different and don't ask me how, it just is," Noble said when she went to argue.

She saw the concern in his deep blue eyes for her and a warm comfort settled over her. She hooked her arm around his. "It is very thoughtful of you not to want to see me suffer any pain, but please believe me when I tell you it is bearable."

"If the pain grows worse—"

"I will tell you. Now let's go see what news your men have brought from Lord Slayer since I know you will not want to delay your search for Lance much longer."

Noble quickly shielded his wife with his body when shouts suddenly filled the air, but stepped aside when he realized they were shouts of joy. Taking his wife's hand, they hurried to see what caused the happy excitement.

Carts piled with sacks of grain and baskets filled with various foods, and one overflowing with cloth rolled into the village. Farm animals followed behind them: cows, pigs, sheep, and chickens. There were two other carts, though they were covered, and Leora wondered what they held, though she caught a peek of something hanging through the wooden slots and knew the cart carried weapons. Lord Slayer not only saw them well fed but had also supplied them with enough weapons to protect themselves.

"I can take stock of this at the keep and see it is distributed fairly," Leora said. "The servants there can help me."

Noble was glad to turn the task over to his wife, her commanding nature could easily handle it. He directed the carts to the keep and Lord Slayer's men as well. Noble instructed the men in the clan who had once tended the animals to take care of the new arrivals and they did with enthusiasm, guiding them to the different pens, some in the process of being repaired.

"I did not expect to see you so soon, Ross," Noble said when the man dismounted and joined Noble and Leora to walk to the keep, his horse following behind him.

"Slayer knew things were bad here and had all this ready for your arrival. He knew it would not take long for you to claim the title, though you did get things moving along fast enough," Ross said, casting a glance all around him at the work in progress.

"I assumed he might, which was why I dispatched a hasty message to him," Noble said.

Leora could not wait a second longer. "My sister, did you speak with her?"

"I did not see her," Ross said.

"But she must walk through the village, talk with people. How could you not see her? Has Slayer imprisoned her?" Leora demanded.

"Nay, your sister is not held a prisoner and she is well cared for. You truly need not worry about her. In time, I am sure Lord Slayer will grant permission for you to see her."

"Grant permission to see my own sister?" Leora said with a sharp tongue. "I need no permission to see my sister, and Lord Slayer will rue the day if he thinks to keep her from me."

"Do not grow angry with Ross, he only follows orders," Noble urged his wife. "Know your sister is well and safe as Ross says and in time you will see her."

Leora bit her tongue to stop herself from lashing out at both men. They did not understand the importance of her seeing her sister as soon as possible, but it would do her no good to be angry with the two men who could help her visit with her sister. In time, however, was not a good enough answer as to when she could see her sister. If a visit proved too difficult, she would find a way to at least get a word to her no matter what anyone told her.

Knowing her husband would dismiss her so he could talk with Ross alone and thinking that perhaps Wendell was one of the men who drove the carts here since they were dressed more like servants than warriors, she spoke before her husband could, once they reached the keep.

"I am sure the people are eager to receive the food items and cloths, so I will leave you to talk while I see to the task," she said with a smile and, with a light squeeze to her husband's hand, took her leave.

"Leora," Noble said with a raised voice after she took only a few steps.

Leora did not stop walking or turn around. She waved her hand in the air as she called out, "I will mind my shoulder, husband."

Noble shook his head.

"She knows what you will say?" Ross asked, surprised.

"Far too often," Noble admitted.

"She is a witch?" Ross whispered.

Noble laughed. "Far from it. She is a knowledgeable woman."

"My sympathy," Ross said.

"It is not as bad as you would think," Noble said as they climbed the keep's stairs.

"But she must be a challenge."

"Aye, and you know how much I love a challenge," Noble said with a smile.

***

Leora organized things quickly enough with the help of Calla, Emma, and the rest of the kitchen staff, all only too eager to help. She did not make the people wait to take their share. She had some of the sacks opened, the baskets lined up on tables, along with the cloth so that people could easily take what they needed. Though she did not offer all of it. She had Emma take what was needed for the keep and some of everything to be stored for future distribution.

Word was sent throughout the village to bring sacks, baskets, whatever was needed to carry their share. Women, men, and children came, and Calla saw that they formed a line and moved along without any issues, though it could have been Noble's warriors who stood watch that kept everyone orderly. But Leora suspected that everyone was far too happy at receiving more food that they calmly, though eagerly, waited their turn.

As things moved along nicely, Leora made her way to the man who had driven the cart. He was busy enjoying a tankard of ale and bread with honey Emma had offered him.

"Do you happen to be Wendell?" Leora asked with a generous smile, though knew he wasn't, Adele's lack of a smile evidence enough that Wendell was not among those who arrived here.

The young man stared at her, his mouth partially open and his cheeks flaming red.

Leora recalled Elsie's advice to her one day. "If you do not want young men frozen silent when you speak to them, then don't smile at them."

She instantly softened her smile and repeated her question. "Are you Wendell?"

The young man lost his dazed look after shaking his head. "Nay, mistress, I am Gower. Wendell was assigned another task today."

"Do you work in the kitchen at Clan Ravinsher, Gower?" Leora asked.

Gower nodded. "I do, mistress."

Leora lowered her voice and let her smile fade some. "I am curious about the woman that Lord Slayer brought to his clan. Her name is Sky. Would you know anything about her? Have you ever seen her?"

Gower lowered his voice as well. "We are not permitted to speak about her."

"Why?"

"Lord Slayer's orders and no one defies his orders," Gower said, a slight tremble in his voice.

Leora continued her pursuit to learn anything she could about Sky, wishing to discover even a scape of information. "So, you have never seen her?"

Gower's glance darted about as if looking to see if anyone watched them or could hear them and that was enough for Leora to realize the young man knew something about Sky.

"You have seen her?" she whispered.

"A quick glimpse, no more, and I should not even have said that," Gower said, shaking his head, realizing his mistake.

"Was she all right? Frightened? Harmed in any way?" Leora demanded anxiously.

Gower clamped his lips shut tightly and worry filled his eyes.

Leora silently cursed herself for frightening the young man with her demanding manner. But if he saw Sky only for a moment, she wanted his honest opinion of how she appeared.

She kept her voice calm and low. "I did not mean to frighten you, Gower, and since you spoke when you obviously fear that you shouldn't have, I will share something with you that no one need know. This way we both will keep what we share here a secret."

His eyes turned wide. "I am not good with a secret."

"I am," Leora assured him and the worry in his eyes faded slightly. "I ask about Sky because she is my sister."

Gower's mouth dropped open.

"People tell me she is safe and well, but how do I know for sure unless I hear it from someone who has seen her or talked with her."

"I did not talk with her, mistress, but I have seen her several times," Gower said.

"Please tell me how she is, Gower. Please. I worry endlessly about her," Leora said, not caring that she sounded like she begged.

"From what I have seen of her, which was from a distance, she appears well. No one harms her, nor would anyone dare to. They would suffer at Lord Slayer's hands if they did," —Gower shuddered— "a horrible fate for sure."

Leora was relieved to hear that, but she was not finished yet. "Was she alone each time you saw her? Has anyone in the clan befriended her?"

Gower stared at her, his silence letting her know he was at a loss for words.

Leora understood without him saying a word. The people feared her because of her affliction and, therefore, avoided her. Her heart ached at the thought of her sister all alone, no one to talk with, no one to care about her, and it made Leora even more determined to see that Sky was returned home to her family.

***

"All goes well with Lord Slayer?" Noble asked as he and Ross settled with tankards of ale at the table in his solar.

"All goes well at the clan, but Lord Slayer will not rest until he finds out who killed his brother and father and revenge their deaths," Ross said.

"How does his search go?"

Ross shook his head. "Not as well or as fast as he would like. But he is wise enough to know impatience can be an enemy at times. His men are spread wide, listening, hoping to hear something that will help."

"His tentacles always stretched wide," Noble said, recalling the many powerful men Slayer was acquainted with, though he did not call them friends.

"The rogue mercenaries bent on killing or abducting your wife or Sky, since one of them could prove the heir to some Lowlander fortune, is what presently occupies his mind. It has Lowlanders arriving here and he does not like their intrusion upon the Highlands."

"Cavell saved a troop of Lowlanders from complete slaughter and intends to escort the surviving ones to the border."

"Then they will likely run into a larger group of Lowlanders who have crossed the border into the Highlands," Ross said.

"Another troop has arrived?" Noble asked, not pleased by the news.

"Someone wants desperately to find the heir to the Lowland fortune."

"My wife remains with me. Under no circumstance will I allow her out of our marriage," Noble said, needing Ross to make sure Slayer understood that.

"Your vows are sealed, your marriage unbreakable?" Ross asked, and when Noble looked away, he shook his head. "Seal your vows posthaste and plant your seed deep so there is no chance of voiding the marriage."

"I will see it done," Noble assured him.

"Immediately," Ross urged. "It will take time for that Lowlander troop to reach us, make sure your wife is with child before they get here."

Noble nodded, annoyed he had not seen to it sooner so that his wife could possibly already be with child, securing their marriage.

"One other thing," Ross said, "we ran into a group of mercenaries on the way here. The fools attacked us or at least attempted to. The ones lucky enough to survive were sent to Clan Ravinsher for Slayer to decide what to do with them. Once they heard where they were going, they couldn't stop talking about their mission and how they were searching for their leader, Kinnel, who a Gallowglass warrior had taken prisoner. I am assuming you were that warrior."

"I am, and his fate is sealed since he attempted once again to harm my wife, a poor attempt at that, his greed ruling his common sense," Noble said, his brow narrowing. "Lance was not with them?"

"Your tracker?" Ross shook his head after Noble nodded. "He was not among them, and I doubt they would have harmed him since he could have led them to Kinnel."

Noble didn't like what that meant. "If Kinnel's men didn't catch him, then what troop does he follow?"

Chapter Thirteen

Noble stood amidst the towering pines deep in the forest, frustrated. He had learned his tracking skills from an early age, his grandfather having taught him.

Patience and a clear mind are the two most important skills of a tracker, he heard his grandfather reminding him. Unfortunately, he feared he would lose the little patience he had left, and then all the skills his grandfather had taught him would be worthless, and he would not allow that to happen.

He took a fortifying breath and remained as he was casting a slow glance but a keen eye on his surroundings or attempting to. His mind had yet to clear, his wife forever popping into it. He had found himself missing her not long after he and his warriors had left Clan Skirling to search for Lance. It was a few days since then and he'd been surprised at how much he not only thought of her but how very much he missed her. She had somehow, in a brief time, become a constant thought that too often twisted at his gut and challenged his heart.

The night before he left to search for Lance, he had gone to their bedchamber long after his wife had, Ross keeping him up with talk and drink. Until finally, and as if he only recalled it, Ross ordered him to go to his wife and see their marriage sealed.

Noble had known when he entered their bedchamber that it would not likely happen that night. His wife slept soundly, turned on her side, her nightdress hanging off her shoulder, exposing the bruise left by the chunk of rock. He cringed at the size of the bruise and how it must pain her, and how sleep could not have come easily for her. He would not couple with her while she was in pain, and he did not like the thought of leaving her the morning after their first coupling. He felt it would not be right or wise since he feared once he did, he would want more of his wife and his mind would be more preoccupied than it already was.

He shook his head. He had to stop thinking about her. He had to concentrate on tracking Lance if he ever wanted to get home and see their marriage protected.

Noble returned his attention to the surrounding area, searching for crushed pinecones, snapped twigs, and disturbed foliage, any signs Lance may have purposely left as markers, but he saw nothing. He worried for Lance as to what that might mean. Had he been found and disposed of without a thought?

He shook his head. What was he missing? He had wondered the same when he had attempted to track Leora from Dundren Abbey after arriving there and finding out she had escaped. He had thought he had picked up her trail, discovering broken twigs and pinecones crushed from footfalls, but they had led nowhere. He had come upon tracks, but the size was far too large for them to be his wife's and too deep as well. Someone with weight had made those tracks and then they had disappeared, not to be found again. So how had she managed to avoid him? It was something he was growing impatient to find out.

Bew approached him appearing as frustrated as he was.

"I can find nothing. How can that be?" Bew asked, annoyed. "Lance would not fail to find me if I went missing. How have I failed him?"

The sudden thought was like a jolt of lightning striking Noble and he smiled as he shook his head. "You haven't, Bew. We are at fault for not considering Lance's skills."

Bew looked confused. "I don't understand."

"We find nothing because there is nothing here to find," Noble said.

Bew still did not understand.

"There are no tracks because Lance continues to track, and he takes no chance of being discovered. That means whoever Lance is tracking he suspects has two trackers themselves, one who follows behind the troop and one who precedes them, similar to what we do.

Bew seemed doubtful, a slight shake to his head. "I cannot believe he would do something like that without leaving us some indication."

"Unless he was left in no position to do so.

Bew's brow quickly drew tight. "That could mean he's in trouble." Then he thought better of his response. "Or he had no time to let anyone know or risk discovery. But what do we do now?"

"We go home and wait for him to return," Noble said.

"What if we have alerted the tracker to Lance's presence?" Bew asked.

"Of that I am not sure, Bew," Noble said. "It is a chance we will have to take, but if Lance does not return home within several days, we will search again."

"Lance is like a hound with a bone when he's tracking, refusing to let go until he's satisfied," Bew said.

Noble gave Bew's shoulder a hardy slap, leaving it to rest there in reassurance. "But a hound forgoes his bone once his master summons him. Lance knows that he cannot delay for long in bringing me whatever he may have discovered. But just to be certain, there is one area we haven't searched yet. We will cover that one and if nothing is found we will head home.

***

Leora looked over the village with Finley. "I do believe the old chieftain did not worry over being attacked. He left the village far too exposed."

"My thought would be that Clan Skirling sits so close to Clan Ravinsher that he figured no one would dare attack his clan, not with Slayer leading the vast troop of Gallowglass warriors in the area. Besides, why would anyone want to attack an insignificant clan like Clan Skirling and risk the Gallowglass's wrath?" Finley shook his head. "It would mean certain death."

"Perhaps, but I'm sure you know well the chaos that ensues when a clan is attacked, and I imagine the Gallowglass even count on it. If the clan knows what to do on the onset of attack, it makes for a better chance of victory." She started walking, casting a glance around and spotting the small black pup sniffing the ground close by. "Keep up, Chief," she called out and the small pup hurried to follow alongside her.

"He has grown strong quickly these last few days," Finley said as he followed along with her.

"That he has," she said, pleased how the pup had added weight and was healing well. "He gets what he needs to grow strong… plenty of food and sleep. Now tell me what you think is the most important thing a clan can do when first under attack?"

"Get to their weapons," he said without hesitation.

"Then weapons need to be kept handy at all times and not just in the home, but in areas where one would never expect them to be located, like the food storage sheds."

"The women and children should be sheltered in the keep," Finley went on.

"I suppose since it is what most clans do when under attack, but I worry that if the clan suffers defeat, then the women and children are left easy prey for the enemy. Wouldn't it be wiser if the women and children appeared to rush into the keep but leave through the kitchen and escape into the woods and make their way to Clan Ravinsher. There should also be a designated person who, at first sign of attack, makes his way to Clan Ravinsher so Lord Slayer can send help."

They continued to walk and talk, formulating a plan that Leora suggested be implemented immediately. Finley agreed and once they finished talking, he left Leora to begin to organize and see the plan carried out without delay.

Leora lingered in the village, speaking to various people, Chief often providing a conversation starter since several people commented on how the small pup followed her so faithfully. She was glad she was getting to know everyone here just as she had done at home. Every day she had walked through the village at home, speaking with young and old alike, seeing if anyone needed anything or simply sharing a conversation with them, and she missed that and she missed—her husband.

The thought surprised her. She had grown accustomed to his presence, found conversation with him enjoyable and challenging at times, and she favored the closeness that had developed naturally between them, an intimacy of sorts that was rather pleasing and something she realized in his absence that she missed.

Thoughts of him always sent a rash of tingles rushing through her or fluttered her stomach. There was no denying she favored her husband, and she wondered if that could be a prelude to love. Could she possibly be falling in love with this man who she had been given in marriage to? Could they have a good life together if she truly gave it a chance?

She glanced around the village. Everyone was busy restoring the village and, in a way, their own lives. Smiles were plentiful as was laughter and easy chatter. This was her new home. She would never return to Clan Murdock. That was Elsie and Cavell's home now. Her life was here with Noble, and it was up to her what she made of it.

"ATTACK!"

Leora turned to see warriors rushing out of the woods on one side of the village, their roars slicing through the pleasant breeze and weapons gripped in their hands.

She watched women freeze in shock, children clinging to them in fear. She scooped up Chief, he having taken a protective stance in front of her, and she ran, yelling, "Get the children into the keep!"

Leora's shouts startled the woman out of their daze, and they rushed to gather the children and hurry them to the keep. She spotted Calla ready to help herd the children and hurried to her.

"Take Chief and make sure he stays in the keep," she ordered Calla.

The lass took the pup, but Chief protested, barking and whining as he was swept away from Leora.

Her next thought was clear. She grabbed a lad's arm, no more than ten or eleven years, a small axe in his hand that would do little good against the size of the warriors descending on the clan.

She recalled the lad's name having spoken to him earlier. "Robert, I need you to go and alert Clan Ravinsher to the attack. Lord Slayer will send help. Can you do that?"

He nodded and his hands trembled. "I can."

"Good. There is no time to get a horse. You need to run like the devil is chasing you."

"I think he is," the lad said, his eyes turning wide as he stared beyond Leora's shoulder.

She released his arm. "Run!"

Leora turned and she froze at the sight of a huge man, a metal helmet on his head with a metal piece covering from the bridge of his nose to the tip and long gray hair hanging from beneath it, standing just on the edge of the village, his many warriors fanning out behind him waiting for his signal to enter. His eyes were ablaze with rage and villagers fled away from him while Gallowglass warriors stood ready to fight.

He raised his hand and pointed his double-sided axe in the distance. "Get him."

Two warriors ran along the edge of the woods, and she knew they chased after Robert, and the speed in which they traveled made it clear they would catch the lad.

Leora stared at the large man's thick hands that gripped the battle axe. A powerful blow from one of his mighty fists would send any warrior who dared to challenge him sailing through the air and his grip on his double-sided axe let all know he was prepared to fight. He appeared unstoppable, and yet he didn't move.

"I am here for the blonde, red-haired woman. Give her to me and no one will die today," the large man shouted, his solid voice booming throughout the village.

Heads turned and glances fell on Leora, though not one Gallowglass warrior looked her way. She could not blame those who had since she doubted many of them had done so on purpose. It was a natural reaction and no doubt a regretful one once they realized their response gave the large warrior what he wanted.

Leora did not hesitate to respond as well. She would not see anyone die today because of her. She walked toward him.

"Stay back," Finley ordered, rushing to stop her.

"Nay!" Leora snapped. "No one will die today."

"Wise woman," the large warrior called out with a nod.

"We have no choice but to fight," Finley said. "A Gallowglass warrior never surrenders and always protects their own."

"I will not see anyone die because of me," Leora argued.

Impatience had the large man walking toward her, and when Finley went to stop him, he swatted him away with one blow of his meaty fist, sending Finley sailing into the air and landing on the ground motionless.

Gallowglass warriors went to rush forward as did the large warrior's men.

"ENOUGH!" Leora shouted. "You will hold your weapons while I speak to this man, and someone go tend to Finley." She walked slowly toward the man. "What do you want of me?"

He tilted his head from side to side, then with two giant steps was in front of her.

"Remain as you are!" Leora ordered, seeing her husband's warriors ready to fight. She raised her chin and looked straight at him. "I will ask one more time. What is it you want from me?"

The large warrior shook his head. "It is not you I seek." He looked past her to the Gallowglass. "Let your chieftain know I have no reason to battle with him. I leave you in peace and will not return. But if he follows out of senseless revenge, then I promise you that all here will die, and I will burn the village to the ground."

His warriors began backing away as did the large warrior, then they turned and disappeared into the woods.

**

Having found no sign of Lance, in the last area they searched, Noble and his warriors headed home. An unsettled feeling plagued him as he rode, and he worried he was missing something. His thoughts continued to linger too often on his wife, not allowing him to pay full attention to the matter at hand. What had he missed?

He could not shake the feeling that there had been something for him to see and he had failed to see it. Lance thought it important to follow whoever he was tracking—why? Had he heard something that caused him to continue to track? Were they to meet up with someone and he wanted to find out who?

Noble shook his head. He often attempted to think like his enemy before going into battle. But this wasn't a battle, this was either an assassination or abduction attempt. What would he do if he led either of these two troops?

Get rid of what would cause the most difficulty in achieving victory.

"Bloody hell!" Noble cried out and his men brought their horses to a halt and instantly drew their weapons.

Bew yelled out, "Lance!"

The tracker was stumbling out of the woods, his breathing labored, sweat soaking his brow, and several scratches marred his face from tree branches swiping at him.

Noble rode his horse over to Lance where he stood bent over, his hands braced on his thighs, his head hanging down while trying to calm his breathing.

"They led you on a chase, didn't they? They counted on me leaving to search for you," Noble said, keeping firm hold of the reins, his horse feeling his annoyance and growing unsettled.

Lance raised his head. "Aye, sir. I heard them talking about meeting someone and I thought it might be the person who is hiring the many mercenaries. I didn't want to chance losing them or their tracks, so I followed. It took me a while to realize that it was a diversion. They knew I was tracking them. As soon as I discovered that," —Lance shook his head— "I have been running to get home ever since, realizing they wanted to get you as far away from the keep as possible and hoping you had not come searching for me yet."

"We need to get home now!" Noble ordered and Lance hurried onto Bew's horse, and they took off.

Their horses pounded the earth and Noble's heart pounded in his chest with anger and fear of what he might find.

Noble knew something was wrong when he got closer to the village. Not one warrior stood guard and he spotted no one on the outskirts or in the fields. He urged his horse forward and slowed him down with some relief when he saw that the clan and most of his warriors were gathered in one section of the village while the remainder of his warriors walked along the edge of the woods, their weapons drawn.

"Chieftain Noble has returned!" someone shouted, and the crowd spread out.

Noble saw what had gathered them together. Finley lay on the ground, his cheek and one eye bruised and swollen and looking as if he was just regaining his wits. Leora sat beside him bathing his head with a wet cloth.

"What happened here?" Noble demanded after dismounting and going to squat down in front of his wife to make sure she was unharmed and to get a better look at Finley.

"Mistress Leora saved us, she did!" someone called out.

"She was willing to give her life for us," another shouted.

One more shout was heard. "Mistress Leora commanded that no one would die today and we didn't, not one of us, thanks to her bravery."

Finley went to sit up, ready to explain.

"Stay as you are," Noble ordered, "until you've regained your strength. My wife can explain what happened here."

"Mistress Leora commanded the Gallowglass to hold their weapons while she confronted a giant of a warrior," Robert, the young lad, called out with pride.

Noble glared at his wife, annoyed that she would do such a dangerous thing and spotted a slight tremble to her hands. The incident had not left her unscathed.

Another person hurried to add to what Robert had said, "That giant threatened to kill us all if the woman with blonde, red hair did not make herself known. Mistress Leora did not hesitate to step forward."

"Mistress Leora also hurried the women and children into the keep before the band of warriors entered the village," a woman said.

"And she thought to send me for help to Lord Slayer, but I wasn't fast enough," Robert said, annoyed with himself. "I couldn't outrun them."

"We were ready to fight," Finley said, managing to sit up with some help from Leora.

"I never doubted that," Noble assured him, knowing his warriors would have died protecting Leora if necessary.

"He was a giant of a man. I never saw anyone with hands the size of his," Leora said, dropping the wet cloth in a nearby bucket and gripping her tunic so no one could see her hands tremble, a delayed reaction to the chance she took confronting the mighty warrior. "He swatted Finley away from me as if he was nothing more than a pesky fly. But in the end, I was not the woman he was looking for."

"He told you this?" Noble asked.

Leora nodded. "He did. He looked at me and told me that I was not the one he searched for."

Penn spoke up next. "He left a message with us for our chieftain. He wants you to know that he has no reason to battle with you. He said he would leave us in peace and not return. Though if you go after him for revenge, then he promises all here will die and he will burn the village to the ground."

"He is a formidable warrior, Noble," Finley said. "I have no doubt he will do as he says but the men stand ready to go after them."

"Nay! Nay!" the crowd shouted. "He left us in peace, let him be."

Noble got to his feet and turned slowly and saw to it that his glare fell on everyone there. "Would you have surrendered your mistress to him to save yourself? Because I know it was not even a thought for my warriors."

Heads hung low and no one would meet his angry eyes.

"Would you have surrendered Robert?" Noble pointed at the lad, then at a woman. "Or Glenna?" He pointed again. "Or Brenda?"

The young woman gasped and gripped her apron, stepping closer to Calla.

"Who would you surrender to save yourself? The Gallowglass are one. Surrender one of us and you surrender us all, which is why the Gallowglass will never surrender one of their own. They would die first. My wife faced death rather than see any of you, her family, die, and not one of you would have done the same for her." His voice grew stronger, angrier. "If something like this ever happens again, you will not have to worry about a warrior returning and making sure everyone was dead and the village burned… I will see to it myself. Return to your chores, NOW!"

Everyone hurried to disperse, though whispers of Mistress Leora's bravery continued to be shared.

Finley got to his feet with only a minor struggle.

"You need to send word to Lord Slayer right away," Leora said anxiously.

"Lord Slayer will be notified of the incident," Noble said, intending to do just that, but he was also eager to speak with his wife alone and let her know she was never to do something so foolish again.

"It must be done immediately," Leora insisted.

"Why?" Noble asked, seeing how anxious she had become.

"I know who he searches for... it is my sister Sky."

Chapter Fourteen

Noble thought he would have to pry his wife's hand off her tunic, she gripped it so tightly, but when he reached for her hand, she hurried to take hold of it and to tuck herself firmly against him.

After issuing orders for Finley to dispatch warriors to Clan Ravinsher with a message, Noble walked to the keep with his wife. Silence reigned as they walked, though he knew his wife would have much to say once they reached his solar. For now, she seemed to take comfort planted against him.

Chief ran to Leora, barking, as soon as she entered the Great Hall as if admonishing her for not letting him protect her.

She scooped him up and as if understanding his annoyance, said, "You are too little to do anyone any damage. Once you grow strong, you can protect me."

The pup licked her face before tucking himself in the crook of her arm.

Noble snatched the pup from her hands when they entered his solar. He held him with one hand and pointed to Leora with the other. "Guard her well, Chief, and you will be rewarded."

The pup's head went up and though he intended a strong bark, his size only allowed for a small woof, and after Noble praised him again, he set him on the floor. The pup ran to where Leora sat at the table, his one leg going out from under him, he was in such a hurry, but he righted himself and rushed to curl up on the hem of Leora's garment, his little head up and alert to all around him.

Noble made haste to the table, his hands going around his wife's hand as she lifted the tankard waiting there for her and helped her to raise it to her lips to sip the hot brew, her hands trembled so much.

"I know you are angry with me. I saw the anger flare in your eyes when all was explained," Leora said after her husband took the tankard from her once she had taken several sips. "But many would have died if I had hidden away like a coward."

"Having grown to know you, I would say you never gave it a second thought. You stepped forward without hesitation," he said and sat beside her.

"I had no other option," she insisted.

"My warriors would have—"

"Fought and some would have died and that I could not live with."

"And what if those warriors were the ones who meant to see you dead?" he snapped abruptly.

"Wouldn't they had simply attacked and seen the deed done? Why stop and announce their reason for being there? I understand their roars and why they rushed at the village, it was to intimidate, frighten, so when they stopped and gave the clan a chance to avoid an attack and possible death—"

"It made for an easy surrender," Noble finished.

Leora shook her head and rested her hand on his chest, relieved to feel the strength of his solid muscles beneath his shirt. "I cannot say I did not fear the situation, but I knew your warriors would have never let them take me. Besides, I had to satisfy my curiosity as to what the large warrior wanted with me." She leaned toward him, her hand pressing firmer to his chest as if weighed too heavily with a burden to bear on her own. "He was looking for Sky's affliction and when he did not see it on me, there was nothing left here for him. So, it is Sky who they search for not me, which is why Lord Slayer urgently needs to be made aware of it."

His arm went around her waist, feeling her strength wane. "He will receive the news soon."

"What I don't understand is how do they keep discovering the different things about the woman they search for? First, it was known that the woman was one of the three Murdock sisters: me, Elsie, and Sky. Then it was discovered that the woman had reddish blonde hair, and Elsie, having dark hair, was a target no more. The search then centered on me and Sky since our hair color is similar. Now it is Sky's affliction that marks her. How was any of this information learned?" The answer came to her quickly. "Inherited traits. Hair color. Affliction. One could inherit them, helping to prove the identity of the woman they search for."

"Whether this man claims you are not the woman he searches for makes no difference, extra caution will be taken with you until this puzzling situation can finally be solved."

"You do not trust his claim?"

"I trust nothing about him since he came here with the intention of abducting or killing my wife, either could have been your fate. I will see that that never happens to you. We have a life to build together, wife,

179

and I will let nothing nor anyone stand in our way. Besides, I am growing accustomed to you."

"I missed you as well," she said with a soft smile.

"You missed me?" He shook his head, having sounded like a young lad pleased by a woman's attention. "I did not say I missed you."

"Of course, you did," Leora argued, and to her, sensibly. "You could have only realized you have grown accustomed to me if you missed me."

"Your reasoning is questionable at times."

"Not this time, since I feel the same as you do," she said.

He slipped his other arm around her waist and drew her gently toward him on the bench. "You truly missed me?"

"Aye, surprisingly so," she said, resting against him without even thinking about it. "It felt strange not having you around to talk with, share a meal with—" She stopped abruptly realizing what she was about to say. She missed his touch, the feel of her hand in his, his arms around her waist as they were now, the strength of his body when she leaned against him, and... his lips, not far from hers, reminded her of how very much she would like him to kiss her again.

Noble didn't need to hear what else she had missed. It was easy to see with the way she looked at him longingly or how her body had easily rested against his. She was ripe for kissing, and he was just as eager to taste her once again.

He didn't hesitate, he kissed her.

The strength of his kiss sent tingles racing through her, and she slipped her arms around his neck, wanting to remain tucked tight against him as he devoured her with his kiss. Her body came alive in ways she had never felt before, sending sensations racing through her that grew as his kiss deepened.

When the tip of his tongue glided lightly over her sealed lips, she instinctively opened to him, welcoming him. It was an intimacy she never knew existed but wanted desperately to explore.

She gasped when he ended the kiss suddenly and rested his brow against hers, his chest heaving close to hers.

"We continue this tonight in our bedchamber," he demanded.

"You need not demand it of me," she said a bit breathless. "I look forward to sharing intimacy with you, though I would have never thought it. But surprisingly, and pleasantly so, I enjoy your kisses, though…"

Noble drew his head back when she suddenly stopped talking and watched her brow scrunch.

"Though what?" he asked.

"Since yours is the only kiss that I have ever known, I have nothing to compare it to, though…"

"Another though?" he asked with a twinge of annoyance and did not wait for a reply. "You need not worry about that since I am the only man you will ever kiss."

"Well, that is a logical assumption since you are my husband, though—"

"Not another though, Leora," Noble warned, annoyed at the thought that she would even think of comparing his kiss with another's.

"But you need to know."

"That you want to kiss another man to see if there is a difference in the kiss?" he asked, his tongue snappish.

"Good Lord, never would I want that," she said, squishing her face in disgust.

That made Noble smile.

Leora shook her head. "The thought alone distresses me."

His smile grew a bit more, seeing how his remark had truly troubled her. "I am pleased to hear that, so if you feel that way, what was your other thought you meant to say?"

Her lovely smile proved she was only too glad to tell him. "Though, I am very pleased to have a husband whose kisses thrill me."

Bloody hell, if her words didn't cause his stomach to knot and to give a squeeze to his heart, not to mention the havoc it caused with his arousal he was just getting under control.

He went to tell her he intended to kiss her often, but she spoke before he could.

"I do hope you feel the same since I would like us to kiss often, I do so enjoy your lips on mine."

He brushed his lips over hers. "Your lips are the only lips mine will touch since I never enjoyed a kiss as much as I enjoy kissing you."

Her smile brightened. "You may turn out to be a better husband than I first thought."

"May? You haven't decided yet?" he asked, giving her waist a light squeeze.

Her smile faded some. "We have much yet to learn about each other. And while we do enjoy sharing kisses, there is more to marriage than just kisses. I saw that with my mum and da, and how time can weigh heavily on a marriage. My mum and da were lucky to have known each other and had fallen in love before they wed. I believe that is what sustained their marriage. Our marriage is not built on love and could easily crumble."

"I care about you, more than I expected to, Leora, and you are right when you say we have much to learn about each other before we know how our marriage will work. But know one thing… as fierce a warrior as I am, I am also that fierce in making certain our marriage will not crumble."

Leora was at a loss for words, unusual for her, but she wondered if he meant that there was a chance for them to find love together.

Chief suddenly barked, which was followed by a rap at the door, ending their conversation, and Finley entered after he was granted permission.

"Lance and Bew are ready and eager, and the men are just as eager," Finley said.

"I do this alone," Noble said.

"The men were ready to fight, sir," Finley said, needing Noble to know.

"I have no doubt they were, but they wisely waited and watched, and I know they would have done whatever was necessary to see my wife was kept safe above all else. But this I must do alone."

"Understood," Finley said. "The men will remain ready. Not one of them will sleep tonight."

183

Leora didn't even wait for the door to close behind Finley when she asked, "Where are you going alone? Tell me you are not being foolish and going off on your own to hunt the warriors who were here."

"I am not being foolish," Noble said.

Leora grabbed his arm, her skin prickling with worry. "Do not play games with me. I want the truth just like you would want it from me."

He disliked causing her needless worry, but he had no choice in the matter. "I do what is necessary as a leader of a Gallowglass troop."

She released his arm and jabbed him in the chest. "You cannot kill them all on your own."

He grabbed hold of her finger. "I don't have to kill them all."

A chill ran over Leora, he spoke with such calm confidence, then fear settled over her. "He was a large man, far larger than you."

"Size does not matter, skill does." He let go of her finger and quickly raised his hand to stop her from speaking. "I am not only the leader of a Gallowglass troop, but I am also chieftain of this clan. I cannot let it stand that my clan was attacked, and I or my men did nothing. My honor is at stake, and I will not see it tarnished."

"You said we would finish the kiss in our bedchamber tonight," she said, knowing it sounded foolish but failing to think of anything else to say.

"I still hope to."

Leora asked the dreaded question. "And if you fail to return?"

Noble pulled her to rest against him. "Finley will take you to Lord Slayer. He will keep you safe along with your sister."

She gripped his arm. "Couple with me before you leave so that our marriage is sealed and there is a chance I can get with child." She could see in his eyes he would deny her. "Do not refuse me this."

"I want nothing more than to give you what you ask, but it will only make my task more dangerous, for my mind will not only linger on our first time together, when I must keep a clear mind, but coupling with you will no doubt be most satisfying and rob me of some of my strength."

Leora could not hide her disappointment or her worry. "We cannot have that."

Noble kept her in his arms. "There is a way you can help me."

"Anything I can do," she said eagerly.

"You, wife, are the only person I was unable to track. I had no trouble finding your tracks from when you left the abbey but afterwards, I lost you several times until you disappeared altogether. I need to know how you avoided leaving tracks since at the time you had no idea that I was tracking you."

"Not knowing who was responsible for me and my sisters being imprisoned in the abbey, I worried someone might be sent to track me, so when an opportunity presented itself, I took advantage of it. You must have picked up on the cart tracks that intersected mine."

"Aye, I did and followed those tracks until I picked yours up again. I figured you hitched a ride with a merchant and then left him to go on your own. I lost you again after that. Your tracks were there one minute and gone the next.

"Those tracks you followed from there were not mine," Leora said.

"You have a distinct track from the shoes you wore, and the weight of the footfall was the same. They were your tracks."

She shook her head. "I came upon a camp of traveling performers. I was starving and they had food. They were kind. I was foolish."

"They were thieves," Noble said, knowing full well that most traveling bands of performers were thieves.

"Aye, they were that and told me I had to repay them for the food they gave me before they would let me leave."

"What did they do to you to make you comply?" Noble asked, fearing the worst.

"There were two men and three women. The one man—" Leora stopped, recalling the pain, and cringed. "He landed several good punches at my stomach and several stinging slaps to my face, and he yanked my hair so hard, far too many times, that he nearly pulled some out of my head."

Noble intended to cross paths with the man one day and when he yanked his hair, he most definitely would lose more than some.

She continued. "I heard the men talking when they thought I was asleep. They planned on using me to collect coins either from whoever I was running away from or selling me to a man who paid them for any women they brought to him, whoever offered them more." She shivered. "I never realized what happened to some women who were taken against their will, and I feared such a horrible fate, which made me more aware of the dangers of traveling on my own and the necessity to escape."

"How did that come about?"

"Too much ale provided by traveling monks who lost a barrel of ale for safe passage. They all drank themselves drunk and forgot to tie me up for the night. I fled as soon as they all were snoring. After that I kept to the woods, not venturing near the well-worn paths."

"You were lucky, Leora," Noble said, trying not to think of what her fate could have been and relieved she was now safe in his arms. "Who copied your tracks?"

"The one woman in the group was my size and she liked my shoes. I had no choice but to give them to her. It was the man in charge who warned her that I probably ran away from a husband who no doubt would search for me. He told her to make certain no one tracked them. She was quite talented, spry, and quick. She was able to leap high and hide in the higher tree branches before dropping down on unsuspecting travelers."

"She led me on a merry chase," Noble said, then asked a question that had him worried. "The men did not harm you, did they?"

She shook her head. "Nay, though if I stayed much longer the outcome may have been different."

He hugged her tight and kissed her brow. "That was of great help, wife."

"You are a wise warrior. You must have confronted enemies who dropped down from trees in a surprise attack."

"Aye, but it is the trees that have low-hanging branches that we watch out for, making it easier to pull themselves up and hide among the branches. That was not so when I searched for you, and it was the reason I never gave the trees thought. It might, however, be how Lance was discovered and tracked."

"You will be careful, husband," Leora said with worry. "You will not think about me. You will keep your mind clear and make certain to return home to me unharmed."

To Noble, there had been only one person who truly cared if he returned home... his grandfather. After he had passed, home hadn't mattered. There was no one there any longer who worried about his return, but now that Leora had expressed her concern, he was beginning to feel that he just might have a home after all.

"You can count on it, wife, since I am looking forward to finishing that kiss," he said and was about to kiss her when he was interrupted by news that a message had arrived from Lord Slayer.

Slayer's message was exactly what he expected since how Noble handled the situation would also reflect on Slayer.

Finley delivered the blunt message. "Finish him."

Chapter Fifteen

Noble waited patiently. He had easily found the tracks of the warriors, which meant they felt themselves safe from retaliation. They did not fear anyone following them. Though the leader was confident, he was no fool. He would have his tracker make certain of it. But Noble was no fool himself, and with his wife telling him about the performer climbing trees that did not have low-hanging branches, he kept watch. Sure enough, he spotted him before the tracker had a chance to spot him. He leapt and scaled the tree with an agility Noble had never seen before now. He climbed high and was able to see a good distance in many directions.

Noble waited and watched and the tracker led him straight to the campsite of the troop that had dwindled in size to just five. He hid on the outskirts of the camp and waited for them all to settle for the night.

Part of tracking was also learning how to walk silently so you would not be discovered when following someone or a troop of warriors. Such a skill allowed a tracker to get close enough to hear talk that would reveal important information that could turn the tide of a battle.

Noble had perfected the skill, another thing his grandfather had taught him, and it allowed him to get close enough to hear, though not be seen, what the group discussed.

"You will give us the promised coins, then join the others you sent ahead?"

"Aye, I wanted to make sure our warning was heeded and no one follows us."

"No one follows of that I am certain."

"Good."

"Will he come himself now to finish it?"

"Aye, he will."

"He goes against a vicious warrior and one who has known endless victories."

"That will not stop him."

"He would not bring an army of warriors here, would he?"

"He is too wise to invade. He will find a way to get her, have no doubt about that. You did well and will get what is owed you."

Talk drifted off and Noble waited in the dark woods. He kept focused on the sounds, the scampering of the nocturnal animals, the hoot of the owls, the moans of the nightly breeze, though many believed it was the spirit of those who died or were left to die in the woods. A tracker learned to recognize them all, even the soft melodies the forest spirits sang at night. He often thought that the forest was more alive at night in the dark rather than during the day in the light. He remained alert, listening.

Snores soon joined the forest sounds and Noble continued to keep watch, his eyes growing used to the dark and his surroundings becoming clearer to him. He maintained his patience and his alertness, having existed on little sleep when necessary, and waited for the moment he knew would come. And it did.

It was not long before dawn when the large warrior woke, stretched quietly, and stood. Noble knew what he was about to do, and it made his own task that much easier. The large warrior drew the dagger from the sheath at his waist and squatted down to clamp his hand over the first man's mouth so he could not call out and alert the others as he sliced his throat. He did the same to the others and watched until he was sure all were dead.

"You will feast today, animals," the man called out as he wiped the blood off his dagger on one of the dead man's garments and returned it to its sheath. Then he stretched again and entered the forest looking for a spot to relieve himself. Noble matched each step the warrior took, so his own steps would be muffled. He waited, positioned himself perfectly, and when the warrior yanked back his garment, Noble took a step that the large warrior could hear.

The warrior turned in a flash, his hand reaching for the dagger at his waist but Noble already had his kirk in his hand and sliced the man's throat from ear to ear. The man's hand rushed to his neck, blood running from it, and his eyes went wide knowing death was not far off.

Noble watched as the warrior collapsed, his big body hitting the ground hard and as he lay there, life fading from him, Noble leaned over him and demanded, "Who sent you?"

He tried to speak but couldn't.

Noble knew after watching him kill the men that he was a warrior dedicated to his leader and would reveal no information no matter what was done to him.

Before standing, Noble said, "Gallowglass always have their revenge."

The warrior struggled as he managed to say, "So does he."

He did as the warrior had done, waited to make sure he took his last breath, then he wiped his dagger clean on the warrior's garment. He left the bodies where they lay. As the large man had said, the animals would feast today. He had wondered why the warriors had come on foot and now he knew. No one would be returning but him. The more important question was… who, like the Gallowglass, would have his revenge?

***

Leora stood looking out over the forest, fearing something had happened to her husband and he would not return to her. She had remained awake last night as long as she could, waiting for his return and thinking endlessly about him. Sleep had finally taken control and she woke alone in bed. With no desire for food and leaving Chief in the kitchen to be spoiled with far more food than he needed, she had rushed out of the keep and through the village. Finley followed her as well as several of Noble's warriors.

Finley had shouted for her to stop, but she had ignored him. Her husband was out there somewhere, possibly hurt, or worse, dead, and her heart felt as if it was breaking. Her mum had been right. Love struck when you least expected it and it had to be love she was feeling, why else would she feel as if her heart was being torn apart?

She had realized when she woke that her feelings for her husband had changed, though why they had she couldn't say, and it mattered not to her. She only knew she felt differently about him, and she wanted the chance to explore what she was feeling with him. She wanted a chance to love him.

"What is my wife doing in the woods?"

Hearing her husband's commanding voice, Leora turned, relieved to see him standing not far from her, and instinct had her running to him. She threw herself at him and he caught her in a powerful embrace. Her arms went around his neck, and she hugged him tight, raining endless kisses on his cheeks and lips.

"I feared something had happened to you and you would not return to me," she said after a quick, final kiss.

He saw relief in her lovely green eyes, and he felt a jab at his heart. She had truly worried about him, a sign that she cared for him.

"It took a bit longer than I expected," he said, keeping tight hold of her, though her hold on him let him know she had no intentions of letting go of him.

"You were not harmed?" she asked anxiously.

"Nay, I suffered no harm," he assured her, her sincere concern playing havoc with his heart.

"I am so glad you are home at last," she said and lowered her voice. "I missed you beside me last night."

They had barely shared a bed, though they had shared many nights by the campfire on their journey here and yet she missed him there beside her and again her words touched his heart.

"Mistress Leora insisted on coming to the woods to wait for your return," Finley said, interrupting the moment.

"And you did not stop her?" Noble asked, with a scowl that turned Finley silent.

"It is my fault," Leora said. "You consumed my thoughts and no warning, no command, no force would have stopped me from entering the woods to watch for your return."

"Mistress Leora was tenacious about it," Finley confirmed.

"With so much yet to be settled between us, husband, I did not want to lose you," Leora said in the way of an excuse for her worry.

Noble waved Finley off and the man hurried away.

"I have not slept since yesterday. We should take this discussion to our bedchamber," Noble said.

"Aye, you need sleep."

"I need you more," he whispered before he lowered his lips to hers.

The blow took them both to the ground, Finley covering them with his body, an arrow lodged in the back of his shoulder. Shouts filled the air and warriors rushed around joined by men from the village. Finley was lifted off them and Noble shielded his wife with his body as he brought her to her feet.

"Send someone with speed to Whitehall Abbey and let them know we are in need of a healer immediately and see who can tend Finley until then, and find the archer responsible," Noble ordered and hurried his wife to the keep.

"News needs to spread that I am not the woman who so many search for," Leora said, keeping hold of her husband's arm. "Did you find out anything that might help us discover what this is truly all about? Is a Lowlander responsible for it?"

"There was little time to get information and it was easy to see that the large warrior was not about to divulge anything."

Their attention was diverted when Finley was helped into the Great Hall.

"Brenda, a woman in the village, is learning the healing ways from the nuns at the abbey. Perhaps she can help Finley, at least until the nuns get here," Leora suggested.

The woman was sent for and as much as Noble did not want to leave his wife, he had matters that required his immediate attention since he presently did not have Finley to rely on.

"Go do what you must," Leora said, eager to keep him by her side yet understanding his leadership was presently needed. "I will help Brenda see to Finley and we will have time later together."

"Do not leave the keep," Noble ordered, a scowl warning her to pay heed.

"You have my word," Leora said, having no wont to cause her husband worry and gave his arm a gentle squeeze before leaving his side and going to Finley.

The day turned chaotic and seemed to go on forever, Leora barely having time to see or speak with her husband. Chief had followed her around, staying close and keeping watch on his surroundings until it became too much for the pup and he sought the comfort of the bed, made from a blanket Leora kept ready for him by the hearth.

News was heard now and again from wagging tongues in the village and Leora was not sure how much to believe since words carried from person to person often changed along the way. She was relieved when Penn brought her a direct message from her husband.

"The man responsible for firing the arrow has been found but the wounds he received from trying to escape capture from our warriors are so severe he would not survive travel. Chieftain Noble hopes to reach him before death does."

"How long do you think he will be gone?" Leora asked.

"It depends, mistress, on what is learned," Penn said. "If it is discovered that he is not the only one in the area, then a search will be necessary and that will take time. But worry not, for I remain here to see you are kept safe."

Leora smiled, not wanting to display her worry. "I appreciate that, Penn."

Penn was so taken by her smile that his cheeks flushed red, and in his hurry to leave turned and bumped into Calla. He grabbed hold of her, his barrel-like chest almost sending her reeling. His cheeks flamed even more and after he muttered an apology, Calla smiled gently. His feet couldn't move fast enough as he hurried to escape the uncomfortable moment.

"It seems Penn does not do well around women," Leora said, offering an explanation for Penn's unease.

Calla continued staring after Penn. "I have noticed that the few times I tried to speak with him."

Leora detected a hint of interest not only in Calla's voice but the way she seemed unable to take her eyes off Penn and that she had tried to speak with him a few times had Leora believing the young woman was interested in him.

"Penn is a fine man," Leora said, hoping to help a budding relationship get started.

"Gentle yet strong as well," Calla said, her eyes still on him as he rushed out the door.

"Mistress!" Brenda called out and Leora hurried to the young woman who was tending Finley.

"Pull it out now and sear the wound," Finley insisted. "I need to help the chieftain."

"I am not sure if it is wise to do that," Brenda said. "I believe we should wait until the nuns get here. They will know what to do."

"I have seen enough arrow wounds to know what to do. You pull the arrow, sear the wound, and send them back into battle," Finley said and went to stand as if to prove himself right.

He cringed and would have collapsed if Leora and Brenda had not rushed to grab him and help lower him to sit on the bench.

"You will stay put," Leora ordered sharply.

"A wise command."

Leora turned along with the others to see Mother Abbess as well as Novice Angelica, who had helped Mother Abbess tend her wound when at the abbey.

"We were on our way here when Chieftain Noble's troop came upon us," Mother Abbess said as she and the novice approached Leora. "Removing an arrow without careful examination could lead to death." She looked at Finley. "Do you want to die today?"

Finley shook his head, words eluding him as he stared at the woman, her firm stance, her strong voice, and her nun habit much too intimidating for him to argue with her.

"I always knew you were a wise man, Finley," Mother Abbess said and got to work on his wound.

Leora remained in the keep as she promised her husband she would, going to the dais to sit while Mother Abbess and the novice, as well as Brenda, tended to Finley. Calla stood by in case anything was needed.

So much had happened and continued to happen in such a short time that it was difficult to make sense of it. It was coming on nearly a second moon cycle since she had left her home and started her journey as a married woman. Not that her marriage status mattered at the time, though that had changed. She had come to admire the man she had been forced to wed and her heart was telling her that it was far more than admiration she was feeling for him.

"You look heavy with thought, Leora," Mother Abbess said, joining her at the table on the dais.

"You are done? Finley will do well?" Leora asked anxiously, wondering how long she had been lost in her thoughts.

"Almost. Novice Angelica is more than capable of seeing to what remains and then she will settle him comfortably in his cottage. She will also make sure that he does what he has been told, allowing the wound to heal before he returns to his duties."

Having gotten to know Finley's dedication to Noble, Leora couldn't help but chuckle. "That will not be easy."

Mother Abbess chuckled as well. "I have no worries where that is concerned. Novice Angelica has the voice of an angel and the nature of a commander and while young, she can be quite formidable." She reached over to Leora and laid a gentle hand on her arm. "You smile but behind it I see concern in your eyes. What weighs so heavily on you, my child?"

"I would share with you, but you are a nun and have no experience with what troubles me," Leora said softly.

"I know of marriage woes, since many women come to me with them."

"You would think I would have many of those since this marriage was forced on me and I have debated remaining in it. But marriage to Noble is far different than I expected."

"Why is that?" Mother Abbess asked.

"That is the odd part." Leora shook her head. "I cannot say for sure."

Mother Abbess patted Leora's arm and smiled. "You are falling in love with your husband."

Leora was surprised by her response. "What do you know about love? You are a nun."

Mother Abbess smiled softly. "I am also a woman… a woman who once fell in love."

Leora's brow shot up. "You fell in love?"

Mother Abbess nodded slowly. "I did."

Mother Abbess looked at her as her hand stroked the beautifully craved cross that hung from a rope around her neck. Leora could tell it wasn't her the abbess was seeing… it was a memory. And Leora did not have to think long to realize what must have happened.

"Your da didn't approve of him?" Leora asked.

The past must have faded, for Mother Abbess nodded and her eyes took on more focus. "He was not what my da wanted for me. I sought the comfort of the abbey after my da made it clear he would never approve of such a union. A few months later I learned the man I loved died in battle. My da intended to arrange a marriage for me but I told him I intended to take my vows to the church. I knew deep in my heart that I could never love another man as I loved him, and I could not stand the thought of having another man's arms around me, holding me, kissing me, demanding intimacy of me. I expected my da to argue and order me to return home, but he didn't, and I was relieved. I often think it was my brother, God rest his soul, who had convinced him to let me be. So, I do understand the joy and sadness of love, and that joy still lives in my heart and memories to this day. If you have found love with your husband, don't deny it, Leora. Embrace it and never let go of it."

"How do I know if it is love? I barely know Noble and yet I feel things I have never felt before when I am with him, and I worry endlessly about him when he is gone."

"Love can't be defined with words, Leora, and even feelings can lead you astray—"

"Then how does one know when one is in love?"

"A question that will be pondered until the end of time. For me, I knew instantly, as soon as I saw him, and I saw the same recognition in his eyes when his glance settled on me. It was like being reunited with a missing piece of myself and once together we felt whole."

Leora could only imagine the sorrow and pain the woman must have suffered losing the man she loved, and her heart broke for her.

"Do not waste a moment, Leora," Mother Abbess urged. "If you are lucky enough to have found love, then love him every day you can before it is too late."

***

It was late. Noble hadn't expected to be gone well into the night, but he had learned that the man who had fired the arrow hitting Finley had not been alone. He and Bew had managed to find tracks, far too many of them, and whether it was sheer luck or skill, he didn't know which, but he was relieved to have found the group. Unfortunately, and to Noble's bewilderment, they all were dead.

He wondered over who had killed them. Had Slayer seen it done? Was it another band of mercenaries? Had the troop of Lowlanders reached here already? But most importantly, was his wife still in danger?

Noble dried his chest and arms with his shirt, he had taken off so he could wash himself, as he entered the Great Hall. He had made use of one of the many barrels filled with rainwater to give himself a quick wash, not wanting to smell of sweat and death when he entered his bedchamber. He was exhausted from no sleep and should be ready to drop into bed, and yet...

He wanted nothing more than to couple with his wife. He knew he had the stamina, having found a willing woman after many a day long battle and enjoying a night with one, and a good sound sleep afterwards. This was different though, his wife was a virgin and though he did not think she would be reluctant, she probably would be somewhat hesitant, shy of being naked in front of him since he intended for her to be naked, not half-clothed like some women insisted on.

Patience, he thought as he climbed the stairs. He would need to take it slow, introduce her to what goes on between a man and a woman so she would feel comfortable with it... with him.

He dropped his damp shirt into the basket outside their bedchamber door, raked his fingers through his hair, took a fortifying breath and opened the door.

She stood in her nightdress in front of the low-burning hearth and turned quickly to look at him. His heart slammed against his chest; she looked like a wanton beauty. The red in her hair blazed like fiery flames and fell in a mass of disheveled waves around her head and over her shoulders, the neck ties of her nightdress lay open enough for him to spy the tops of her full breasts and her lips looked ripe for kissing. She stood staring at him, not moving, as if she were frozen in place.

He could see she knew what he intended, and he worried she was frightened. He reminded himself to be patient and he turned and closed the door. When he turned back around, his wife was stripping her night dress off, then she dropped it to the ground and looked as if she was not quite sure what to do next.

Noble didn't hesitate, he started walking toward her, stripping his garments off as he went.

Chapter Sixteen

Noble couldn't take his eyes off his wife as he approached her. She was a rare beauty, her body perfectly sculpted in curves that he ached to touch. The flames in the hearth highlighted the red in her hair, making it appear as if the waves that fell around her face and over her shoulders to skim the tips of her puckered nipples looked to be ablaze, though not as fiery as the blaze of passion in her lovely green eyes.

"I know not what to do," she confessed softly, staying as she was, a bit anxious yet eager to discover the intimacies between a husband and wife.

"I do," he said, and his arm curled around the curve of her waist to draw her against him as he brought his lips down on hers.

His kiss did not demand, it coaxed her to join him in pleasure and she did. But it was not only the kiss she enjoyed but the feeling of his naked body against hers. There was a heat to it that drew her and made her want to explore every part of him, and his hard muscles reminded her of his strength and fierceness. But with the tender yet possessive way his arm remained firm around her waist, there was no doubting he was in command. And that was fine with her since she had no idea what to do, though whether it was passion or curiosity or both, she could not stop herself from stroking his chest. She even dared to let her hand wander over his muscles moving lower and lower until her fingers brushed along a nest of hair.

He halted their kiss, took a calming breath, and met her eyes with his. "Touch me anywhere and everywhere, wife, I welcome it, and know that all of me belongs to you now, just as all of you belongs to me."

His remark left Leora feeling a bit empowered and as he settled his lips on hers once again, she continued exploring him, her hand resting on his manhood briefly before she removed it.

He hurried his lips off hers. "Do not stop. I enjoy your touch."

She slipped her hand over his manhood again, reveling in its size and strength.

"It throbs," she whispered.

"For you," he said, lost in the pleasure of her inquisitive strokes.

"It is so large."

"We will fit perfectly... I will make sure of it."

His fierce confidence had her saying, "I trust you completely, Noble."

Her complete faith in him and her innocent touches had him tilting his head back to release a groan of pleasure as her hand stroked under his manhood to cup his sac and weigh it gently in her hand before giving it a tender squeeze then slipping around his manhood to stroke it once again.

Noble's hand fell off her waist as he took a step back away from her, forcing her hand to slip off his shaft. If he let her continue much longer the night would be over before it began.

"Your turn, wife," he said and scooped her up into his arms and carried her to the bed.

A pleasurable excitement raced through her and she ached with anticipation.

He lowered her down on the bed then moved to hover over her, placing his hands at either side of her head on the mattress and kissing her lightly before saying, "You are nothing like I thought you would be."

Leora ached to touch him again and rested her hand against his chest. "And you, dear husband, are far more than I expected."

Her hand fell away as he kissed her and lowered his body to skim his chest lightly over hers. Her hard nipples teased his chest and fueled the passion that already riddled his body from her intimate touches. He felt her shudder and was pleased she was feeling the same. He added to their mounting passion by moving the tip of his shaft to tease between her legs so she would welcome him when the time came. She surprised him when she spread her legs eagerly welcoming him without hesitation. And while he could easily slip into her and pleasure them both, there was more he wanted to introduce her to first.

Leora gasped when his mouth settled over her nipple, and he rolled his tongue over it and nipped at it playfully.

Never had she known such pleasure existed or how easily she could surrender to it, but she would not deny her body what it craved or deny the pleasure she shared with her husband. She couldn't if she wanted to, her desire was far too strong and her trust in her husband even stronger.

He was gentle with her, though there was a demand in his kisses and his touch that could not be ignored. He was letting her know he was in command, and she did not have to worry about anything but enjoying this time with him.

She gasped as his lips continued to explore her body and his hands joined in as well, touching her in places she herself had never touched and never knew could create such a fiery pleasure within her.

Her hips lifted instinctively when his fingers entered her, shocked by the intimate intrusion and yet finding it igniting her passion even more.

His name slipped from her lips in a gasp. "Noble!"

He moved to suddenly brush his lips across hers. "You are a beautiful woman, Leora, in body, mind, and heart."

People endlessly commented on her beauty but never had anyone, not once, had seen beyond her facial beauty. Never had anyone complimented her mind or seen any beauty in her heart and at that moment she knew without a doubt that...

I love you, Noble.

The words were loud in her head, but they never reached her lips. Did she worry he did not feel the same? Or was she not sure herself?

He kissed her in such a way that it made her feel as if they were sealing something, and they were. Their coupling would seal their vows tying them together forever, and she returned his kiss in kind sealing her fate.

After that Leora was lost in endless touches and kisses until neither could delay any longer.

"I do not want to hurt you, wife," Noble said as he made ready to enter her.

"You won't," Leora assured him far too eager to feel him inside her and she smiled softly. "Though you will cause me more pain if you delay much longer."

"Hold tight," he ordered, and she gripped his arms.

He entered her swiftly, not because he was impatient to do so but because he believed she would feel less pain if he did it quickly. She cried out with pleasure, and he knew he did not have to temper his thrusts. She met every one of them enthusiastically and demandingly.

Leora was not sure what was happening to her, did not know where this overwhelming pleasure would take her, but she was eager to find out. She kept a good grip on her husband's arms, his muscles taut as he held himself slightly above her delivering thrust after exquisite thrust.

She suddenly felt as if she stood on the edge of some high precipice about to fall off into—she screamed her husband's name as she tumbled off the edge into unbelievable pleasure that consumed her body over and over again until she was completely spent, her hands falling away from her husband's arms too weak to grip them.

That was when Noble dropped his head back and let out a groan as he exploded in a pleasure that had him thrusting into his wife until his climax faded and left him with a satisfaction that he never experienced until now.

Noble shuddered one last time, then dropped down to rest on his wife a moment before rolling off her and onto his back.

Leora remained on her back, waiting for her breathing to calm down and she was pleased when his hand reached out to take hold of hers. He felt as she did, wanting to remain connected to each other.

When she had enough breath to talk, she turned on her side to face him, slipping her hand out of his to rest it on his chest. "I had no idea how unbelievably amazing it would feel to couple with you and how I can now envision spending my life with you." She shook her head. "If I did not know any better, I would think you cast a spell on me."

Noble placed his hand over hers, the warmth of her palm seeping into his tired chest muscles and easing them. "Or you spellbound me. Whatever it is between us, I am glad for it, for I too envision a good life with you." He could not prevent himself from yawning as he turned on his side and rested his hand on the curve of her waist. "The beautiful sight of you naked, offering yourself to me without hesitation will live long in my memory, especially when I must go into battle, for it will give me a reason to live and return home to you." He kissed her gently, then turned on his back, a yawn escaping him.

"You need sleep," Leora said.

"Aye," he said, and another yawn escaped him.

Leora sat up and reached for the blanket at the end of the bed to pull over them. She thought he was asleep, his eyes closed, when she finished tucking it around him and went to lie on her back, but his arm hooked around her waist.

"I want to feel you naked against me," he said, his eyes remaining closed as he tucked her against him.

Leora was surprised that his strength hadn't waned with the way he held her firm against his side as if he feared letting go of her. He wanted her there and she wanted to be there beside him, a thought she never expected to have, but found comfort in.

She cuddled against him, knowing like him that tonight would live long in her memory. She recalled what Mother Abbess had said to her about feeling whole when she had discovered love. She had not quite understood what the woman meant, yet now, after coupling with her husband, she could understand that there had been a part of her she had never known was missing. Whole. Complete. Love? She shook her head more confused than ever and closed her eyes, hoping tomorrow would bring clearer thoughts.

***

Leora groaned, the dream so real that she was certain she would soon burst with pleasure and the scent of coupling was strong in her nostrils. Her husband's intense rhythm was demanding, and her passion grew with his every thrust.

"Open your eyes, Leora!"

Her eyes sprang open at her husband's commanding tone. It wasn't a dream. It was real and Leora couldn't have been any more pleased. Her passion soared, seeing him kneeling on the bed between her spread legs, his hands gripping her bottom, holding her firm as he pounded into her.

It wasn't long before she screamed his name that she exploded with pleasure, her husband joining her. He lingered in her for a while before he slipped out of her to drop down on his back beside her. He didn't say a word when he turned, slipped his arm beneath her, and brought her to rest against him when he turned onto his back.

It was a few moments later when he said, "Here is where I want you and here is where you will stay… always."

He was letting her know he wanted her always, could he possibly love her?

***

Leora had a burning question for Mother Abbess the next day, but the woman was busy tending to the many people who sought her healing skills, and she did not want to disturb her. Mother Abbess had been generous in sharing her experience with Leora yesterday about love, but she had failed to ask how a woman knew if the man she loved, loved her in return. How could a woman be sure?

She shook her head, annoyed that she was wasting thoughts and time on questions of love when there were more important matters at hand. She had never gotten to ask her husband what had kept him so long last night. What information had he discovered?

He was gone when she woke this morning and selfishly, she would have preferred he had waited for her to wake before he took his leave. But he was chieftain and had his duties to see to, and no doubt he wanted to see how Finley was doing. She also wanted to discuss with him some thoughts she had on securing the safety of the clan. At least she had not wasted all her thoughts yesterday on love, she had spent some time considering safety precautions that would benefit the clan.

Love, however, had remained a constant question and all else had been forgotten, but not today. Today she would speak to him about a few pressing issues.

Leora leaned down and scooped up Chief, who was waiting patiently by her feet to see where they would go next. "We are off to find, Noble, Chief."

The pup barked as if approving of her decision and licked her face. With food and rest he had improved quickly and learned just as quickly, his head perking up any time her or Noble's name was mentioned, being protective of them both.

Leora smiled and kissed the top of the pup's head. "Sky would love you and be proud of me for looking after you since I was never the animal lover she is and has been since she was young. It is amazing how animals are so trusting with her, but then I always thought they could sense her extremely kind soul and knew she would not harm them."

Chief barked and wiggled to get out of her arms. She placed him on the ground, thinking he needed to see to his duty, but hurried after him when he took off running. People moved out of his way, chuckling as they watched Leora chase after the racing pup.

He was fast and tumbled when he took a turn too sharply, but righted himself quickly enough, and he had Leora nearly breathless when he finally disappeared into one of the barns that housed the horses.

"Now I've got you," she said to herself a bit breathless before entering the barn.

She stopped once inside, the overcast day not providing enough light through the partially open door to see the whole place clearly. Darkness and shadows lingered in spots as did silence, and no horses snorted or stomped their hooves.

"Chief," she called out and heard his puppy bark and a snarl from somewhere deeper in the stable. She stepped further inside. "Come here right now, Chief!" The pup barked again, then whined and she worried that he had somehow gotten himself stuck. "What have you gotten yourself into now?" she said, moving deeper into the stable.

She jumped when the stable door suddenly slammed shut, the dark quietly consuming her. She pressed her hand to her chest, her heart racing, and gave her eyes a chance to adjust to the sudden darkness before making any sudden move. Darker shadows shifted around her, and she turned to walk to the door to hurry and open it, the darkness a bit frightening, but she stopped when she thought she heard a sound. Was someone in here with her or had she imagined the sound.

Chief whined, then let loose with a soulful, puppy howl.

"Chief, what's wrong?" she called out and worried he was hurt.

She hurried forward to find him. Her feet caught on something, and she fell forward and quickly cushioned her head with her arm before it hit the earthen floor.

Chief was at her side licking her face and she was relieved to know he was not hurt.

"I am good, Chief, but we need to leave here," she said a bit dazed and struggled a bit to get to her feet.

Chief agreed bouncing around her as if anxious to leave, but when she went to step forward, he jumped in front of her, barking.

"You see something I don't," Leora said, paying heed to his warning bark. "I probably tripped on a sack that fell over or someone forgot to move."

She eased her foot forward and felt it, but it didn't feel like a sack to her. Curiosity had her wanting to see what had tripped her and she eased her steps to find a way around whatever blocked her path.

"Let's see what tripped me, Chief," she said and when she reached the door, she swung it open so that enough light would fill the stable.

Leora froze, shocked to see the body. It was a woman's body she had tripped over and she was lying face down. She hurried to see who it was, praying the woman was all right.

As soon as she saw the red hair, she called out, "Adele!"

She dropped to the young woman's side and turned her over gently to make sure it was her, though she was confident it was. She gasped, shocked and upset to see that it was Adele and blood covered the front of her garments. Leora feared she was dead and leaned her face close to see if she was breathing. It was a faint breath, but she caught it.

Chief started yapping as she stood and stripped off her tunic, then dropped down beside the young woman again to press the rolled garment against where there was the most blood, unable to see exactly where the wound was located. Her hands were soon covered in blood.

She gave a hasty glance around, something she should have done before going to Adele to make sure no one else was there with them, but then Chief would have barked, alerting her if there was anyone else here.

"We need to get help. Go find Noble, Chief. Go find Noble," she urged the pup. "Go, Chief, Go find Noble," she urged again, not willing to leave the young lass alone, and the pup took off.

Chapter Seventeen

Noble had thought of waking his wife before he left their bed this morning, but she had been sleeping so soundly that he had not wanted to disturb her, especially after having woken her in the night to couple with her again.

He could not get their first time together out of his head. It was the most pleasurable coupling he had ever had, and he looked forward to many more. She had shocked him when she stood naked in front of him and that had pleased him more than she would ever know. It had also soared his desire for her tenfold.

If he didn't stop dwelling on last night, his manhood was soon going to salute him since it was already stirring. He forced his thoughts on Finley as he walked through the village, which had him smiling. He felt for his friend. The first thing he had said to him, in a conspiratorial whisper, was to beg Noble to free him of the commanding novice, a sweet looking lass who was anything but sweet. Noble didn't believe the novice could be that bad, but when she ordered him to leave not long after he arrived, insisting Finley needed to rest, he thought to do as Finley asked. Novice Angelica had turned a stern eye on him and wasted no time in telling him all the things that could go wrong with Finley's wound if he did not rest and heal, death topping the list.

Noble had bowed to the novice's wisdom and Finley's pleading eyes followed him out the door. He had to admit that Finley looked better than he expected and if in battle he would probably be back on the battlefield by now, though if Novice Angelica was there that might prove differently. He wondered if the novice could turn the tide of battle with just one of her stern looks.

Noble turned his head, thinking he heard Chief barking. The pup was young and had yet to grow into his bark. He continued to listen and sure enough he heard the pup's yap. He hurried toward the yapping sound.

When he rounded a cottage, he spotted Chief racing wildly around people, though he skidded to a stop, tumbled over, and righted himself. When he was on his feet, he stayed where he was and barked at Noble.

"Is something wrong with Leora, Chief?" he asked, rushing toward the pup.

The pup barked, turned, and took off.

Noble followed, calling out as he did for some of his warriors to follow him.

The pup kept barking and disappeared into one of the barns. His gut twisted in fear that something had happened to his wife. He was relieved when she suddenly appeared, and he almost came to an abrupt halt seeing her hands soaked with blood, but he didn't. He ran faster toward her.

"Are you hurt?" he called out as he drew near.

"Nay. Nay," she said, shaking her head. "Adele is hurt badly. Send for Mother Abbess."

Noble called out for Mother Abbess to be brought to him and for two warriors to follow him into the barn. He hoped his wife would agree to wait outside since she appeared dazed and his worry for her soared, even more so when she continued shaking her head and as if it cleared away her daze, she hurried toward him before he reached her.

Leora spread her arms wide, not wanting to get any blood on her husband, but desperate to feel his arms around her. He didn't fail her. His arm hitched her around the waist and yanked her against him.

"There is so much blood. At first, I thought she was dead." Leora shuddered. "But there is breath left in her." She rested her face against his chest, the smell of blood heavy in her nostrils, and worry that the young woman would not survive weighing heavily upon her.

Noble felt her body slump a bit in his arms and he ordered gently, "Take a few deep breaths, Leora."

She did as he said, regaining the strength that only moments ago seemed to be slipping away.

"Mistress Leora, what happened to you?" Mother Abbess asked anxiously.

Noble turned and Leora turned with him since he kept her tucked against him, relieved to see Mother Abbess. "A young woman in the barn needs help."

"There is so much blood that I could not tell if she was bleeding from her chest or stomach," Leora said. "Hurry, I will show you."

"Nay, you will remain here with me and let Mother Abbess tend to Adele," Noble ordered.

"Your hands need cleaning if you wish to help me. See to that first, then join me if your husband allows," Mother Abbess said with a slight nod to Noble.

Leora took a deep breath before saying. "I am not one to say please often or to plead, so I strongly request that you allow me to help Mother Abbess."

"After we see to cleaning your hands," he said, realizing Mother Abbess was allowing time for Leora to calm from the shock of finding the young woman.

Leora nodded, knowing her husband would have it no other way and at least he was not refusing her.

Mother Abbess hurried her steps inside the barn, two of Noble's warriors waiting outside, having signaled to him that there was no worry for anyone to enter.

People started gathering to see what was going on.

"Penn," Noble called out, and Penn hurried to him. "See that our warriors keep everyone at a distance."

Penn nodded and began issuing orders to the other warriors, who quickly formed a line to keep people from coming any closer.

Noble took his wife to the rain barrel that sat at the corner of the barn, Chief following close to Leora. He reluctantly released her to scoop up one of the few buckets sitting around the barrel and filled it with the rainwater that had accumulated there. He held the full bucket in front of his wife, and she hurried her hands into the water, scrubbing the blood off them.

Tears threatened her eyes, her heart aching for Adele. "This is my fault. Someone was after me and got the wrong woman."

"It is not your fault," Noble commanded firmly.

"Trouble and death follow me," Leora said, upset and fighting to keep her tears from falling.

"Trouble and death follow the fool who thinks to take you from me. Something that will never happen."

Chief yapped as if in agreement with him.

Her husband spoke with such confidence, and the way the little pup stood ready to protect her eased Leora's worry some.

"Besides, we have no idea why Adele was left bloodied. She could have been providing someone with information about you or the clan and the person decided she was no longer needed. We cannot jump to conclusions."

Leora dried her clean hands on her tunic as her husband tossed the dirty water away and as soon as he dropped the empty bucket to the ground, she reached out for his hand.

Noble's hands took hold of both of her hands, and he glanced over her palms, then turned her hands over and glanced at the back of them as well. Satisfied and relieved they showed no signs of harm, he released them, then took one of her hands in his and curled his hand firmly around it, needing to keep hold of her.

"Are you sure you want to help Mother Abbess?" he asked, thinking death may have claimed Adele by now and though he doubted death was a stranger to Leora, it being part of life in any clan, it still was a disturbing and sorrowful part.

"Aye, I want to do all I can to help her," she said, unable to stop feeling responsible for what happened to Adele no matter what her husband said.

Noble leaned down and scooped Chief up to hand to Leora. "He will not leave your side and I do not want him getting in the way."

Leora tucked Chief in the crook of her arm, and he settled content against her. She remained close to her husband's side as they entered the barn and her stomach roiled seeing the blood on Mother Abbess's hands as she tended to Adele. Novice Angelica had joined her, and they both worked feverishly over the young woman.

"Move out of what little light we have," Mother Abbess ordered. "I will need her moved as soon as I make sure the bleeding has stopped."

"When you are ready let me know and I will see it done," Noble said, as he eased his wife out of the way and studied the scene as he stood there watching.

He was glad Novice Angelica had joined Mother Abbess, no doubt a relief to Finley, and his wife's help wasn't needed. He disliked seeing a tear roll down his wife's cheek, but Chief's small tongue was quick to lick it away, though there was something in her eyes that made him think she was not looking at this scene but a memory of another. And it made him think she had not shared all of what she had gone through after her escape from Dundren Abbey.

He felt she needed rescuing now from whatever memory had control of her and he leaned his head down toward hers and whispered, "Tell me what happened here."

She shook her head briefly before she recalled the incident. "I told Chief we would go and find you and he took off and something brought him here. I didn't see

Adele at first, and then the door shut suddenly, and I thought someone might have entered, but someone could have left," Leora said, just realizing it. "I tripped over her in the dark when I went to search for Chief, worried something might have happened to him since he whined then howled."

Noble's stomach churned hearing that and he looked at the two warriors there. "Why was there no guard watching my wife?"

Leora went to defend the men but the fierce warning scowl her husband turned on her had her holding her tongue.

One warrior offered an excuse, poor as it was. "Finley usually assigns the men."

Noble silently berated himself, his thoughts having lingered far too much on his wife this morning and not spending enough time with Finley discussing what needed to be seen to.

Another warrior spoke up. "I can speak with Finley and see that the guards are assigned daily positions."

"Wise offer, Dyle," Noble said, planning to talk with Finley himself about guard duty and other things he might need to be made aware of since Novice Angelica had prevented him from talking with Finley extensively. Something he would not let happen again.

"What can you tell me about the wound, Mother Abbess?" Noble asked.

"I would say a dagger of some kind," Mother Abbess said without taking her attention away from Adele.

Noble turned quiet, leaving the nun to tend Adele and saw that his wife's glance lingered on the wounded

222

young woman. He wondered what she was seeing and surmising, so he did the same.

Endless questions circled in Leora's head. Could Adele have been meeting someone here? Her garments were not out of place nor were they torn. Could she have been surprised by someone? Would anyone in the kitchen know why she would have been here when she should have been tending to her duties in the kitchen?

"I should go tell Emma and the others in the kitchen before they learn of it from anyone else," Leora said.

Noble had seen the way his wife had studied Adele and he had felt her strength return to her, no longer leaning close to him as she had been doing since entering the barn. He was getting to know her well. She would be concerned for those in the kitchen hearing about Adele, but she was also eager to ask them questions, as was he.

"We will go together," Noble said and turned to his warriors. "Two of you will wait here and do as Mother Abbess instructs. Dyle, go now and speak to Finley and see that his orders are carried out immediately."

Noble barely walked a few steps from the barn when Lance came rushing toward him.

"Do you need me to track anything, sir?" Lance asked.

"I have given it thought, but with so many tracks in the area around the barn, I believe it would be a useless task, but have a look and let me know if you spot anything that might have some worth to it," Noble said.

"He wants to please you because he worries that he failed you and caused the clan to almost be attacked,"

Leora said, watching Lance rush off and drop down in front of the barn to study the ground.

"It was my failure not his. I should have known."

"It is impossible to know everything," she said.

"I lead. I better know or I put my men and now my clan at risk."

Noble… his name suited him so well, Leora thought and placed a restless Chief on the ground.

Chief remained at Leora's side as they walked but when he realized the kitchen was their destination and not the keep, he took off yapping all the way there.

"They give him endless treats. It is no wonder he grows strong so fast," Leora said, watching the pup disappear through the open kitchen door.

"I am glad he has taken to you. He will protect you with his life."

"And I will protect him as well," Leora said, realizing how much the pup had come to mean to her and finally understanding her sister's love of animals, and eager to have Chief meet Sky.

The kitchen staff froze when Noble followed his wife through the door, though not Chief. He was too busy lapping up a bowl of food he'd been given.

Noble spoke before Leora could say anything.

"Where is Adele?" Noble asked.

"Gathering wild onions for supper tonight," Emma said and took a slow step back.

Noble pursued her with questions. "Did she go alone? How long has she been gone? Was she instructed not to waste time?"

Leora saw the alarm on Emma's face and no doubt she worried that something was amiss. But questions had to be asked before the news was delivered, or the shock of Adele's attack might have them too upset to answer.

"Aye, she went alone, sir. She has been gone a while and should be returning soon. Is there anything I can help you with, sir?" Emma asked, a tremor of fright in her voice.

Noble's glance fell on each of them as he asked, "Did Adele say if she was meeting anyone?"

Heads shook except for one plump lass. Her head remained still.

"You, lass," Noble said with a nod at her. "What do you know?"

The lass paled, worry filling her eyes.

"Speak up, you have nothing to fear," Noble urged.

Her hands gripped her apron as she hurried to speak. "I heard her tell Calla that she hoped to see Wendell today."

"Did anyone see Wendell?" Noble asked.

They all shook their heads.

Emma finally got the courage to ask, "Is Adele all right, sir?"

"Unfortunately, she isn't, Emma," Noble said. "Adele was attacked and left badly wounded in one of the barns. She now fights for her life."

"Good Lord," Emma gasped while most cried out in shock and others froze at the terrible news.

"Mother Abbess and the novice are with Adele and doing the best they can to save her life," Leora said, hoping it would help them to know that everything that could be done was being done to help save their friend.

"That is a relief to know, mistress," Emma said through her tears, and the others nodded.

"If any of you recall anything Adele may have said to you this morning or yesterday that you feel may help us find out who did this to her, come to me or Mistress Leora immediately," Noble ordered, knowing they would more likely be willing to talk with Leora than with him.

His hand went to his wife's back to nudge her out of the kitchen, eager to find Calla and discover what she knew. It didn't take a nudge since her steps were quick. Chief, having finished eating, hurried alongside her.

"We need to find Calla," Leora said.

It should no longer amaze him that they thought so much alike, but it did. He never felt such a strong connection to anyone as he did to Leora. It was as if a part of himself that he had not even realized had been missing had returned to him.

"There she is," Leora said with a gentle poke of her elbow at her husband as they entered the Great Hall.

"Calla," Noble called out and she turned and hurried toward them.

Noble intended to seat his wife and himself at the dais to speak with Calla, but his wife thought differently and followed Chief to the table by the hearth. She sat while the pup went and curled up in the bed kept there for him. He noticed she hugged herself as if chilled and realized that what had happened had finally taken its toll on her.

He tossed two logs into the hot embers left in the hearth and it did not take long for them to spark with flames.

"You are chilled, mistress," Calla said when she reached the table. "I will bring you a hot brew."

"Nay," Noble said, stopping her from rushing off. "I wish to speak with you. Have another servant bring a brew for my wife."

"Aye, sir," Calla said and turned, calling out orders to a lass. When she turned back to see that Noble had remained standing, she quickly asked, "Is something wrong, sir?"

Noble had no patience left, he wanted answers. "Adele spoke with you about meeting Wendell today."

Calla didn't hide her surprise. "She hoped he would visit, sir, though she was not certain of it."

"What made her think he would visit with her today?"

"He had not visited her in a while, and she believed he missed her as much she missed him and would find his way here today. It was probably why she volunteered to gather wild onions, a chore she doesn't favor. It would take her into the woods, and she could go to the spot where they usually meet."

"Do you know where that is?" Noble asked.

"Adele never said, sir, but she would tell you if asked."

Hearing her husband's impatience in his short, rapid questions, Leora spoke before he delivered the harsh news too bluntly. "Adele has suffered a heinous attack and fights for her life."

Calla gasped.

"We are trying to find out all we can so we can catch the culprit and see that he pays for what he did," Leora said.

"Adele was so happy when I spoke with her, so sure Wendell would come see her today. She was sure he loved her as much as she loved him."

The servant returned with tears in her eyes and placed a tankard in front of Leora. A jug of ale and a tankard was carried in by another servant who was teary-eyed as well, the sad news beginning to spread.

Seeing that Calla was anxious to leave and go speak with the other servants, Leora dismissed her and was glad her husband didn't object.

Noble sat beside his wife on the bench. "I do not like that the morning brought such sorrow after a night of pure happiness, though the memory will live long in my heart and mind, and I look forward to the memories we have yet to make."

Leora kissed his lips gently. "Words I appreciate hearing from you, and I too will long cherish the memories we made last night, and I am eager for the ones we have yet to make. And as much as I want to dwell only on that, we have a duty to the clan and to Adele to discover what happened."

"I agree and we will, but there is something I need to discover right now."

"What is it? How can I help?' Leora asked eagerly.

"You can tell me where you drifted off to when we were in the barn. You were seeing someone else when you gazed at Adele on the ground, and it has caused even more upset for you."

She turned her head away from him.

Noble eased her head around, with his finger to her chin, to look at him. "Share what troubled you, wife, and free yourself of the disturbing memory."

Leora gripped his forearm, eager to rid herself of the upsetting memory that returned too often. "On my journey home after my escape, not only from the abbey but from the performers as well, I came across three men dead in the woods. They were torn apart and there was blood everywhere. I stood frozen, staring at limbs strewn about. I couldn't tell what happened to them. Had men done such horrible things to the three or had it been wild animals or a combination of both? I never felt so vulnerable, so frightened, so alone. I hid for almost a whole day fearing I would cross paths with the savages that had done that to those men, frightened to death of what my fate might be at their hands. It made me realize the evil that lives among us, and I was determined more than ever to return to the safety of my home. But seeing Adele like that and in her own home made me think that there is no place that is completely safe from evil. That if it wishes to touch you, it will find a way."

"I give you my word that I will never let evil touch you, that I will see you kept safe," Noble said, feeling her fear and knowing its strength since he had put such fear himself into men and women during and after battle.

"I have no doubt you will try, but you cannot be with me all the time and the attacks that have happened, and not just today, prove that." She silenced him before he could speak with a gentle kiss. "I trust completely that you would rescue me if ever necessary. It is my fear that I would not be strong enough to survive until you reach me."

He chuckled. "I believe it would take little time for anyone who abducted you to return you since they would quickly grow tired of your endless questions, arguments, and challenges." He was glad his attempt at humor brought a slight smile to his wife's face. "But seriously, Leora, if I had to go to hell to rescue you, I would go without hesitation. So, know I will always, without a doubt, rescue you and you will remain strong until I do."

"Is that an order?" she asked, the promise she saw in the depths of his blue eyes soothing her soul.

His tone turned commanding. "Aye, it is, wife, and you will obey it without question."

"As will you, if it is ever necessary that I need to rescue you," she said.

That she was serious was obvious and his gut twisted. "Never. Not ever will you jeopardize your life for mine."

He kissed her to diffuse the argument and lingered in it to please them both.

Leora pressed her brow to his when the kiss ended much too quickly for her, and her heart fluttered much too rapidly. She drew her brow off his and stared silently into his deep blue eyes, trying to look deep inside him and see if it was possible to see what was in his heart, for she was sure her heart was filled with love for him.

"Be careful, Leora," Noble warned. "There is a fierceness inside of me you do not want to see."

Leora could not stop herself from asking, "Is there room in there for love?"

His wife's unexpected response had him at a loss for words. Did she wonder if he was capable of loving her, or was she asking if he had room for the love she felt for him?

"Sir!"

Penn's shout had them both turning to see the warrior rushing toward them.

"A young man, Wendell, has arrived and is asking for Adele."

Chapter Eighteen

Noble grabbed Wendell by the arm when his legs looked about to fail him, after being told that Adele was badly wounded. He hurried the young man to sit on the bench at the table where Leora sat.

Wendell shook his head, repeating. "She can't die. She can't die." His words faded and he stopped shaking his head. "We are going to get married and have lots of bairns—" He didn't stop his tears from falling, he let himself cry. "I love Adele so much."

Leora choked back her tears, feeling his pain and realizing the horrible pain she would suffer if she thought Noble was close to death, and it made her think that only love for another could have someone suffer so much.

"I worried when she wasn't at the spot where we usually meet," Wendell said, tears flowing down his cheeks.

"Had you planned to meet there today?" Noble asked.

"It was never certain for me, since my chores changed from time to time, but Adele never failed to go to our appointed place by chance I would be able to meet her. She volunteered on foraging days even though she disliked gathering wild onions because it gave us a chance to be together. When she wasn't there today, I knew something was wrong."

"Had she met anyone else at that spot while waiting for you?" Noble asked.

Wendell shook his head. "Nay, she was careful when in the woods and would hide if she heard footfalls and wait until they passed by. But she always told me she could recognize my footfalls since she was so eager to hear them."

His eyes were filled with worry as well as tears and Leora worried along with him.

"Did you see anyone in the woods on your way here?" Noble asked.

Wendell's head drooped. "Nay, sir, it was quiet."

The way the young man glanced away as he hung his head told Noble he was lying, and he didn't hesitate to confront him on it. "You're lying to me, Wendell."

Leora wasn't surprised by her husband's accusation since she thought the same as soon as Wendell lowered his head.

"You would be wise to tell me," Noble urged.

Wendell raised his head. "I fear Lord Slayer more than I do you, sir."

Noble nodded. "I can understand that, and it is wise that you do, but you will tell me and accept any consequences that comes of it… like the man I am sure Adele believes you are."

"I failed her, sir," Wendell said, fighting not to sob. "I told her I would always protect her, and I did not keep my word."

"You still have a chance not to fail her by telling me all you know so we may find who did this to her and see that he suffers for it," Noble encouraged.

Wendell tried to stem his tears, pressing his sleeve-covered arm against his eyes for a moment. He was somewhat successful, the tears continuing to only trickle from his eyes.

"I watched and learned where Lord Slayer stationed his warriors, so I wouldn't be spotted leaving the clan without permission."

Men and women could be irrational when in love and Wendell was certainly wrong for not obeying clan rules. They were there for a good reason, yet Noble could also understand the risk the young man took for love, and that startled him since he always obeyed Slayer's commands. But the thought of not being able to see Leora would not be something he would tolerate. And that thought had him thinking about when his wife had asked if there was room enough inside him to love? If she had looked a bit deeper, she may have seen what he was feeling for her.

His wife asked what he should have.

"You would want to avoid the sentinels here as well, so no one would report your visits here to Lord Slayer. How then did you avoid the sentinels here?"

Wendell was reluctant to respond.

Noble didn't need his response, he knew. "Adele told you, didn't she."

"Aye, sir," Wendell admitted.

Leora turned a quizzical look on her husband. "But Wendell has not been here in a while so how could Adele—" She stopped speaking abruptly and looked at Wendell. "She snuck over to visit you at Clan Ravinsher, learning where the sentinels were here once we arrived, and you informed her of the ones there, and she kept it all a secret."

"We had to, or we would get in trouble," Wendell confessed.

"That was how she learned to avoid footfalls in the woods, by going to see you," Leora said.

"I didn't like it when she came to see me. I feared for her safety, but we were so desperate to see each other that she insisted on taking the chance," Wendell said and raised his chin some when he looked at Noble. "I was about to speak with Lord Slayer about wedding Adele and making Clan Skirling our home. Adele and I both prefer our home to be here." He wiped away his trickling tears. "Please, sir, please let me see Adele. I want her to know how much I love her so she will fight hard to live so that we get to share a good life together."

"As soon as Mother Abbess permits it, you can see Adele," Noble said. "And when you return home, you will tell Lord Slayer yourself that you have been leaving the clan without permission. Though I would not be at all surprised if he already knows."

Wendell's surprise showed in his wide eyes. "But if Lord Slayer knows, why does he let me continue to do so."

"To see what you're up to, who you may be meeting, what you may be planning, and taking his time in deciding your fate," Noble said.

Wendell paled.

Mother Abbess entered the Great Hall and Wendell hurried to his feet and ran to her, bombarding her with questions about Adele.

"Wendell!" Noble called out firmly.

He turned, his eyes turning wide once again, realizing his actions had been improper. He lowered his head as he approached Noble.

Mother Abbess walked alongside him and spoke in favor of the young man. "He cares deeply for Adele, and I believe it would be wise for him to go and sit with her, hold her hand, let her know he is there, and encourage her to survive."

Wendell kept silent and let his eyes do his pleading.

Mother Abbess continued to speak. "Novice Angelica is tending to Adele. She is needed there more than with Finley, who insists he is fine and needs no fuss made over him. Though it would be wise of him to rest for at least another day or two before resuming his duties."

"I will see that he does and, Wendell," Noble said, turning his attention on the young man and seeing hope gleam in his tear-filled eyes. "You may go sit with Adele. I will send word to Lord Slayer explaining what happened and request that you be allowed to remain here until the issue can be resolved."

"Bless you, sir, bless you," Wendell said, bobbing his head and looking more hopeful.

Wendell rushed from the room as soon as Mother Abbess explained where he could find her.

"Sit and I will have a brew fetched for you," Noble offered.

"I cannot stay. My knowledge of wounds far surpasses any of the nuns here with me. There is much that needs doing if Adele has any chance to survive. I wanted to make you aware of what I know so far."

Mother Abbess paused briefly before she continued. "Adele has not regained consciousness yet, which is far better for her since she would be in tremendous pain if she woke. There is only one wound and, thankfully, it does not go as deep as I feared, and I do believe nothing vital was damaged inside her but only time will confirm that."

"So, she was stabbed only once?" Leora asked.

"Aye, only one wound," Mother Abbess said.

"No wounds elsewhere?" Leora asked.

"I looked but there is only one. Now if that is all I really must return to Adele," Mother Abbess said.

"Keep me apprized," Noble said, and the nun took her leave, and he joined his wife to sit at the table. "I can almost see your thoughts churning."

"Yours must be as well," Leora said, eager to share her thoughts with him. "Adele had no wounds on her arms or hands meaning she didn't try to defend herself, which could also mean that her attacker could have surprised her. But what had taken her to the barn in the first place when she was so eager to get to her secret meeting spot in hopes of seeing Wendell?"

"Or Chief's barks and sudden entrance into the bern could have stopped the attacker from finishing what he started," Noble suggested.

"Or he realized he had the wrong person," Leora scrunched her brow. "But if that was so, and I was the one he intended to find, why not attack me when I entered?"

"Fear the pup's barks had drawn attention or—" Noble turned silent.

"Or what?" Leora asked, impatient to hear what sudden thought had turned him silent.

Noble didn't respond right away, his mind still working on a possibility.

"You have me breathless with anticipation," Leora said, growing more impatient.

Noble lowered his face near hers to whisper, "I would prefer to have you breathless another way."

She gave his lips a faint kiss. "That can be arranged later... if you no longer keep me in suspense."

"You make my thoughts drift, wife," Noble complained and shook his head to clear it. "With how many sentinels I have stationed around, it is unlikely the attacker got past them, which means the attacker is here among us. And that he did not attack you when you entered could mean only one thing—"

"He would be missed if gone too long from his chore," Leora finished. "Let's go find out who may have been missing."

Noble grabbed his wife's arm when she went to stand. "I will not chance your safety on this."

Leora tapped his chest. "Need I remind you that I am a lot safer being with you than without you."

Bloody hell, why did she always have to make sense? How many times had he thought that now? When was he going to accept that his wife not only had a quick mind but a sensible one?

She tapped his chest again. "I can tell by your silence that you realize the wisdom of my words."

"How lucky am I that I have such a wise wife," he said with a touch of sarcasm.

Her smile bordered on a laugh. "I am pleased to see you finally realize it."

He tapped the tip of her nose as he reminded, "I am in command, wife."

She rested her cheek against his and whispered, "I love it when you are in command."

"Bloody hell, Leora!" he scolded, drawing his head back. "You know what those words of yours do to me?"

"I have no idea," she said with playful innocence and slipped her hand between his legs and grinned, feeling his arousal.

He grabbed her hand and tore it off him, though he would have much preferred her hand to remain there, however, now was not the time or place—unfortunately.

"Behave," he ordered.

She frowned. "Is that what you truly want of me?"

He placed her hand on the table, then quickly gave one of her nipples a squeeze.

She gasped and cast a quick glance around the room, grateful no one was there to see his improper behavior, the servants still congregated in the kitchen over the news of Adele.

"What if someone was about to see that?" she scolded. "No one could see what my hand did beneath the table, whereas yours—"

"Play with me, wife, and I play back, so be prepared to accept the consequences of your actions. And nay, I prefer you not behave."

She smiled sweetly. "That is good to know, and I believe I will have no trouble accepting the consequences of my actions."

"I will count on that," he said and gave her a quick kiss. "Now let's go see if we can find if anyone was spotted missing from their chore."

***

Leora slipped quietly out of bed, not wanting to disturb her husband, who was sleeping soundly. Chief's head popped up from where he slept by the hearth, but she gave him a quick pat and told him to go back to sleep and he did. Her mind was jumbled with thoughts that she was trying not only to make sense of but to fit together, preventing her from sleeping. She grabbed her nightdress off the chest near the bed and slipped into it. They had coupled shortly after entering their bedchamber, both eager and needy. Noble had fallen asleep soon after while she remained awake. Knowing sleep would not come soon to her, she decided to seek a spot where she could think. She eased the bedchamber door open slightly, just enough for her to slip past, then left it as it was for her return. She made her way to the bedchamber that was meant for her, but Noble forbade her to sleep anywhere but beside him in *their* bedchamber.

Her bedchamber was dark, and she lit one of the candles from the blazing torch in the sconce on the stone wall outside her door. She used it to light a few other candles in the room and to set the dried logs in the hearth to burn and chase the chill in the room that had her shivering. She did not intend to remain there for the night. She would return to their bedchamber since she did prefer sleeping beside her husband. She simply needed a place to pace and to think.

It had been disappointing to discover that all the prisoners who had been brought there had been accounted for today. Noble's warriors had assured him that the men were watched and never let out of their sights. Did that mean someone in the clan had attacked Adele? Could her attack have had nothing to do with Leora? She had also found out that the troop of men her husband and his warriors had tracked down had been found dead, every one of them. Had the two fractions hunting the reddish blonde-haired woman come to blows? Was she and Sky still being hunted by them? But what of the man who looked at her and knew right away she was not the woman he searched for? Was that someone who was only looking for Sky and had nothing to do with the Lowlanders who searched?

Leora kept pacing in front of the hearth unable to clear her mind. She worried about Sky and when she got a chance she intended to speak with Wendell and see what he could tell her about her sister. But from what she had learned thus far, Sky appeared safe where she was, and until this matter could be resolved, she might be better off remaining at Clan Ravinsher. She just wished she could visit Sky and see for herself how her sister was doing.

Her thoughts drifted back to Adele. The young woman had yet to wake, and the nuns were doing all they could for her. Wendell remained by her side when the nuns permitted. The incident had caused worry in the clan with speculation that someone among them had been the one to attack Adele, leaving everyone suspicious and on edge. It was imperative they discover who attacked Adele and why.

Several tiny barks caught her attention. It seemed that Chief had not gone back to sleep after all. Before she could open the door, it opened, and her husband entered along with Chief, who ran over to her and barked at her as if scolding her for leaving the bedchamber.

"Silent, Chief!" Noble ordered and the pup stopped and plopped down beside Leora.

Her husband hadn't bothered to slip on a stitch of clothing, he was stark naked. He said not a word as he approached her or when he scooped her up in his arms and carried her out of the room. Chief followed along to their bedchamber, where he immediately returned to his bed.

Noble didn't even say a word when he yanked her nightdress off after setting her on her feet next to the bed. He said nothing until he lifted her and dropped her down on the bed and came down over her.

"This is where you belong, and this is where you will stay."

"Do I belong here?" she found herself asking, not only him but herself.

"You are my wife," Noble said as if it explained it.

"Aye, and is it the only reason I sleep beside you?"

He moved off her onto his back. "What is it you ask of me, wife?"

"It does not matter. My mind is chaotic tonight and the reason I sought solitude." She went to turn on her side, thinking herself foolish for proposing a question that he wasn't ready to answer.

Noble turned, his hand settling on the curve of her waist, preventing her from turning away from him. "It matters very much to me. You matter very much to me."

With so many questions languishing, she wanted one, just one answered. Setting her apprehension aside, she asked, "Do you think there will come a time you will ever love me, Noble?"

"Nay."

His quick, blunt response had her feeling as if her heart had shattered into a million pieces.

His hand moved off her waist to grip her jaw. "How can there come a time I will love you when I already love you? It was my fierce love for you that I feared you would see when you attempted to look deep inside me. I worried it would not be returned, worried you could not love me with the same intensity that I love you. But I realize it matters not, for I will love you with a fierceness for the rest of my days whether you love me or not."

He kissed her, leaving no doubt how much he loved her.

She had to tear her lips off his, eager to tell him she felt the same, that she could love him with just as much intensity, but he captured her lips again, preventing her from speaking. His demanding kiss sent her passion soaring, though so had his words. That he loved her made all the difference.

He eased her onto her back with his body and she spread her legs, welcoming him, eager to join with him, eager to make love with her husband, eager to let him know she loved him. But no words were exchanged between them as he settled his manhood inside her. It was a need she felt, and she knew her husband did as well. A need for them to seal their love as they had done with their vows, only this meant so much more. This would truly join them as one and no one could ever break this seal.

Noble never wanted anything so much in his life as he did now, wanting to make love with his wife. Her love was all he needed. She was all he needed. It was but a small moment in time but would last a lifetime within him.

He joined his wife, soaring together in their passion, reaching the precipice together, and tumbling off it together in a shattering climax wrapped in love.

"I love you, Noble," she whispered in his ear as he lay collapsed on top of her.

He raised his head. "You need not say it—"

She pressed her finger to his lips. "I say I love you because it is what I feel in my heart and in my soul. You have become an integral part of me, one I cannot, nor do I want to live without. I have a fierce burning love for you, husband, that will burn forever within me."

He kissed her, then rolled off her taking her with him to rest against him, his arm strong around her. "We were meant for each other, wife. We are much alike, and fate found a way to bring us together."

"And I am forever grateful that fate did."

"As am I," he agreed. "Now tell me what chaotic thoughts keep you from sleeping."

She smiled as she cuddled against him. "They are all gone now."

"I chased them, did I?"

"They fled in fear," she said chuckling.

"Good, now you can sleep comfortably."

"As long as I sleep beside you, I will sleep comfortably," she said and kissed his chest.

"Good then, no more sneaking off to that other bedchamber. I will have the bed removed and you can make it your solar."

"I think the bed should remain."

Noble glared at her.

Leora smiled. "It is a good place for me to deliver our bairns—of which we will have many."

"That I can guarantee you, wife."

Noble remained awake until sleep claimed his wife, which did not take long, only then did he sleep, content she would stay put in his arms.

He did not know how long they had slept when his wife suddenly jolted up in bed and said, "I know how Adele's attacker got here without being seen."

Chapter Nineteen

Noble watched his wife walk through the village, not that she got much walking done, stopping to chat with almost everyone or someone stopping her to chat. It had been weeks since Adele had been attacked, and since his wife had jolted up in bed and told him she knew how the attacker had managed to enter the clan unseen. And damn if it hadn't made the most sense. She told him someone had to have been in the woods and spotted the couple and started watching them and realized they knew how to avoid the sentinels.

He got annoyed he hadn't thought of it right away. It was one of the reasons, when trouble was brewing, that a chieftain or lord forbade anyone to leave the clan without permission. Lance, after much tracking, had proved Leora's theory to be true. He had found tracks that had taken him to a campsite where a small troop of warriors had camped. They were gone now, dispersed in three different directions. Noble had alerted Slayer, and more sentinels were stationed in the area.

The clan was relieved to know the attacker wasn't among them, but they remained alert and ready, knowing it was not over yet. All were pleased that Adele was growing stronger every day, under the watchful and commanding eye of Novice Angelica. Mother Abbess had returned to her duties at the abbey, leaving the novice and another nun to care for Adele. Wendell spent much time with her, and many believed his strong love for her was what helped her to survive.

Adele settled the question as soon as she was able to as to what she was doing in the barn. It was a simple enough explanation. She had gone to fetch a larger basket she had seen there since she had squirreled away some food for her and Wendell to enjoy together. She never reached the basket, hearing a sound and turning to face a shadow and felt a stab to her stomach. The next thing she knew she was waking in her cottage in horrible pain, but she was relieved to see Wendell sitting beside the bed and Mother Abbess hovering over her.

Noble surmised the culprit believed he got his target and feared being caught upon hearing Chief's barks, he hurried off when the chance permitted. Another reason why Lance came upon a cold camp. The mercenaries had left thinking their mission successful.

Noble smiled, seeing Chief tumble over his own feet as he chased the young bairns around, yapping at them. The pup had grown quite a bit, though he was still only a pup, and he forever followed Leora around. He was glad the pup did since he barked if someone got too close to her, though not when Noble did.

Life had become more pleasant with the passing days, the weather proving even more pleasant, the warmth of summer beginning to take hold. He favored being chieftain of a clan, and he was pleased the clan was flourishing under his leadership. Several cottages were close to being completely built with more continuing to be built, fields and gardens were flourishing, sheds were nearly filled to the brim with food, and people were hungry no more.

Noble was also glad his marriage was flourishing. He and Leora talked much, laughed often, and made love almost every night, which meant she would be with child soon, and that filled him with joy. He often thought of having a wife one day, but he had never thought of his wife as someone he would turn to when he needed counsel. He found himself doing that more and more. Surprisingly, even Finley sought her opinion at times. His wife had become an essential part of his leadership, and he often felt blessed that fate had brought them together.

His wife waved when she spotted him and ended her conversation with two women to hurry to him, Chief following at her heels, and she hooked her arm around his when she reached him.

Noble leaned down to steal a quick kiss. "I miss you when you are gone too long from my side."

Chief barked as he wound his way between their legs.

Noble glanced down at the pup. "I missed you too."

She smiled, loving her husband for loving the pup as much as she did. "You read my mind, husband, for I miss you just as much."

Her beautiful smile never failed to lighten his heart and others as well, seeing those around them staring at her. "You steal everyone's heart when you smile."

"There is only one heart that matters to me," she whispered.

"And you already stole that one," he said and began to walk toward the keep with her.

"I didn't steal it, you surrendered it."

"I never surrender, wife."

"There is always a first time."

"How did I know you were going to say that?" he said with a hint of laughter.

"Because you know I am right more times than I am wrong, just as I am right that you are headed to the keep to sneak me to our bedchamber and make love to me."

"Spoken with such confidence."

"Spoken with impatient passion," Leora said. "So, we should hurry… to get there but not hurry once we are in our bedchamber."

"So, it is a slow love making you desire."

"Very much," she said, urging him along with a tug.

"Then I will see you pleasured more than once."

Leora grinned. "I do love how you indulge me, husband."

"Believe me, wife, it is not a chore," he said with a grin of his own.

They both laughed and hurried to the keep, Chief keeping pace with them… until a shout brought them to an abrupt stop.

They turned to see Finley rushing toward them.

249

"The troop of Lowlanders we were warned was headed this way will arrive soon," Finley said. "They arrived far sooner than expected. A mercenary troop is escorting them here."

"All is ready for battle if necessary?" Noble asked.

"Aye, all are prepared, ready to fight if needed," Finley confirmed. "And a troop waits, ready to meet them when they reach a certain point and escort them here the rest of the way. Penn leads them."

"Good, then there should be no problem. I will hear what they have to say and send them on their way," Noble said.

Finley nodded. "I will wait on the outskirts of the village with more men, so they see our strength and it deters any foolish notions."

After Finley departed, Leora's smile faded, leaving concern in its wake. "You should alert Lord Slayer. If I am not the one the Lowlanders search for, they will continue to Clan Ravinsher."

"I do not think they will go there," Noble said. "We have spoken about how when the hunt for a woman who had been given away at birth began, all that was known was that she was one of the three baby girls given to your da and mum. Then it was discovered that it was a woman with reddish blonde hair they searched for, excluding Elsie from the search, and now we have learned that someone searches for a woman with an affliction. It is either one woman who is hunted or two different people hunt for two different women. We will learn which one it is when the Lowlanders arrive. And Slayer probably already knows of the Lowlander's arrival and will await word from me."

250

Leora nodded. "That seems most likely, though if it is two different people who search for two different women, I fear this dilemma will take forever to end."

"It will end here with the Lowlanders, for I will make it known that neither you nor your sister will be going anywhere," Noble said with a fierceness that left no doubt he would have it his way.

Leora stepped closer to her husband. "I have no doubt you have the strength and ability to see it done, but I worry about the consequences it could inflict on the clan."

Noble took his wife in his arms. "The clan is family, wife, and family fights for family no matter the cost, just as you do for Sky." He kissed her quickly. "Though, it turned out far better for you since you got me as a husband."

She laughed. "I cannot argue with the truth. Now I should go and see that food and drink is made ready for our guests since the Lowlanders look upon the Highlanders as savages and I will see them proven wrong."

His deep blue eyes swirled with anger. "If they attempt to take you away from me, they will feel firsthand just how savage a Highlander can be."

***

Leora stood by her husband's side, Chief alert by her leg, as a small troop of Lowlanders and, surprisingly, an elderly woman brought their horses to a stop in front of the keep. Noble had only permitted a handful of Lowlanders to enter the village. The others, along with the small group of mercenaries with them, were made to wait on the outskirts of the village.

One of the Lowlanders helped the elderly woman off her horse.

"Good Lord, it is a relief to finally arrive here," the woman said and walked to stand directly in front of Noble. "I am Lady Elizabeth MacMurray, and I am in need of a hot brew and a soft cushion." She turned to Leora and looked her up and down, her aging eyes finally lingering on Leora's hair. "And you, dear, are the reason I made this dreadful journey. We must talk." She took hold of Leora's arm, leaving her no choice but to help her up the stairs.

Chief let loose with a puppy bark and rushed a few steps ahead of them before plopping down and waiting for them to catch up.

"Be gone with you, you mangy animal," Lady Elizabeth ordered, shooing at the pup with her hand.

Leora stopped on the next step, forcing the older woman to stop as well. "That handsome animal is Chief, my pup. He goes where I go whether anyone likes it or not."

Chief barked as if in agreement and Noble hid his smile, hearing the reprimand in his wife's voice. Lady Elizabeth would learn soon enough that Leora was not one to hold her tongue.

Lady Elizabeth glanced over Leora with an approving smile and said, "As you say, my dear."

When the two women proceeded to climb the stairs, the Lowland warrior went to follow.

Noble stepped in front of him. "You will wait out here."

"Simmons goes where I go," Lady Elizabeth called out.

"Not here, he doesn't," Noble ordered firmly.

Lady Elizabeth turned. "You would deprive an elderly woman her request?"

"That was no request, it was a demand, and I am the only one who demands and commands here," Noble said with authority.

"I know not if I deal with savages," Lady Elizabeth snapped.

Noble's voice turned fierce. "Either do I."

Lady Elizabeth was taken aback and left speechless.

"Come with me, a hot brew awaits, and I will see a cushion brought for you," Leora said to end the confrontation.

Lady Elizabeth stared at Leora as she said, "Proper manners are inbred in the aristocracy, my dear. I am pleased to see you have them."

Leora hurried the woman along, knowing her husband's temper had been more than sparked, it was close to being set ablaze.

Lady Elizabeth was soon settled at the dais, a soft cushion beneath her, a hot brew in hand, and food aplenty on the table, and Chief went to his bed by the hearth and sat, keeping a careful eye on the old woman.

"That man," Lady Elizabeth said but Leora did not let her finish.

"Chieftain Noble, my husband," Leora said.

Silence followed for a few moments before Lady Elizabeth asked, "Your marriage vows have been sealed?"

"Many times over, and she is probably already with child," Noble announced as he approached the dais.

"That doesn't matter," Lady Elizabeth said dismissively. "The child can be raised in the Lowlands and given a good life."

"My wife and child are not going anywhere, and I would kill anyone who attempts to take them from me. Now speak your piece and leave my home!" Noble ordered, furious that the old woman would dare speak such nonsense.

A quiver of fright could be heard in Lady Elizabeth's voice when she spoke. "You would deprive your wife of her inheritance? A fortune awaits her in the Lowlands and a man who would take her as his wife even though she has been touched by a savage."

Noble lunged at the table, gripping the edge, and Chief rushed to his side, growling as ferociously as a small pup could at Lady Elizabeth, and she paled and drew back in fear.

"You will feel the wrath of a savage firsthand if you dare mention taking my wife away from me again," Noble threatened.

The elderly woman regained enough courage to say, "She is my granddaughter, and I will see that she inherits what is rightly hers."

Leora hurried to speak before the confrontation between the two worsened. "How do you know for sure if I am your granddaughter?"

"My only son, only child, Henry, told me on his deathbed that he had gotten a young, noble woman pregnant and refused to wed her since it was nothing more than a minor indiscretion to him. She feared what would happen to her and the child if her father found out. My son knew of a woman who could help her and so he sent her to the woman. He never heard from her again and assumed she chose not to return home. My son's death left me without an heir to a sizeable fortune and estate. I want my blood to inherit it and so I decided to see if I could find the child he had out of wedlock. I was able to find out that it was a granddaughter and that she had reddish blonde hair like her mother."

"You must have another relative who could inherit, a nephew perhaps?" Leora suggested, trying to see any resemblance to the woman but failing to see even a smidgen.

Lady Elizabeth sneered. "A nephew who wishes to rob me blind and see me in an early grave."

"So, he is the one who hired the mercenaries to kill my wife," Noble said, feeling the pieces of the puzzle beginning to connect.

"There have been attempts on your life?" Lady Elizabeth asked, her eyes widening in anger.

"Aye, there have been," Noble confirmed.

"That would be Hedley. He is a weasel and always has been. He has always been jealous of my son Henry. I caught him smiling the day of the funeral. He believed all of what I have will be his. I will see him dead before that." She rested her hand on Leora's. "Don't you see how important it is that you come home and inherit what is rightfully yours?"

"Don't you care to find out if I am truly the granddaughter you search for?" Leora asked.

"You fit all that I have been told of the bairn."

"What is that?" Noble asked and walked around the table to sit in the chair beside his wife, Chief following him to make himself comfortable at Leora's feet.

"My son told me that a few women were helping women deliver bairns who could be in danger if the child's birth was discovered or if they feared for their own life for getting pregnant by someone they shouldn't have. Unfortunately, one of the women was caught and forced to reveal those involved. She managed not to reveal the names right away, giving the other women time to get away and save themselves. One came to the Highlands and continued her work here. I paid dearly to find out that my granddaughter was one of three bairns given to the same family to raise. I discovered Hedley had a spy at my home who told him all of what I had learned and, unfortunately, he managed to hire unscrupulous men to travel to the Highlands before I could gather a troop of Lowland warriors to send here and fetch you for me. I left not long after the troop of Lowlanders with another troop and hired mercenaries along the way. It was a good thing I did since the first troop was attacked and suffered many losses."

"You took a chance with your advanced age traveling here," Noble said, and though the woman was far too commanding, he did admire her courage.

"I may not have the physical strength I once did, but my mind is as keen as ever and so is my determination to have my granddaughter inherit what is rightfully hers."

Noble scowled. "You would be a fool to challenge me."

"I was a fool for making this journey, and yet here I am," Lady Elizabeth said. "And I am not going anywhere without my granddaughter."

"Then welcome to Clan Skirling. A cottage in the village will be your new home."

Lady Elizabeth glared at Noble. "Beware, Highlander, I never fail or surrender to a challenge."

His response was instinctive. "There is always a first time."

"Aye, and you would be wise to remember that," Lady Elizabeth said.

"And you, Lady Elizabeth, would be wise to remember that this is my decision to make," Leora said, and reached out to take hold of her husband's hand. "While I understand your dilemma, you must understand that I love my husband very much and he loves me just as much—"

"More. I love her more, and here is where she stays," Noble interrupted, squeezing her hand while reaffirming his stance that he had no intentions of letting go of his wife.

"Wealth is far greater than love," Lady Elizabeth said, "and with wealth comes power."

"Love has brought me more wealth than you can offer, and I have no need or wont of power," Leora said and saw a flicker of disappointment in the elderly woman's eyes. "No amount of wealth or power would be worth more to me than the love I have for my husband. That will never change. Besides, you do not know if I am truly your granddaughter, and I wonder if you really care."

"You have the courage to question me. That is something I would do," Lady Elizabeth said. "You are a strong woman like me. I will accept the cottage you offer me, for I intend to remain here and prove you are my granddaughter, and when I do, I will petition the King to have you returned home."

"The King's authority is worthless here," Noble said. "And he is not foolish enough to go to war with Highlanders over such a trivial matter."

"Either would the Highlanders," Lady Elizabeth warned. "But we could find a solution if it comes to that, perhaps I can entice you, Chieftain Noble, into accepting a title far more relevant and powerful title than that of Chieftain."

"The Highlands are our home," Noble said, realizing the woman was a wise manipulator and he would have to be far more aware of her words and intentions.

"Home is where you two are," Lady Elizabeth said with a cunning smile.

"And that is here in the Highlands," Leora said, agreeing with her husband. "But tell me, how do you intend to prove I am your granddaughter?"

"By visiting the abbey where I believe you were born and seeing if there is anyone there who can tell me about the unwanted bairns who were delivered there."

"And where is this abbey?" Noble asked, thinking he already knew.

"Not far from here."

"Whitehall Abbey?" Leora asked, not hiding her surprise.

"Aye, that is the one," Lady Elizabeth confirmed with a firm nod.

Chapter Twenty

Noble wanted to speak with his wife privately. Unfortunately, the day continued to be too busy for them to catch any time alone together. With Lady Elizabeth refusing to leave until she could prove Leora was her granddaughter, lodgings had to be made for her and a campsite set up for the troop of men who escorted her here as well as the mercenaries who would not receive further payment until they escorted Lady Elizabeth and her men back to the Lowlands.

"The mercenary group is on edge. They did not know this mission involved the Gallowglass," Finley said, standing beside Noble as they looked over the campsite.

"Good, it will make them think twice before doing anything foolish," Noble said, his glance stern and his arms folded across his chest to let them know that he was in command and that his word ruled.

The mercenaries quickly turned their glances away in haste and after whispered warnings to Lady Elizabeth's troop of men, those men avoided glancing Noble's way as well.

"The old woman must be offering a substantial sum for the mercenaries to tolerate her demanding demeanor," Finley said. "I am surprised that her nephew didn't just offer them more coin to see she never left the Highlands."

"I wondered the same. He probably has no wealth of his own, which is why he is so set on inheriting hers."

Finley turned a concerned look on Noble. "That can make for an extremely dangerous situation. It would mean he is promising the mercenaries coins he does not yet have."

"No doubt he has enough to entice them and has somehow made known the wealth that awaits them if the mission proves successful."

"She must be one wealthy woman," Finley said.

"I am."

Noble and Finley spun around, Finley unable to hide his shock at seeing Lady Elizabeth standing not far from them.

"You keep good control of yourself, Noble, unlike your man there, who cannot hide his surprise on seeing how I approached you both without being heard," Lady Elizabeth said and cast a stern eye on Finley. "You may take your leave. I will talk with Noble alone."

"Chieftain Noble," Finley corrected, scrunching his nose in an annoyed sneer.

"*Lady* Elizabeth," she said, letting him know her status far exceeded Noble's.

"We will talk later, Finley," Noble said to prevent any more discourse between the two.

While Lady Elizabeth took it upon herself to lead them in a walk, Noble noticed that she leaned heavily on him for support. She had to be exhausted from her journey, yet she did not surrender to it. She was one determined woman and that made him think how determined his wife could be and wondered if there could be any truth to Leora being the woman's granddaughter.

"I am no fool, Noble. I know you heard my approach by the way your head tilted slightly, and hearing my meager footfalls you knew I was of no threat. I learned at a young age that it was to my advantage to temper my footfalls, though age is making that more difficult. It helped me to discover things I wasn't meant to know and to prepare for things to come, like a marriage to a foolish and selfish man. If it wasn't for me, Clan MacMurray would not have the wealth it has today and it is the reason I will not see the clan destroyed by a man much like my husband, foolish and selfish."

"I can understand that, Lady Elizabeth, but it will not be at the cost of my marriage," Noble said.

"I never knew the love of a man for a woman nor a husband for a wife, and rarely did I see it in any marriages. So, it surprises me to see it with you and Leora."

Noble was pleased that not only his love for his wife could be seen so easily but also that her love for him was obvious. "You also see how stubborn my wife can be—"

"Much like me."

Noble continued, not wanting to admit the woman was right. "Which means you know Leora will not leave me and go with you."

"Which leaves me no choice but to bring you along and see you granted the title of Lord Noble of Clan MacMurray."

"You waste your breath with such an offer. I am a Highlander as is Leora. The Highlands are in our blood and will be in our children's blood. Leora and I will never leave the Highlands," Noble said with a tone of warning in his voice.

"You would deprive her of wealth and status?" Lady Elizabeth asked with annoyance.

"As Leora told you, all the wealth she needs is here as well as status, for she is wed to an elite and respected Gallowglass warrior."

Lady Elizabeth released a heavy sigh. "My friend warned me how stubborn Highlanders can be."

"Prideful, not stubborn," Noble corrected with a slight smile.

"I do not give up easily," Lady Elizabeth said.

"Defeat is difficult to accept."

"I am not defeated... yet," she snapped and walked away.

Noble knew where she was headed... to speak with Leora. She refused to give up and she was wasting no time in seeing that she got her way. He was eager to hear from his wife what the woman had to say to her and to share what Lady Elizabeth had said to him. He was also eager to get his wife alone so they could talk, among other things, but that would have to wait until later.

He went to find Finley and to further discuss what might need attention with the arrival of their unexpected guests.

***

"Take your leave," Lady Elizabeth snapped upon entering the cottage provided for her and seeing a servant there with Leora.

Chief popped up from where he was sleeping by the hearth and hurried to Leora, snarling at the older woman as he went.

Calla looked at Leora. "You may leave now, Calla, and go see Penn and find out if anything is needed at the campsite and take Chief with you. No doubt he's hungry." She looked down at the pup. "Go with Calla, she will feed you."

Chief didn't hesitate to rush to the door and bark with impatience.

Calla smiled and nodded. "Aye, mistress."

The young woman's smile wasn't for the pup and it warmed Leora's heart to see it. She had been finding ways to bring Calla and Penn together often since Penn, while a fearless Gallowglass warrior, was frightened to death of approaching Calla. And yet, it was obvious he wanted to.

"You should rest after such a strenuous journey," Leora suggested when she turned her attention to Lady Elizabeth after Calla and the pup left, and saw the exhaustion on her face and the slump of her shoulders. "Sit," she ordered and helped the older woman to sit on the bed that had been prepared with clean bedding.

"I am grateful to find that you are not like your father or his father," Lady Elizabeth said, "foolish and selfish, thinking only of themselves and their own desires."

Leora had learned well about manipulation. Her mum had taught her what to watch for and how to spot it and learn how men and women used it time and time again to gain advantage. So, she recognized what Lady Elizabeth was attempting to do... make her believe that she spoke about her father and accept him as such.

"Henry, your father, agreed to the arranged marriage his father and I made for him, but it was a complete failure. He barely paid attention to his wife and after three miscarriages, she refused to allow him in her bed, not that he was in her bed often. He much preferred seeking his pleasure elsewhere. She died not long before he did, and I was making plans for another marriage for him when he took ill. That was when he told me about the possibility of him having a child out of wedlock." She shook her head. "More than one child."

That surprised Leora. "Then why look for me and not the others—" She smiled softly. "You did search for them and since you are here now, I can only assume you found no other child your son had but me."

"I had an extensive search done and after weeding out the liars and reprobates, I found four possibilities. Two had died, leaving you and who you believe is your sister Sky. I ruled her out as soon as I learned of her affliction."

"What if her mum had had such an affliction?" Leora challenged.

Lady Elizabeth dismissed the suggestion with a wave of her hand. My son was a handsome man and would have never touched a woman with such an affliction. Besides, he remembered your mum more clearly than any of the other women and I thought he may have loved her, but he didn't. He enjoyed her because he claimed she was the most beautiful woman he had ever seen, and you, dear Leora, are the most beautiful woman I have ever seen."

"That does not make me your granddaughter," Leora said.

"Not yet, but it brings me a step closer to proving you are," Lady Elizabeth said. "Now I am ready for a meal, which you can have brought here, then I will retire for the evening. A good night's sleep will refresh me so I may go to the abbey tomorrow and see what I can learn."

Leora would see done what the woman commanded and made her way to the keep. She preferred the woman did not join her and Noble for supper and cause more upset than she already had. She, herself, was upset more than she cared to admit. There was no way she would ever leave Noble or the Highlands. Her life was here, her sisters and da were here, and the family she was just beginning to build with Noble was here. All the wealth in the world could not replace what she had here, and she worried that Lady Elizabeth would find a way of taking it all away from her.

The disturbing thought made her even more determined to make sure that would not happen, and Mother Abbess might be able to help with that. She knew her husband would not permit her to go to the abbey tomorrow with Lady Elizabeth, so she intended to send a request for Mother Abbess to come to Clan Skirling. She would not be left out of the talk Lady Elizabeth would have with Mother Abbess. She would hear the truth for herself if the truth could be found, though she worried Lady Elizabeth might not care.

"You're upset."

Leora startled at her husband's voice and welcomed his arm that circled her waist to gently ease her to rest against him. "Bothered more than upset. I wish this was done, settled, so we could get on with our lives. I worry that Lady Elizabeth already believes that I am her granddaughter, whether I am or not. Her need to save her clan comes before the truth, and I am her last chance to see her succeed."

"I thought the same myself," he agreed, feeling her body tense with worry.

"I think it would be best to have Mother Abbess brought here to speak with Lady Elizabeth. I want to hear their conversation for myself, and I know for safety's sake you will not permit me to go to the abbey."

"You are right. I won't permit you to go to the abbey, which is why I sent a message to Mother Abbess requesting her presence."

Leora smiled and rested her hand on her husband's chest. "You know me too well."

"I want to know you even better," he said and winked, "in more ways than one." Her smile faded and he was quick to ask, "I said something that upset you?"

She shook her head gently. "Nay, I was thinking how I never expected to have a husband who I could talk with so freely, so openly, and who I could trust so unconditionally."

"I never expected the same of a wife. I look forward to talking with you each and every day, to hear your opinion on matters, to consider your wise suggestions, to offer counsel when I don't realize I need it, and to see your love for me shine so brightly in your eyes."

She kept her voice to a whisper as if what she was about to say was a secret kept between them. "We truly have fallen madly in love with each other."

Noble smiled and kissed her brow. "That we have, wife, that we have. I would love to rush you off to our bedchamber and spend the rest of the day there with you but—"

Leora sighed, disappointed that that was not about to happen. "But there is too much for the both of us to see to."

"We will retire early tonight," he said in way of compensation.

"I look forward to our time alone together," she said and cringed upon hearing her husband's name shouted. "You are needed."

"Am I?" he whispered.

Leora's eyes met his and she smiled softly. "I am in need of you more than I believe is proper and I love you more than I thought possible."

He kissed her gently. "I need you more and I love you more."

She chuckled softly. "We are a needy pair."

"A perfect pair, wife." Noble kissed her again. "Until later."

His reluctance to leave her coupled with hers, overwhelmed her and she turned away, tears springing up in her eyes. Whatever was the matter with her? There was no reason for her to tear up at his departure. He had his duties to see to and she had hers. She would see him—she was suddenly swept up into a tight hug.

"What's wrong? Why are there tears in your eyes?" Noble demanded but didn't wait for an answer. He scooped her up in his arms and carried her into the keep and straight into his solar.

"You have your duties to see to," she reminded after he kicked the door closed with his foot.

"Aye, you. Now you will tell me what is wrong. Are you not feeling well?"

She was truthful with him. "You leaving my side upset me, though I don't know why since it is a common thing you do, and it should not have bothered me. It was foolish and how did you know I grew teary-eyed when I had turned away from you?"

"It is for that very reason I knew. You never turn away until I am almost out of your sight and when I turned to see you as I usually do and saw you had already turned away and your shoulders were slumped, I knew something was amiss." He walked to a bench and sat, settling her on his lap.

She rested her brow to his. "It must be Lady Elizabeth's arrival and talk of me leaving you and the Highlands that is disturbing me. Even though I know it will never happen, the thought alone frightens me."

He captured her lips in a strong kiss and Leora realized how hungry she was for him and returned the kiss, fearing it wouldn't be enough.

And it wasn't. When he ended the kiss, she whispered, "I have a hungry need for you, husband, a need to join with you, become one with you, and know nothing or anyone, not now… nor ever, can separate us."

"As always our thoughts are one," he said and stood, walked to the table with her in his arms, and gently placed her to lie down on it.

He took hold of her hips and pulled her bottom to the edge of the table, shoved her garments out of the way, her legs spreading open to welcome him. He pushed his plaid aside and entered her swiftly, her legs hugging his waist as he leaned down over her bracing his hands on the table at the sides of her head.

"Hold on, wife," he ordered, and her hands gripped his taut arms.

She expected it to be fast, over and done since they had duties to see to, but this duty presently took priority. The hard rhythm he set sent a wicked passion racing through her that had her moaning with pleasure and had her urging, "Don't stop. Please don't stop, Noble."

He continued pounding into her and though her pleasure built, she still wanted more and continued to plead with him not to stop. She gasped when he suddenly stopped and withdrew from her, but in the next instant his arm went beneath her waist and he flipped her over and bent her over the edge of the table, shoving her garments out of the way.

"Grab the table's edge. You are going to need something to hold on to," he ordered.

She stretched her arms out and gripped the edge, crying out with delight as he entered her and drove in and out of her with a fierceness that took her pleasure to new heights.

Her passionate moans heightened his own desire that felt completely out of control. His need to give her what she desired overwhelmed him, for he needed it as much as she did. He wanted to feel them locked together, joined as one, forever in love, never to be parted.

"Noble!" she cried out, letting him know she was close, ready to erupt in pleasure.

"You're mine. You will always be mine," he said with a powerful passion and with several hard thrusts sent her tumbling off the edge to follow soon after.

Leora's face scrunched as she cried out, exploding in a fiery passion that consumed every part of her and it flared again when her husband roared with his own release. The ripples of pleasure seemed never-ending and she basked in every exquisite ripple.

Noble dropped down over her, pressed his cheek to hers and with labored breath said, "Damn if I don't love you beyond reason, wife."

Leora smiled, feeling far happier than she ever felt.

The door rattled with a knock and Finley shouted. "You are needed, Noble."

"A moment," Noble called out.

"I will be in the Great Hall."

Noble eased off his wife, adjusted his plaid, then her garment, running his hand over her naked backside as he did, relishing the feel of her warm flesh, then hurried his hands to her waist and eased her up off the table and into his arms.

"I wish I did not have to leave you so soon after coupling with you," he said.

"Nonsense. You put me first and gave me what I needed, indulging me yet again.," she said with a smile. "Now you must see to your duties as chieftain."

"I love indulging you," he said and gave her a quick kiss before releasing her and heading to the door.

"Good. Keep that in mind, for I may need more indulging later tonight," she said with a teasing smile, and his laughter followed him out the door.

Leora took a few moments for herself in the blessed silence to think. With so much going on and falling in love with her husband, she had had no thoughts for her sisters or da. That was not true. She did think about them but not as frequently as she had done since her arrival here. She had had such grand plans to go see her sister for herself even if it had meant sneaking off and journeying through the woods alone. But reason had made her see the foolishness of such a thought and learning how well-protected Sky was with Lord Slayer, she had realized her sister was safe where she was for now. Eventually, Noble would take her to see Sky and arrangements could be made for her return home.

She did not have to worry about Elsie. She was safe with Cavell, and he loved her. And as for her da, he had been doing well when she had left home and would only get better with Elsie's loving care. It seemed the time had come to have their own families and live their own lives just as their mum had told them they one day would do, except for Sky.

Though their mum always believed that a good man would find Sky and be unable to resist her loving and unselfish heart. She hoped her mum was right. She hoped her sister Sky would find love.

Chapter Twenty-one

"I have been waiting three days for Mother Abbess," Lady Elizabeth said, her arms crossed over her chest. "And I am tired of waiting. I will go to the abbey and talk to anyone there that may be able to help me."

"Mother Abbess was sent word to come directly to Clan Skirling when her task was done. You may miss her if you go to the abbey," Noble said, the three days the old woman had been there feeling more like three moon cycles with her demanding ways and constant questions. Thinking the respite her absence would bring had him adding, "But if you want to go, I will not stop you."

"You have no right to stop me. I will go where I please," Lady Elizabeth said with a sharp lift of her chin.

"Then go," Noble said and turned and walked away from her before he put her on a horse himself.

Chief ran at him yapping and tumbled over his own legs as he did but righted himself fast enough as usual, jumping around him in joy when he reached him.

"I worry he will not grow into those legs of his, he tumbles over himself so much," Leora said, worry creasing her brow as she stopped in front of her husband.

"Chief will do fine, worry not. We all find our footing eventually," he said, bending down to give her a quick kiss.

"Do we?" Leora asked, thinking about her sister Sky. How does one do that when given a burden to bear? The thought had her asking, "Any word from Lord Slayer since his last message?"

"Nay, he is aware of the Lowlanders arrival and the demands Lady Elizabeth is making and offers any support I need, but we agree that it is someone else entirely who searches for Sky. He will keep us apprized and let me know when we can visit."

"I hope it is soon," Leora said, worry growing heavier in her scrunched brow. "I will feel better when I can see Sky and know for myself that all is well with her and, when safe, make arrangements for her return home."

"Sir! Sir, forgive my interruption," Wendell said, running toward Noble, wearing a wide smile. He stopped a short distance from him and leaned over, his hands on his thighs while he caught his breath. He straightened up suddenly, a smile on his face. "I heard and I had to thank you, let you know how very grateful I am, and to tell you that I will serve Clan Skirling well."

"It is Lord Slayer you should be grateful to," Noble said. "It is only because of his consent that you can call Clan Skirling your new home."

"Aye, sir, I am grateful to Lord Slayer as well, truly I am," Wendell said with a tremble.

Leora stepped forward. "You fear Lord Slayer so much that you quiver when you speak his name?"

"There are not many who don't quiver when his name is mentioned, mistress," Wendell said. "He is a powerful warrior."

"You have duties. Go see to them," Noble ordered, knowing such reference would only make his wife worry more about her sister.

"A moment," Leora said. "How is Adele doing? She looked quite well when I saw her two days ago."

Wendell's wide smile returned. "Adele is doing well, mistress. She still must rest, and Novice Angelica warned that she is still not allowed to lift anything, and it will be a few more weeks before she can return to her kitchen chores. But that is all right, Emma says I do Adele's chores well enough and without complaint. I do my own as well. Atworth is teaching me how to fashion weapons and I quite enjoy it."

"Then go and see to your chores," Noble ordered again.

"Aye, sir, and thank you again, sir," Wendell said and hurried off.

Leora tilted her head and turned a questioning look on her husband. "It is obvious that Wendell is relieved not to be living at Clan Ravinsher any longer. Is it not a pleasant place?" Leora asked, thinking she had been too quick to assume her sister was doing well there.

"I have seen no discontent when I have been there," Noble said.

"Wendell obviously fears Lord Slayer," she said and turned at the sound of Chief yapping to see him chasing after a small group of young, squealing bairns with delight.

"He should be, he disobeyed him."

"And yet Lord Slayer allowed him to remain here," she reminded.

"A wise decision on his part."

"How so?" she asked, curious as to why he would believe that.

"He rids himself of someone he cannot trust, someone who does not obey rules, someone who could put his clan in jeopardy for failure to obey him."

Leora got upset upon hearing that. "Has he no heart?"

"A question many ask," Noble said, "but he never questions his duties and seeing your sister safe would be a priority for him. But worry not about that, we have reason to rejoice." He smiled.

Leora looked puzzled. "Why is that?'

"Lady Elizabeth decided to go to Whitehall Abbey and see what she can learn there. We are free of her for a while."

"That is nonsense. Mother Abbess will come here. There is no reason for her to go there. You need to stop her. It could prove dangerous for her," Leora insisted.

"She will not listen to me, and I cannot stop her. Besides, I do not care if she leaves. She is annoying. I wish her departure was permanent," Noble argued, wanting to be rid of the woman.

"Annoying or not, she is not familiar with the Highlands, and can she truly trust the mercenaries?"

"What does it matter to you?"

"I feel sorry for her. She has no family left. She is all alone and fighting for her clan. We should at least respect her for that."

Noble leaned his head down and kept his voice low and touched with a hint of annoyance. "Do not tell me you believe her foolish tale about you being her granddaughter."

Leora rested her hand on his arm, for comfort or in need of his strength, she wasn't sure. She only knew she needed to touch him and feel she was part of him.

"I don't know what to believe anymore," she said. "I believed I was part of my parents and my sisters, only to find out I am not. Their blood does not run through me, and I wonder who my true parents might be. Who I truly am. I suppose that makes me curious to know for sure if I am or am not Lady Elizabeth's granddaughter." She shook her head before Noble could speak. "I am not leaving you or the Highlands no matter what is discovered about my birth. My heart would shatter if we were ever separated, and I cannot live in any other place but the Highlands. Whether in my blood or not, the Highlands is my home."

Noble eased his arm around his wife. "I am selfish, my only thought was of myself and not wanting to lose you. I never gave thought to how this news might make you feel or knowing the parents who raised you and loved you are not your true parents." He gave her waist a gentle squeeze. "That would have been something I would not have minded hearing about my own parents." His teasing got the response he wanted... his wife chuckled. "We will do what we can to find out the truth."

"I truly appreciate that, husband, and hopefully, Mother Abbess can shed some light on the problem," she said, pleased she could count on her husband's help, but then he had been helpful from the beginning even if she had not realized it until now.

"I will go stop Lady Elizabeth from leaving."

"You told me you couldn't stop her," she said with a slight grin, knowing full well he could if he wanted to.

"My clan. My rules," he said with a wide grin.

"I thought you might say that, so I believe it would be better for you and Lady Elizabeth if I talk with her," Leora suggested, already imagining the altercation that would take place if her husband forbade the woman to take her leave.

"I will not argue with you over that," Noble said with relief. He had no desire to spar with the old woman yet again.

Leora kissed him lightly. "Please keep Chief with you. Lady Elizabeth is not a dog lover and Chief does not tolerate her well."

"Chief is one wise animal," Noble said and watched the pup stumble over his feet once again but right himself quickly and continue to play with the bairns.

Leora went to walk away, but her husband's arm remained hooked around her waist.

"You call what you gave me a kiss, wife?" he asked, a spark of passion flaring in his eyes, which sparked even more when she turned a smile on him that poked at his heart.

She leaned close to his face to whisper, "My light kiss was meant to tease and be a promise of things to come, for if I kissed you any more than I did, I would grow wetter for you than I already am."

She hurried, with reluctance, to step away from him, knowing what consequences her words would bring.

"I will find you when you are done with the old woman, then you are mine… mine and mine alone."

She shivered at the strength in his command, for it meant he would see it done and she could not wait. She hoisted the hem of her garments to make it easier to hurry her pace and ran to find Lady Elizabeth.

Leora reached the woman just in time, a troop of Lowlanders already to ride.

"You cannot go," Leora called out to stop Lady Elizabeth from mounting her horse.

The older woman turned, her face pinched with annoyance. "I am tired of waiting. I want answers now."

"A day or two more will not matter," Leora argued, then thought of something that might deter the woman. "There is a novice here from the abbey. Why don't we speak with her and see if she knows of anything of the past at the abbey. Nuns do talk among themselves, and an older nun may have spoken to her about what went on at the abbey years ago. Besides," —she pointed to the dark clouds overhead— "the sky does not look promising, and you do not want to get caught in the rain. It could bring on an illness and have you stuck in the Highlands longer than you anticipated."

Lady Elizabeth shivered at the thought. "I will talk to this novice, but I will not rule out visiting the abbey, though it will not be today." She held out her arm to Leora.

Leora wrapped her arm around the older woman's and walked at a tempered pace with her.

"You have a wise mind like mine, and you do not fear speaking your mind. I am impressed that you express your opinion so freely to your husband, even though he is a mighty warrior. I am also impressed that he considers your opinions and does not reprimand you for speaking when and how you wish. The more I learn about you, the more I realize you are much like me," Lady Elizabeth said. "Though I am pleased to see that you have a far better husband than I did and that you are not selfish, reprobate like your father. No matter how hard I worked to deter him, Henry followed in his father's footsteps, to my great disappointment. It would be a great relief to me to have a strong granddaughter to replace me and see that Clan MacMurray continued to thrive and remain strong and prosperous."

Leora was well aware that the woman continued to convince and manipulate her into believing she was the granddaughter she searched for, even if it was not the truth. She would not remind the woman again that she would not be returning to the Lowlands with her no matter the outcome of her search.

As they neared Adele's cottage, where novice Angelica could be found, Leora spotted her outside hanging freshly washed sheets on a low-hanging tree branch to dry.

"May I be of help, Mistress Leora," Novice Angelica asked when Leora was not far from her.

"I have questions for you about the abbey," Lady Elizabeth called out even though they were close enough to be heard without her raising her voice.

Novice Angelica folded her arms across her chest and asked, "And what interest do you have in the abbey, my lady?"

"You do not question my interest. You provide me with answers," Lady Elizabeth reprimanded.

"I beg your pardon, my lady, but you are not a patron of Whitehall Abbey and, therefore, I am not obligated to answer any of your questions, according to the rules of the abbey. Unless, of course, our patron permits it."

"And who is this patron?" Lady Elizabeth demanded.

"Lord Slayer of Clan Ravinsher, leader of the largest troop of Gallowglass warriors in the Highlands," Novice Angelica said with pride.

"Is that supposed to frighten me?" Lady Elizabeth asked, unfazed by the announcement.

As if it was simply a fact, Novice Angelica said, "It would be wise of you to."

Leora was all too familiar with how commanding Novice Angelica could be and she hurried to jump in before a battle of wits broke out between the two women. "Lady Elizabeth is interested in the abbey's past when unwanted bairns were delivered there. We were hoping you might know something about that time."

"That was far before I came along," Novice Angelica said.

"There must be many a tale about that time the nuns share," Lady Elizabeth said.

"We do not gossip," Novice Angelica said.

"I am not looking for gossip. I am looking for facts," Lady Elizabeth snapped impatiently.

"Facts I can offer you," Novice Angelica said. "It is no secret that many unwanted bairns were brought to Whitehall Abbey and parents found for them."

"I was told the bairns were delivered there," Lady Elizabeth said.

"Then you were given a false fact," Novice Angelica said. "The abbey was much smaller years ago than it is today and there would have been little room to house expectant mums and their bairns and insufficient food to feed them. Whitehall Abbey was simply a waiting place for the bairns until their prospective parents could collect them."

"Are you saying that Whitehall Abbey contains no vital information about the bairns? Their birthplaces? Their true parents?" Lady Elizabeth asked, the news upsetting her.

"There are no such records at the abbey, and I would know since I tend to the abbey's present records and also the archived ones," Novice Angelica said.

"It is ludicrous to believe the abbey would keep no records of the bairns brought there," Lady Elizabeth insisted.

"Actually, it would be wise of the abbey to do so," Leora said. "The bairns who passed through the abbey needed to be protected, keeping records would have offered them no protection."

Lady Elizabeth continued to disagree. "I understand that, but many churches and institutions keep secret documents mostly to protect themselves. I do not believe that whoever the abbess was at that time would not have thought the same and kept records somewhere."

Leora was about to respond when Chief's frantic yapping caught her attention and she turned to see the pup and her husband rushing toward her.

"TAKE COVER!" Noble shouted, as warriors came rushing from all around the village toward the woods just beyond Adele's cottage.

Leora turned and saw the first line of archers, their bows raised, their arrows ready to fly, and all were pointed at where she and Lady Elizabeth stood.

"Get in the cottage!" Leora screamed and hurried to shield Lady Elizabeth as she urged the old woman toward the door.

Novice Angelica reached the door first, shoving it open and turning to grab Lady Elizabeth's arm and yank her in. Leora shoved her from behind and nearly made it through the door when she heard something hit the doorframe then felt a sting to her backside as she stumbled into the cottage.

***

"Go to Leora now, Chief!" Noble commanded, seeing the door close behind his wife after she stumbled while rushing into the cottage, and the pup took off.

With so many arrows flying at the three women, it was easy to surmise that his wife and possibly Lady Elizabeth were the targets. He was impatient to run to his wife and make sure she hadn't been wounded, but he needed to quell the attack before he did that. He was relieved to see the door open to let Chief inside and his wife wave to him. Seeing her allowed him to put aside his worries for her and see a quick end brought to the attack. He had sensed something was wrong, an unease that had far too many birds taking flight in the woods closest to the village. He had sent Lance and Bew to see what they could find, and they had confirmed what he had suspected when they both came running to let him know that a troop of archers was in the woods and had killed two sentinels and were about to hit the village.

Noble had the word spread throughout the village of an immediate attack instead of sounding an alarm so that his warriors could reach the woods and attack the troop from behind. Unfortunately, they were unable to stop the first barrage of arrows, but they were able to make it be the last barrage of arrows.

"All but three are dead," Finley said, specks of blood on his face. "The fight was quick, the archers unprepared to face Gallowglass warriors. I don't think the troop of archers were native to the area."

"Not native to the area and unprepared can mean only one thing… they had not been told who it was they were hired to attack. They paid a dear price for their ignorance," Noble said and looked to where the three surviving archers were having their hands tied behind their backs and forced to kneel.

"They did, which means they may be more than willing to talk. I will wait with the captives while you go speak with your wife," Finley said.

"You surmise I will speak to my wife first before questioning the captives?" Noble asked, which, of course, he intended to do, but he was surprised Finley had known his intentions.

Finley shrugged. "Mistress Leora would be at your side by now if something wasn't stopping her."

"I see I am not the only one who has gotten to know my wife," Noble said.

"Mistress Leora has made herself known to everyone throughout the clan and our warriors. There isn't a person here who doesn't return her smile. Even that cranky old man who does nothing but complain smiles when he sees your wife and stops to talk with her when he barely says two words to anyone else." Finley lowered his voice. "That is why Mistress Leora cannot be the granddaughter of that cranky old woman, she is far too pleasant."

Noble had to smile. "You have a point there, Finley. Leora took shelter in Adele's cottage with Lady Elizabeth, so I believe all is well with her. As soon as I make sure, I will return here to speak with the captives."

It was with a hasty pace Noble left Finley. He was glad Finley had shared his thoughts on the unlikelihood of Leora being Lady Elizabeth's granddaughter. It made him feel more confident that Leora was no relationship to the cranky woman.

He hurried to Adele's cottage, confident that Leora was busy calming Lady Elizabeth and did not bother to knock on the door. He flung it open, and his heart slammed against his chest, and his eyes rounded in shock. His wife was bent over the small table, her garments hiked up onto her back and her backside red with blood that ran down her leg.

"What are you doing? Go away! Go away now!" Lady Elizabeth screeched and slammed the door in his face.

Chapter Twenty-two

Fury replaced the shock that had gripped Noble, and he kicked the door open and stepped inside and with an anger that permeated the small room, he ordered, "Get out!"

Lady Elizabeth spoke up with a tremor in her voice. "This is most inappropriate."

"Another word from you and it will be your last," Noble warned with controlled fury.

Novice Angelica hurried to take hold of Lady Elizabeth's arm and rushed her out the door. Chief didn't move from where he sat near Leora.

"Do not dare move!" Noble ordered when his wife was about to stand.

His angry command stilled her as well as sending a chill through her. She had seen anger swirl in his deep blue eyes on occasion but what she saw now in his eyes appeared more of a raging storm about to break loose.

"It is nothing more than a minor and inconvenient wound," she said, hoping to quell his anger as he approached her.

"That's a lot of blood on your backside and running down your leg," he said as he stopped just behind her and pressed his hand on her lower back when she went to get up. "I told you not to move."

Leora did not bother to argue since she knew it would do her little good. She let herself relax, releasing a soft sigh as she balanced herself on her elbows and kept her head turned toward him as best as she could, from the position she was in, while she spoke with him. "There is not as much blood as there appears to be. It is because water mixes with the blood. Novice Angelica was cleaning the wound when you entered unannounced."

"I do not need to announce myself anywhere in the clan, I am chieftain," he said, snatching up a clean cloth and gently wiping her backside dry to get a better look at the wound.

Anger lingered in his voice but had quelled some and Leora hoped to quell it more. "I believe the arrow hit the cottage, then grazed me, my garments and my quick response to your command preventing a far worse wound."

His hand followed where the cloth had been, and his intimate touch sent a slight shiver through her.

"Novice Angelica believes a thick coating of honey should seal it well enough, though she did warn that sitting might prove uncomfortable for a day or so." She shut her eyes tight trying to ignore his hand gently stroking her backside. His touch, one of concern, still managed to spark her desire for him, and if he didn't stop soon…

"Keep touching me like that and you will soon need to satisfy the passion you are fast igniting in me," she warned, and his hand fell off her, to her disappointment.

"Bloody hell," he mumbled.

She smiled. "Good, I am not alone in what I feel. You feel it as well."

"You are wounded," he said as if needing to remind himself. "And I have prisoners to talk to."

"Prisoners? We need to speak with them." Leora went to stand and once again his hand prevented her from doing so.

"I need to speak with them. You need to remain here and let Novice Angelica finish tending your wound."

"It just needs a thick coating of honey, and you can do that," Leora said and stretched her arm out to reach for a small crock not far from her on the table.

Noble grabbed it.

"Hurry. I am eager to hear what they have to say," Leora said impatiently.

"You have been wounded and to—"

"A minor wound to the backside does not require rest. Besides, it is better for me to stand with the wound so new, giving it a chance to heal. Now hurry and be done with it."

"Are you dictating to me, wife?"

She gasped lightly as she smiled. "I am hurt, husband, that you would even think that of me." She gasped again, though this time the gasp was when his hands hit the table on either side of her head as he dropped down over her, planting his cheek next to hers.

"My heart still hammers in my chest as it did when I first saw all that blood on you, reminding me how I could have lost you today," he whispered softly, though with a twinge of harshness. "And seeing that a mark was left on you in a place that is for my eyes only infuriates me."

Unable to do anything else, she pressed her cheek against his. "You stopped the attack quickly and prevented it from being far worse than it could have been, preventing the warriors from reaching me, which I had no doubt you would. My minor wound should leave no scar, but by chance that it does, then it should be a reminder of the day you saved my life." She kissed his cheek. "You are my champion, Noble, and always will be, and I love you more today than I did yesterday, and tomorrow I will love you even more."

A rap at the door had Noble yelling, "Go away!"

"The one captive is anxious to talk with you," Finley called out.

"We must not delay," Leora urged.

"I will be there shortly," Noble called out, standing.

The door creaked open.

"Open that door, Lady Elizabeth, and I will see you locked in your cottage until you depart, which will be tomorrow," Noble threatened.

"It is not proper for you to tend your wife's wound in such a delicate spot," Lady Elizabeth said, keeping her voice tempered so Noble could hear but not those outside.

"And why not when I touch her there often?" Noble called out.

"Savage!" Lady Elizabeth gasped and shut the door.

Leora went to get up. "That wasn't very—"

His hand shoved her down gently. "Stay put until I paste your wound with this honey."

"That was not nice. You should not have said that to her," Leora scolded.

"Nice is not a word one would use in describing a Gallowglass warrior. Besides, what is wrong with speaking the truth? I quite enjoy touching you there and often."

Leora continued to scold. "You were being ill-mannered."

He chuckled. "What do you expect from a savage?"

Noble wiped his hand clean of the honey and quickly cleaned the blood off from where it ran down his wife's leg before easing her garments over her backside, then slipping his arm beneath her waist to help her to her feet.

Chief came alert with a stretch, having fallen asleep under the table while the two had talked.

"This savage loves you very much, wife," he said and kissed her with more enthusiasm than planned, leaving them both a bit breathless.

"We need to go before we don't," she whispered and took his hand to tug him to the door, the passion that surged through her begging her not to leave.

He went to stop her, to yank her back in his arms but she stopped him.

"We can't, not now, even as much as I want to feel the strength of you move inside me, it must wait." She sighed heavily. "We cannot put our own needs above the safety of the clan."

"It is good that I have you by my side. I will count on your counsel, for you will help me lead wisely."

Surprise captured her face, widening her eyes. "Truly, you trust my counsel?"

"Trust and respect it more than anyone."

Her heart was filled with joy that he trusted and respected her word, though more so what it meant. Theirs would be a good, loving marriage and she looked forward to spending endless years with him.

Once outside, Leora spotted Lady Elizabeth busy conferring with Simmons, and she paid them no mind, except for a strong wrinkle of her nose, a small protest of their improper behavior. Novice Angelica was busy helping the wounded along with Brenda.

All called out praise to their new chieftain for his sharp instincts, quick actions, and for saving them from a brutal battle. The clan had lost two men and suffered several wounds, thankfully none were serious. So, it was smiles that continued to greet them as they made their way to the captives.

"Who wanted to speak with me?" Noble demanded, his voice strong with authority.

The middle archer of the three men tied with hands behind their backs and kneeling raised his head. "I speak for the three of us. And offer no excuse but beg for your mercy. We were sent here to the Highlands to make sure Lady Elizabeth of Clan MacMurray never returned to the Lowlands. We have no fight with the Gallowglass."

"It is one thing to think me a savage, another thing to think me a fool to believe your lies," Noble said, a harshness not only in his voice but on his handsome face as well. "You did not come here ignorant of what you would face, but you did come here believing you were more skilled than the warriors you would face... a deadly mistake for sure. Now tell me who sent you."

One of the other men was quick to respond. "Lord William of Clan Braverman."

"So that's who is financing Hedley's quest to gain control of my clan," Lady Elizabeth said with fierce anger as she hurried her steps toward Noble and Leora.

Noble turned to snap at the older woman. "You have no business being here."

"It appears we both have a penchant for being places we shouldn't be," Lady Elizabeth countered.

Leora hurried to intervene and to prevent the squabble between the two from escalating. "Why would Lord William finance Hedley's efforts to gain control of your clan?"

"Lord William has long desired to unite our clans, though his true intentions are to gain control of my clan. He can do that with me out of the way and by marrying his only daughter to Hedley." She shook her head. "Lord William will tolerate Hedley until his daughter produces an heir to Clan MacMurray, then he will see the fool disposed of quickly." She shook her head again. "I knew someone had to be helping Hedley. He does not have the finances nor the intelligence to do this on his own." Her eyes went wide. "Good Lord, I forgot that William has skilled archers." She turned to the prisoners. "You're part of his elite troop of archers, aren't you?"

The man in the middle who had claimed to speak for the three of them kept silent, not so the one who provided Lord William's name.

"We are and—"

"Shut up, Neville!" the man in the middle ordered.

"Why? We are damned no matter what we say. Lord William would see us punished for failing to do as he ordered, and that is if we ever make it home, nor would he care if he learned we were captured, and the Gallowglass are not known for being kind to their captives. So, my best choice is to cooperate and hope that provides me with a quick death."

"Neville's right," the other prisoner said.

"What if I offered you a different choice?" Lady Elizabeth asked.

"You have no authority to do so," Noble warned.

"Then give me the authority," she snapped.

"Nay!" Noble commanded. "Nothing less than death awaits them for attacking my clan."

"That is nonsense," Lady Elizabeth said with a dismissive wave of her hand. "Killing serves no purpose. Use them to your benefit."

Noble laughed. "You are naïve to think they could be of any benefit. They cannot be trusted and—"

Lady Elizabeth was quick to correct him. "Maybe the middle one can't be trusted but the other two I believe will do whatever is necessary to survive."

The two men nodded vigorously.

"You fools!" the man in the middle shouted at each of them. "You will still lose your life in the end."

"Not if given the chance to run," Leora said, looking from one to the other of all three men and all of them avoiding her glance. "Lowlanders who would brave the Highlands for the clan they serve would fight to the end to see their mission accomplished. They would not want to return home defeated, the only survivors of their troop. That would be worse than defeat. It would make them appear cowards."

"Wise words, wife," Noble praised, seeing the look of defeat on the three men's faces.

"Hmmm," Lady Elizabeth said, glaring at the three men. "I should have considered that. Willaim's warriors are loyal to him. William would not be stingy with the amount of men he sent. Are there more men than those who attacked today?"

Leora spoke up before her husband could explode at the woman. "It is my husband's duty to question these men, not yours, Lady Elizabeth. You either remain here holding your tongue or take your leave now." And when Lady Elizabeth went to respond, Leora added, "Or be forcibly removed."

Lady Elizabeth smiled. "Aye, you are much like me." She folded her arms across her chest and pressed her lips tightly together.

"Lord William said we would be doing the Lowlands a favor in getting rid of the foolish, old hag," Neville said as if the woman had proven Lord William's words true.

Leora's hand shot out to grip Lady Elizabeth's arm, a warning to hold her tongue, though Leora did not hold her tongue.

"It would appear Lord William was remiss in his remark since it appears Lady Elizabeth is not the fool here and, unlike her, you will not be surviving the Highlands."

Lady Elizabeth grinned from ear to ear while the men seemed to just realize their fate and looked at Noble.

"I will tell you anything you want, if you will just spare my life," Neville pleaded. "I have a wife and small bairn—"

"He lies. He has no wife and bairn," another said. "He is one of Lord William's cherished spies he has among his men."

The man in the middle turned so quickly to look at Neville that he almost tumbled over. "You spy on your fellow archers?" He turned quickly to look at the other man. "And you did not warn me or others about this?"

"And get falsely accused of something and get punished for it like others did?" The man shook his head. "I am no fool, though I was for not making my escape as soon as we entered the Highlands, something I have been desperate to do." He looked to Noble. "Lord William is determined to claim Clan MacMurray for his own and will do anything to make sure of it. Lady Elizabeth is right about Lord William marrying his only daughter to Hedley. The marriage celebration is already being planned. Lady Elizabeth, the woman who is believed to be her granddaughter, and MacMurray warriors will not make it back to the

Lowlands alive. And with word spreading among the mercenaries that it is the Gallowglass they will face leaves few willing to sign on to the mission."

"How do you know this?" Noble asked.

"I followed Neville when he met secretly with a man that was not known to me once we arrived in the Highlands and heard them talking. I hoped to gather information that would provide me with some leverage when I made my escape."

"He lies! He is the spy!" Neville shouted.

The two other men joined in and shouted amongst themselves, each accusing the other.

"SILENCE!" Noble shouted and Chief stuck his head out between Noble's legs and let loose with a puppy bark as if doubling the command.

Complete silence followed.

"The three of you will tell me all you know and detail your arrival here in the Highlands and who you met and talked with, as well as what you know about Hedley," Noble demanded.

"What will we get in exchange for our help?" Neville asked.

"A quick death," Noble said.

"Then why should we tell you anything?" one of the three asked.

"To avoid torture," Noble said and turned to his wife. "Leave this to me and go make sure all in the clan do well. I will share with you later." He leaned his head down to whisper, "If you are in any discomfort make certain to rest." She smiled and looked about to speak, and he warned, "Do not tempt me when I have my duties to see to."

"Do not forget all your duties," she reminded and turned away.

Noble watched her walk off with Lady Elizabeth, Chief following behind them and wondered how he was going to avoid making love with his wife tonight so that her wound would have time to heal. She was not easy to resist and not one to be denied, and though her wound was minor, it still required healing. He would retire well after she did this evening and deal with her annoyance in the morning, making sure to leave their bed before she woke.

Annoyed he would deprive her and himself, he turned his frustration on the three men. "You will tell me everything without delay or suffer the pain of torture."

Chapter Twenty-three

Leora paced the floor in the Great Hall frustrated and impatient and if something did not change soon her temper was going to burst, something that rarely happened.

Chief watched her anxiously, his eyes following her every move, ready to leap into action.

Seeing she had the pup anxious, she dropped down and gave him a hug and a kiss. "Go rest. Everything is good."

The pup did as she said, plopping his small frame down not far from her and keeping his attention focused on her.

Her thoughts went to her sister. That she had yet to see her since arriving here still disturbed her. She could reason all she wanted to that Sky was safe but until she saw or at least heard from her sister, she could not be sure how Sky fared. Then there was Mother Abbess, who had yet to arrive or even send a missive as to when she might arrive. That alone warned that something was amiss. And then the least thing that should concern her but was the most frustrating was that her husband had avoided intimacy with her the past four days, claiming she had yet to heal. Annoyed by his claim, she had sought the advice of Novice Angelica, not about intimacy, something that would be unknown to the novice, but about how her wound was healing.

It hadn't surprised her to learn that the wound was doing well, since the area was not as tender as it once had been, and the novice had assured her that with how well the wound was healing it would be only a few days until it was completely healed. Her husband was being overly cautious and though it was thoughtful of him, it frustrated her that they hadn't made love. The closeness and pleasure they shared when coupling and the contentment that followed was something she cherished, and she missed it terribly.

Her husband had purposely avoided any talk of it with her and that frustrated her even more since there was nothing they didn't share. It was another thing she cherished about her husband, that he shared everything with her. They kept no secrets and she intended to make sure that never changed between them, which was why he would not talk with her about their lack of intimacy so frustrated her.

"Good news!"

Leora jumped as she turned, and Chief barked, her husband's booming announcement startling her out of her musings. Good news was always worth smiling at, but her smile was all for her husband. His shirtsleeves were rolled up and the swath of plaid that usually fell over his shoulder and chest hung down along his side and the veins in his arm muscles were pronounced, meaning he had been engaged in physical labor. He never looked more inviting as he did now, although it might have been their lack of coupling that made him more appealing than usual.

It was when she spotted the man who followed behind her husband that she got excited for the news.

"Ross has brought a message from your sister," Noble announced, his smile growing, happy for his wife.

All thoughts of anything but her sister vanished, and she rushed toward the two men, Chief keeping pace with her.

Noble was quick to catch her around the waist, fearing she would collide with Ross in her eagerness to hear the message and he sent the pup a stern look that had him plopping his butt down with haste.

"Tell me," Leora said, her glance anxiously on Ross but before he could respond, added, "You received this message directly from my sister and not through Lord Slayer?"

"Your sister said you would ask that, and she told me to tell you that she has found the love with the animals at Clan Ravinsher that Snowball had given her at home."

A tear trickled down Leora's cheek and she smiled softly. "Snowball was a kitten Sky befriended when she was just a bairn. They were inseparable. Snowball died a few months before we were sent to Dundren Abbey."

Noble did not care to see his wife cry but at least it was happy tears she cried. And the trill on her lovely face in anticipation of the message filled his heart with joy for her.

Ross continued. "She also said to tell you that she is doing well and being well cared for, though she misses you and Elsie terribly. She says you are not to worry over her, though she knows you will ignore her words, but trust that she is safe and well-protected, and that when it is safe, the three of you will reunite and have much to discuss and that she looks forward to that time. And you should know that your sister made me repeat the message over and over until I remembered every word since she said you would know by the words alone if the message was from her."

Tears continued to trickle down Leora's cheeks, though she chuckled. "My sister knows me well, and I thank you, Ross, for delivering her exact words."

"Words I don't think I will ever get out of my head now." Ross shook his head as if trying to rid himself of them.

"Come sit, drink, and eat if you are hungry," Leora invited and led them to a table that had been set with drinks.

"Who is this? Does he bring news of Mother Abbess?" Lady Elizabeth demanded upon entering the Great Hall.

"I am no concern to you, woman," Ross said dismissively as he filled a tankard of ale after sitting.

"Lady Elizabeth," the elderly woman corrected with a lift of her chin. "And you, sir, are ill-mannered."

Ross raised his tankard. "I appreciate the compliment."

Lady Elizabeth shook her head. "Savages, the bunch of you." She turned to Noble. "Does he have any news?"

Noble assisted his wife to sit opposite Ross before he joined her at the table. "He has no news that is of interest to you."

"I will never understand you Highlanders, but then how do you understand a savage?" she asked more of herself than those there as she seated herself beside Ross and waved at a servant lass. "Bring me and Leora a hot brew."

"Mistress Leora," Ross corrected.

"I will not refer to my granddaughter that way," Lady Elizabeth said haughtily.

"From what I hear, that has yet to be proven," Ross said.

"I see news travels fast in the Highlands, and what is it you hear?" Lady Elizabeth asked bluntly.

Ross was just as blunt. "That you are on a fool's mission. That there is no way that it can ever be proven that Mistress Leora is your granddaughter."

Anger shined in Lady Elizabeth's eyes and the heat of it stung her cheeks. "All I need to do is claim it so."

Ross laughed. "Maybe in the Lowlands but not here in the Highlands."

Lady Elizabeth glared at Ross. "I can promise you that when I leave this savage place that it will be with my granddaughter."

Ross raised his tankard as if toasting his words. "Then I hope you find her because Mistress Leora will not be going anywhere, and Lord Slayer told me to make sure that you understood that."

"So, you knew who I was all along," Lady Elizabeth said in an admonishing tone.

"I only knew that a foolish, elderly woman was causing problems here and you fit that description perfectly," Ross said, with a smile and raised his tankard once again.

"You are a rude and ignorant man," Lady Elizabeth said, "which means this Lord Slayer is just as rude and ignorant or perhaps more so than you and let me tell you," —she shook her finger in his face— "I have bested more rude and ignorant men than you, so neither you nor Lord Slayer frighten me."

Ross placed his tankard on the table and turned a glare on the elderly woman. "A word of warning, Lady Elizabeth, but first, shake your finger at me again and you will lose it. Now for the warning, Lord Slayer is a man of few words, but when he speaks, everyone wisely listens. So, ignore his words at your own risk, for one word from him and you will have a permanent home here in the Highlands."

"Do you threaten a grave here in the Highlands for me?"

Ross shook his head. "Not at all. You would be left for the animals to pick your bones clean."

Lady Elizabeth laughed. "You think that frightens me?" Her laughter quickly faded, replaced by a sneer. "If there is one thing that I learned in my many years, it is that there isn't a person alive who will turn down substantial coins and the power such wealth brings."

"I believe you have already met one," Ross said with a nod to Noble.

Lady Elizabeth nodded. "Noble is a stubborn one, but I am more stubborn, and I will have my way."

Ross burst out laughing. "Woman, you are blind when it comes to Highlanders."

Noble ended the squabble. "Enough from the two of you, and you, Lady Elizabeth, would do well to accept the fact that Leora will never leave me or the Highlands. You waste your time here and I grow tired of your company."

Lady Elizabeth's chin went up once again. "I would be only too happy to leave this barbaric place with my granddaughter. So, the sooner I get to speak with Mother Abbess, the better."

Noble wanted to strangle the stubborn woman. "What difference would it make? Whether Leora is or isn't your granddaughter, she is not going anywhere with you."

Before Lady Elizabeth could continue to argue, Finley rushed into the room and didn't hesitate to deliver the news. "Two nuns have arrived from Whitehall Abbey… Mother Abbess has been abducted."

***

Noble and Ross had vacated their seats at the table so that the two upset nuns could sit as well as Novice Angelica, who was also distraught by the news.

Lady Elizabeth stood, though more paced anxiously near the table and when she went to speak, Noble stepped in front of her.

"One word from you, Lady Elizabeth, and I will have you removed from the room, forcibly if necessary."

The elderly woman glared at him but clamped her mouth shut tight.

Noble turned and looked from one nun to the other. "Tell me all you know."

The one nun who was just beginning to wrinkle around her eyes spoke up. "I am sister Benedetta. I was helping Mother Abbess tend to Mayer, an old farmer at one of the outer crofts who had taken ill. The old man was not doing well no matter the efforts of Mother Abbess. His son and daughter-in-law were worried he would not make it, and Mother Abbess and I feared the same. But he lingered, which is what kept Mother Abbess from answering your summons. Mayer finally passed peacefully in his sleep, and it was when prayers were being said over his grave that a group of men suddenly arrived and threatened our lives if Mother Abbess did not go with them. Mother Abbess did not hesitate to go with the men. She told me not to worry that they were probably mercenaries and no doubt looking for a healer to help one of their men who had been injured and she would be released soon enough. But she did tell me to come directly to you and let you know what happened. It makes no sense though that Mother Abbess would be abducted to tend to an injured mercenary. All mercenaries know they can seek healing at the abbey, so why abduct her?" She brushed at the tears trickling down her cheeks. "I fear for her life."

"It could be a trap," Ross said, drawing everyone's attention. "Someone may be using her to draw you away from your clan to rescue Mother Abbess while they come for—" He looked from Leora to Lady Elizabeth, then back at Noble.

"Of course, it is a trap, you fool," Lady Elizabeth admonished and received a scowl from Noble. "I will not remain silent when I can be of help. Hedley does not have the intelligence to plan such a trap. He would make a mess of it. This is Lord William's doing. He grows as impatient as I do to see this done."

"Then let's finish this," Ross said. "I will alert Lord Slayer. The abbey is his responsibility, and he will want to send men to help find and rescue Mother Abbess."

"Now you are making some sense, for a savage that is," Lady Elizabeth complimented and condemned in a few words.

Leora could tell when her husband's mind churned with thoughts. He appeared focused, listening to all that was being said, yet his deep blue eyes shifted along with the ideas running through his head. So, she wasn't surprised by his suggestion.

"Unless we set a trap for them."

"An excellent idea," Ross said, nodding.

"As long as it is executed wisely," Lady Elizabeth cautioned.

"My husband always plans wisely," Leora said with a smile and pride for her husband.

"That he does," Ross agreed, his eyes narrowing as he looked at Lady Elizabeth waiting for her to dare disagree.

The elderly woman ignored Ross, turning her attention to Noble, and he raised his hand in warning for her to hold her tongue.

"I have no time to exchange barbs with you, Lady Elizabeth. You would be wise to make yourself useful and stay out of my way." He turned to Finley. "Bring Lance and Bew here," he ordered, and with a nod Finley took off. "Sister Benedetta, when Finley returns with my trackers you will tell them how to reach Mayer's croft."

The nun nodded, brushing away the last of her tears.

"We will take this discussion to my solar," Noble said and reached his hand out to his wife for her to join them.

Ross went to follow, and Lady Elizabeth hurried to step in front of him.

"Where do you think you're going?" Ross snapped.

Noble did not glance back as he spoke, though Chief glanced back as he kept pace beside him. "As much as I would prefer not to have Lady Elizabeth privy to this discussion, it is a necessity. She knows who we fight and can provide us with necessary information."

"An intelligent savage," Lady Elizabeth said as if she did not quite believe it.

"Who will relieve you of that sharp tongue of yours if you continue to fail to curb it," Noble threatened.

"Your wife would never allow it and you love her too much to intentionally upset her," Lady Elizabeth said, "which I must say I admire the abundant love you have for her. It is so very rare to see, and it is why I am confident you will see that no harm befalls her."

Noble caught, out of the corner of his eye, the soft smile that spread across his wife's face, knowing the woman's words were true. He would never, not ever, cause her intentional pain and he was annoyed that the elderly woman realized it, making his threat worthless. But he could not allow that to pass.

"You're right, Lady Elizabeth, my wife would not approve, and I would acquiesce to her request that you not be harmed." Noble stopped abruptly at the solar door, forcing everyone to come to a halt and he glared at the woman. "I can, however, exclude you from this discussion and also forbid you from seeing and speaking to my wife for the remainder of your time here and that command she would not deny me." He did not turn to his wife for her to confirm it. He was confident she would do it on her own.

"And I would do as my husband commanded," Leora said.

Lady Elizabeth smiled. "You both are perfect to rule my clan and make it even more powerful and influential than it already is." She marched into the solar, calling out for drinks and food to be brought there.

Ross shook his head and followed her into the room.

Noble scowled. "I cannot wait for her to take her leave."

Leora shocked herself with her response since she had no intention of saying such a thing to him, at least not now. It was not the time nor the place. So, why did she whisper, "And I cannot wait for you to make love to me."

Frustration. Pure frustration, she thought and turned away from her husband to enter the room.

Noble snagged his wife around the waist and snatched her back before she could enter and called out before shutting the door, "We will be a moment."

Chief barely escaped having the door hit him as he hurried out of the room he had barely entered to remain with Leora and Noble.

"I should not have said anything now. It is not the right time, and I don't know why I said it." She shook her head, her remark an unintentional lie that she would not let stand. "I do know why. I am frustrated, completely frustrated that you have shown me not an ounce of intimacy in the last few days, and I cannot express enough how much I miss it. How much it means to share something so precious with you."

Noble spoke low, though with a strength that could not be missed. "I would kiss you now, but it would only flare my arousal that has lingered for days, waiting for you to heal. I have missed the precious time we share, miss feeling one with you, loving you, cherishing you." He took a deep breath, fighting to calm the passion that flared so quickly. "But I wanted to make certain you had healed—"

"I have healed," Leora said, interrupting him quickly, "and you will keep me... keep *us* waiting no more. And I will have your word on that."

Chief stood close by, his small head swiveling back and forth from Leora to Noble as they spoke.

"You have it, wife," he said and went to kiss her, but she turned her head away and he scowled.

"I want you to kiss me, I truly do, but if you do, it will not stop there. I will drag you, if I must, to our bedchamber where I will keep you imprisoned for the rest of the day and night and force you to make love to me. And we cannot do that now. Duty calls."

"You would not need to drag me or imprison me. I would go most willingly and see you—us—satisfied repeatedly." He stepped away from her and took another deep breath. "You are right, though I wish otherwise, duty calls."

Leora opened the door before they both surrendered to their passion.

"Tonight, I promise you," Noble whispered just before they stepped into the room and Leora's smile turned to one of utter surprise seeing Ross and Lady Elizabeth laughing.

"Are we dreaming or am I actually seeing this?" Noble whispered to his wife.

Ross spotted them and raised his tankard. "The woman is a good storyteller."

Chief trotted over by the hearth to curl up in front of the small fire lit there, a wide yawn escaping him before he rested his head down to get some sleep.

The discussion went easier among the four than Noble expected. Suggestions were tossed around, some with potential, some dismissed, and some accepted as a plan started forming.

Their discussion continued to go well when the door burst open, and Finley rushed into the room without knocking. "You need to come now!"

Chapter Twenty-four

Lady Elizabeth rushed around Noble toward a tall, slim man standing in the Great Hall looking quite distraught. "Hedley, you sniveling weasel you."

Hedely took several steps back, fear vivid in his wide eyes. "The plan has gone awry. Completely awry."

His hasty retreat did not help the man, Lady Elizabeth walked right up to him and poked him repeatedly in the chest. "Never! Never would I allow you to get even a small portion of the MacMurray wealth, let alone the title."

Lady Elizabeth was forcibly pulled away from Hedley and shoved down to sit on a bench at a nearby table, Ross's hand resting heavily on her shoulder as a warning she was not to move.

"How dare you—"

"I rule here, Lady Elizabeth, and it is time you obey my rule. Move or speak again and I will see you remain in your cottage until your departure home," Noble warned, and when she looked ready to speak, he warned again. "One word, just one and you will be deposited in your cottage with a guard outside your door, and you will know nothing of what goes on from this moment on."

"She is an evil witch, she is," Hedley said, pointing his finger at Lady Elizabeth. I am the sole male heir to Clan MacMurray. It is rightfully mine. Her refusal to see me inherit it all caused me to seek help from Lord William, and now that has gone all wrong." Hedley shook his finger at Lady Elizabeth. "This whole debacle is your fault."

Lady Elizabeth sneered at Hedley but wisely held her tongue.

Leora joined her husband, walking over to where he stood in front of the dais to stand by his side, with Chief taking a protective stance at her side. She had seen how upset the two nuns had become with the situation, having shielded themselves behind Novice Angelica, who stood fearlessly protecting them. She had gone to them suggesting the novice take the nuns to the village to see if anyone was in need of their care since they did not need to be privy to what would be discussed, and busy hands would ease their worry.

When Hedley saw her, his mouth dropped open and, for a moment, he was speechless. Then words rushed out of him. "Good Lord, you are beautiful."

Noble saw how Lady Elizabeth smiled, and her chest expanded with pride, but again she wisely held her tongue.

"Leora is my wife and will remain my wife. There is no proof that she is Lady Elizabeth's granddaughter," Noble said. "You have traveled to the Highlands for nothing, and I will see that you and Lady Elizabeth leave the Highlands with nothing."

"As long as I leave with my life, I do not care," Hedley said, wringing his hands. "But you should know your wife is not safe. The mercenaries Lord William hired intend to abduct and ransom her for more coins than agreed upon. They claim they are not being paid enough for going against the Gallowglass."

"What leverage do they have for such a demand? It would be foolish of them to kill her for then they have nothing to bargain with," Ross said, and Lady Elizabeth nodded anxiously as if it was the question she would have asked.

"That is an easy answer," Noble said. "They will sell her to the highest bidder."

Lady Elizabeth looked puzzled.

Ross' eyes went wide.

Leora reached for her husband's hand and as soon as hers touched his, his hand devoured hers, clutching it firmly, and she looked directly at him when she said,

"An enemy of the Gallowglass, of which I imagine there are many."

Lady Elizabeth gasped.

Hedley nodded. "She is right. That is their intention."

"So, they abduct Mother Abbess believing Noble will go rescue her, send you ahead under the pretense that you fear them and just want to go home—"

Hedley interrupted, "I do fear them. They are savages and now that they have banded together—"

"Banded together?" Noble asked.

"Aye," Hedley said, nodding. "Three troops have joined together to demand more coin from Lord William, though some favor selling her to one of your enemies, feeling they will get more coin from them."

"May I speak, Chieftain Noble?" Lady Elizabeth requested.

"I know what you will say. You have the coin to meet their demand," Noble said.

"I do and I will pay whatever it takes to see my granddaughter safe, and she will be safe in the Lowlands. Both of you come home with me where you will not have to worry about losing her. A home where she will finally be safe."

Leora could see her husband question the wisdom of such a decision since she knew he would do anything to keep her safe. Lady Elizabeth needed to be reminded of what Leora and Noble had told her on endless occasions and her husband also needed to hear her say it again as well.

"That is generous of you, Lady Elizabeth, and I and my husband are most grateful for your generosity, but we do not even know if I am your granddaughter. And as we both have told you time and again, neither of us will ever leave the Highlands."

Noble squeezed her hand, her reassurance that nothing would have her leaving the Highlands chasing away any thought of even considering the older woman's offer.

Noble turned his attention on Hedley. "So, you have come here today seeking my help, seeking protection from the mercenaries hired to kill my wife so you can inherit Clan MacMurray, and you expect me to believe what you say?"

Hedley returned to wringing his hands as he spoke. "I never wanted your wife dead, that was Lord William's doing. He gave those orders. I did not even want to come here but Lord William insisted I see it done. But no inheritance is worth my life. I want nothing more than to go home."

"And after trying to kill my wife, I should simply let you go?" Noble asked.

Hedley's whole body started trembling. "I wanted no part of that."

"And yet you were part of it," Noble accused.

A quiver ran through his every word. "Please, I beg you. I just want to go home. I mean your wife no harm."

Noble turned to Finley. "See him held prisoner until I decide otherwise."

"I am guilty of being a fool, nothing more. Please, I beg you have mercy," he cried as he was led out of the Great Hall.

"It is imperative that Mother Abbess is found," Leora said. "She may be able to tell us something that will help end this dilemma."

"If she knew something, wouldn't she have said something by now?" Ross asked.

"Nuns see much but say little," Noble said.

"The very reason many a nobleman is a benefactor to an abbey," Lady Elizabeth said. "The nuns keep their secrets." She was quick to glance at Noble. "It is not easy for me to hold my tongue, but I will do my best."

"I would make certain of it if I were you since you will not like the promised consequences," Noble reminded. "Now go and do your part in the plan, an easy task for you since it allows you to do as much talking as you like."

Lady Elizabeth stood. "And talk I will, spreading the word of your departure tomorrow, letting everyone know you go to find Mother Abbess."

"I will go and do my part as well," Ross said and took his leave with Lady Elizabeth, the two bickering as they went.

"I have to go and make sure all is ready as well, and you, dear wife, will not leave the keep," he said firmly and kissed her lightly.

"When do you think they will attack?" Leora asked, worried about her husband's safety and for the clan.

"When they are sure that we are a distance enough away from the clan but worry not. The tree perches you suggested we build in the higher branches of the tall trees will see them coming from a distance and we will be well prepared."

"And you will leave in the morning?"

"Aye, the morning but the night is ours." He pressed his cheek to hers to whisper in her ear, "And I look forward to it." That she did not respond with some tempting remark told him something was on her mind. "What troubles you, Leora?"

Her thoughts were so heavy, she sighed. "I do not know if Hedley speaks the truth or if he is an unwilling or willing pawn in this game and plays his part well. Does he truly regret the part he played in it or does his part continue? Or is it Lord William who is to blame for all of it?"

"Either way, this will all end soon," he assured her, intending to see that it did. He had had enough. He would see those responsible dead so his wife's life could never be threatened again. He gripped the back of her neck and pressed his brow to hers. "You have my word on this, Leora. I will see it done."

She brushed her lips over his. "You will take care, husband, for I will not lose you. I love you and we have a whole life yet to live together."

He couldn't explain it but somehow his heart felt full. He'd been missing something yet never knew it until Leora entered his life and now… life was far different, far better than it had ever been.

"And I look forward to every day I get to spend with you," he said.

"That is a lot of time, husband, since I intend to make sure we grow very old together. You may even grow tired of me."

Noble laughed. "Never, wife. Your bold nature keeps things far too interesting."

"I am not bold, I am determined," she corrected with a smile.

He laughed again. "Call it what you will. It is your nature, part of who you are, and I love all of you."

Her smile grew and his heart felt as if it slammed against his chest, her beauty blossoming with her smile.

Leora slipped her arms around his neck and rested her cheek close to his as she whispered, "I cannot wait for you to slip inside me tonight and love me."

He stepped away from her, shaking his head, her words creating an image in his mind that aroused his manhood. "Bloody hell, Leora, this is no time to tempt me."

She scrunched her brow as if confused. "When is a good time to tempt you?"

His smile was wicked. "You play with me, wife."

"I very much want to play with you."

He gripped her chin and brought his lips close to hers. "I will do the playing tonight, wife."

She waited for his kiss, but he released her chin and walked away.

"Noble!" she called out in a scolding tone, annoyed he had left her lips aching, not to mention other parts of her.

He released a hardy laugh. "Now you know how it feels, wife."

***

Leora waited impatiently in their bedchamber. She had left the Great Hall in hopes that her husband would soon follow but it had been some time now since she had slipped on her nightdress and Chief had fallen asleep in his favorite spot by the hearth, and he still hadn't joined her. She should not expect it of him when they were on the verge of a probable attack on the morrow, though perhaps that was the very reason it was so important to her that they made love. One never knew what the future held, but she did know her husband would do anything to keep her safe.

She had realized just how much he would sacrifice for her when she saw in his eyes that he had considered Lady Elizabeth's offer of returning to the Lowlands and ruling her clan. That he would leave the Highlands to keep her safe let her know the depths of his love for her. She would never let him do it, of course, but to know he considered it had made her love him even more.

The door opened and her husband entered. He smiled at her after closing the door and by the time he reached her, he was naked.

He tugged at her nightdress. "We need to rid you of this. I want you as naked as I am." That she hesitated and her brow creased had him asking. "What troubles you, Leora?"

"This probably isn't the time—"

"That never stopped you from saying what you will," he said, rubbing at the creases that deepened in the spot between her eyes.

"Never again are you to consider going to live in the Lowlands to keep me safe." She tapped his lips before he could speak. "And do not tell me you did not consider it. I saw it in your eyes when Lady Elizabeth offered it again."

"Briefly, but only briefly and just as briefly dismissed it," he confessed. "The thought of knowing you would be safe was too appealing to ignore."

"I forbid it. We will never leave the Highlands. It is our home and here is where we will live our lives."

His brow went up and his tongue was sharp. "Is that an order?"

"Must I make it one?" she countered, drawing her shoulders back and tilting her chin stubbornly. Her bravado faded before he could respond, her shoulders drooping and her chin dropping. "I cannot believe that you love me that much that you would leave the Highlands to keep me safe. It fills my heart with joy and pain at the same time."

He lifted her chin and met her eyes with his. "I briefly considered it, wife, but your words, your refusal yet again of her offer, reminded me that our hearts are here in the Highlands and neither of us would be happy anyplace else, and such a move could very well destroy the love we have for each other and that I will not allow."

She smiled, relieved. "You are a wise man."

"I know my wife well," he said, with a devilish twinkle in his blue eyes.

"That you do," she agreed unable to take her eyes off his.

"I know your needs as well," he said, easing her nightdress up along her body.

A shiver of anticipation ran through her as her nightdress slipped slowly along her body, teasing her skin and rushing gooseflesh over it.

"I have gone too long without you," she said and gasped when she felt his hard manhood brush against her.

"We have all night," he reminded.

She gasped again, a realization hitting her, and hurried to step away from him, shoving her nightdress down. "We cannot do this tonight."

Noble looked bewildered at her. "Why not?"

She shook her head. "I should have realized, but I am selfish and only thought of myself, my own needs. I will not see you depleted of your strength when battle awaits you tomorrow."

"I have enough strength for both," he said and stepped toward her and got annoyed when she stepped away from him again.

"If anything should happen to you because I was too selfish to forgo my needs for your safety," —she shook her head— "I would never be able to live with myself." She raised her hand, warning him off. "We will not couple tonight."

Noble shoved her hand aside, grabbed the neck of her nightdress and ripped it down the middle, ridding her of what was left of it. His wife gasped, shocked, and before she could respond, he hooked his arm around her waist and yanked her hard against him.

"Need I remind you yet again that I am in command?" he asked, a fiery passion blazing in his deep blue eyes and in the strong timbre in his voice. "But you are right about one thing, wife. We will not couple tonight. We will make love and more than once on that you have my word. And tomorrow I will battle with the fierceness I am known for and end the danger to your life."

He kissed her with an intense passion that left no doubt he was in command, and she surrendered to her own passion, her intense need for him, her overwhelming love for him.

He walked them to the bed, not breaking their kiss, and dropped down on it. He loved that her hands instantly began to explore him, lingering in spots before she settled on his manhood to caress with pleasure.

He wasted no time in doing the same, his hand brushing over her breasts to tease her nipple with his palm and playful squeezes. But his mouth was hungry for it as well and he tore his mouth off hers and, with his hands at her waist, lifted her, bringing her breast to his face and his mouth captured her nipple.

Leora gasped as her husband's tongue worked its magic and she ran her fingers through his hair, holding tight to his head as he sent waves of pleasure racing through her.

"I am going to taste every part of you tonight," he said, "leave my mark on you so that you know every part of you belongs to me."

"And I will do the same to you."

His laugh was wicked. "You will not have the strength by the time I get done with you."

Noble pushed her onto her back and proceeded to do as he said.

Leora thought to prove him wrong, that she could mark him with her kisses as he did her, but he would have none of it. He commanded their love making, her own passion forcing her to surrender to the strength of his love.

He kept her lingering on the edge of pure pleasure, pulling her back when she thought she would tumble off, only to tease her back to the edge again. She was lost in a thick haze of passion, barely able to think until she could do nothing but beg.

"Please, Noble! Please!"

He entered her swiftly, his thrusts overpowering, and she knew she would not last. She did not want to. She needed to tumble over the edge and get lost in the abyss of passion, and she did, crying out her husband's name as she burst into endless pleasure.

She heard him roar and felt the strength of his release and it sent her tumbling over the edge once again, devouring her.

Out of breath after his intense climax, Noble moved off his wife to drop on his back to lie beside her. Never had he experienced anything like what he had just shared with his wife. He could have sworn he had felt their hearts beat as one, their bodies join together as one and when he released... he felt as if they breathed as one. Never had he known such exquisite pleasure.

He reached beside him to take his wife's hand and bolted up when he felt it limp, lifeless. Her eyes were closed, and she was not moving. His heart pounded in fright.

He tapped her cheek several times. "Leora! Leora! Bloody hell, woman, open your eyes!"

Her eyes shot open, and she let out a long sigh. "I was lingering in the pleasure that continues to trickle through me."

Noble collapsed back on the bed. "You frightened the hell out of me."

"Why would I frighten you?" Leora laughed lightly. "Did you think you killed me with pleasure? If I had to die that would be a glorious way to go."

"That's not funny," he warned.

"Nay, it isn't for I would not go alone." She rolled on her side to cuddle against him. "I would take you with me."

Noble chuckled, his arm going around her to hug her tight. "You better, for I will not be left without you."

She lifted her head to look at him. "Something we agree on."

"We agree on things more lately than when we first met," he said. "I believe we are more alike than we first realized."

"So, you finally admit that you are as determined as I am," she said with a playful poke to his chest.

"Are you telling me that I'm stubborn, wife?"

"Determined," she corrected and went to slip out of his arms, but he stopped her. "I need the blanket. I am growing cold." He released her. "And since someone tore my nightdress, I need the blanket to keep me warm."

"You don't need your nightdress. You have me to keep you warm." Noble pulled her back into his arms and settled her snug against him, then pulled the blanket over them. "Besides, I prefer you sleep naked beside me. It makes it that much easier to have my way with you during the middle of the night or early morning."

"Not tonight or tomorrow morning though," she cautioned softly. "You have exhausted yourself enough tonight, please sleep well and be strong for tomorrow."

"I know you, wife, and I am warning you right now, if you slip out of bed after I fall asleep so that I cannot make love to you if I should wake during the night, then I will come find you and make love to you until the sun rises."

"You do know me too well," Leora said, annoyed. "If I stay, will you promise if you wake during the night, you will go right back to sleep?"

"I will try and that will have to do," he ordered.

"Try hard," she said.

He kissed her brow. "Go to sleep, tomorrow will come fast enough, and it will be a busy day."

Noble was glad he did not promise his wife, since he woke just before dawn with a need for her and though it was a fast coupling, it was just as satisfying. It was the perfect way to start the day and face the battle that was to come.

Chapter Twenty-five

Noble kept one hand on the reins of his horse and his other hand rested on the curve of his wife's waist as he held her close. His head was bent close to her face as if whispering to her and appearing to all that he was bidding her farewell before going off to find Mother Abbess.

"You conjure tears to make it appear that I will be gone, wife?" he asked, seeing her eyes glisten with tears. "You know the plan well. I will be waiting close by to quell the attack before it can even take place while Ross and his men, appearing as if they left for home last night, are no doubt, close to finding Mother Abbess. Therefore, there is no reason for worry. All will go well if you attend to your part and remain in the keep along with Lady Elizabeth." He smiled. "Now I understand why you are teary-eyed. You are stuck with Lady Elizabeth."

Leora poked him in the chest, pleased he wore a leather chest shield to give him some protection. "She fights as tenaciously for her clan as you do for ours."

"Unfortunately, she will not be the victor in this battle." Noble kissed her, leaving no chance for a response. "Go in the keep now, so I know you are tucked safely away." He glanced at the pup. "In the keep with Leora, Chief, and keep her safe."

The pup barked and started up the stairs, stopped, turned back, and barked at Leora as if commanding her to follow him.

"He is a brilliant dog," Leora said with pride, then kissed her husband, lingering a bit in it before reluctantly easing her lips off his. "That is so you keep in mind what awaits you and take no foolish chances."

He grinned. "It is the very reason I will take foolish chances, so I make certain I return home to you."

She poked him again. "I forbid you to take any foolish chances."

He glared at her, though kept grinning. "You dare command a Gallowglass warrior?"

"I command my husband," she shot back. "And you will obey me on this or else!"

"Or else what?" he challenged and laughed. "Do not think to say you will deny me the pleasure of intimacy with you since we both know that will never happen. You favor your wifely duties far too much to threaten that." He continued, a chuckle in his voice, "And do not bother to say there is always a first time or that miracles do happen, for those words are worthless in this situation." A tear trickled down her cheek and Noble's grin and laughter faded. He brushed the lone tear away. "Leora—"

"I cannot lose you," she said and grabbed his hand to kiss his palm. "The strength of my love goes with you so that you have the power to conquer all foes today."

He cupped her chin. "You will not lose me today. You have my word on it."

Chief barked impatiently.

Leora turned to the pup. "I'm coming, Chief." She turned back to her husband. "Go and be done with it." She was about to turn and race up the steps when Finley came running toward them.

"Signals were received from two tree perches," Finley said, when he got near. "Two sizeable troops of mercenaries approach from two different directions. And Ross's troop was spotted returning."

"Ross must have found Mother Abbess. He and his men will be caught unaware," Noble said.

Finley nodded. "And far too outnumbered and though Ross sent word to Lord Slayer, his warriors have not yet been spotted. They will attack from two sides as we leave the village."

"While a smaller troop attacks the village to fight less-skilled men," Noble said and thought a moment. "We remain here. Send a man to warn Ross and another to Lord Slayer, letting him know we need more warriors, though hopefully they are already on their way."

Finley ran off to see it done.

Noble turned to his wife. "You need to go into the keep and prepare for the women and children to shelter there, and you are not to leave until I come for you— me—no one else. Now go."

She nodded and turned, racing up the steps, Chief running right alongside her yapping all the way. She had no time to linger on thoughts of her husband, though he flitted through her mind, worry for his safety never leaving her. She called out to Calla, and they were soon busy settling the women and children as they entered the Great Hall. It wasn't until nearly all were settled that Leora realized that Lady Elizabeth was not in the room. She knew she was to come there, it had been part of the plan she agreed to, so where was she?

"Calla," she called out and the young woman hurried to her. "Have you seen Lady Elizabeth?"

"Nay, mistress. I have not seen her," Calla said and gave a hasty look around.

Leora did the same though she had checked twice already and had not spotted her. She would go look for her herself, but she had given her husband her word about not leaving the keep.

"Is something amiss, mistress?" Novice Angelica asked.

Leora was grateful for the novice and nuns' help with the women and children. Some women even took the opportunity to speak to them about wellbeing concerns.

"I wonder what is keeping Lady Elizabeth. She should have been here by now," Leora said while she continued to glance around the room, hoping she had missed spotting her, though that was unlikely.

"I can go see what is keeping her and escort her here," Novice Angelica said.

Leora was relieved to hear that. "I would be most grateful and no matter how difficult please do not let her refuse to take shelter here."

"Worry not, mistress, I will return with her."

"She is a formidable and fearless young woman," Calla said as the novice hurried through the room and out the door. "And from what many say, an exceptional healer. All are amazed at how well Adele has recovered."

"Mother Abbess has taught her well," Leora said and silently recited a prayer for the woman's safe return.

A horn suddenly sounded, echoing through the Great Hall, announcing that the attack had begun.

Leora worried over the novice and Lady Elizabeth. They could very well not make it back to the keep or they could be harmed trying to get here. She grew even more concerned when Novice Angelica returned not alone, but with an injured clan member.

"Forgive me, mistress, but I could not find her," the novice said, "and the fighting worsens and the injured need help."

Leora had no time to worry about Lady Elizabeth. She quickly began clearing an area in the Great Hall for the injured to be treated. She could not stop Novice Angelica and Sister Benedetta from repeatedly going out into the fighting to help the injured back to the keep. She actually envied them, wishing she could do the same but knowing it would upset her husband if he saw her. So, she kept her word, difficult as it was, and remained in the keep doing her part, confident in her husband's skills as a Gallowglass warrior.

The nuns kept returning with injured clansmen, all remarking on the bravery, skills, and fierceness of their chieftain and the Gallowglass warriors. Though there were some who feared there were not enough warriors to stand against another wave of mercenaries and that frightened Leora knowing more than one troop of mercenaries was out there.

Leora did her best not to worry, keeping herself busy so she did not know how much time had passed when she spotted Simmons, his glance hurrying over the room and his eyes going wide when he saw her.

They both hurried toward each other, Chief following along with her.

"You must come quick, Mistress Leora. Lady Elizabeth has been injured," Simmons said, clearly upset.

"I will go and help you bring Lady Elizabeth here," Novice Angelica said, having heard and offered her help.

"Nay, it may already be too late, and Lady Elizabeth begs to see Mistress Leora. Please, there is not much time," Simmons pleaded.

"I will not let you go alone. I will go with you," Novice Angelica said, stepping closer to Leora.

"Then come, we must go now," Simmons insisted anxiously.

The foolishness of rushing off with Simmons was not lost on Leora, so to be cautious she asked, "How do I know this is not a trap?"

Simmons's eyes widened. "She said you might say that and that I should remind you that the only thing important to her is your safety and she would never put you in harm's way. I can assure you, Mistress Leora, that she waits in a safe spot."

Leora remained skeptical, something not seeming right to her, and then there was her word to her husband that she would not leave the keep until he came for her—him—no one else.

Simmons glanced down at Chief. "You should leave the pup. It is safer here for him.

His remark added to her unease and made it less difficult for her to decide. "Tell Lady Elizabeth I am sorry, but I gave my husband my word not to leave the keep until he comes for me, and I intend to keep my promise."

"She thought you would say that as well," Simmons said.

The next thing Leora knew, the tip of a blade poked at her side.

"I fear you have no choice," Simmons warned. "You are coming with me and you as well." He nodded at Novice Angelica. "Say a word and it is not a light poke she will feel."

"Stay, Chief," Leora ordered, fearing for the pup's safety.

He protested with a bark and a growl, sensing something wasn't right.

"Wait for Noble, Chief," she ordered, the pup barked, not at all pleased with her command and prayed the pup would not follow but instead go find Noble.

Leora did not know if anyone paid any mind to their departure or even noticed, but what would it matter with the fighting going on? She would not waste time and worry over what awaited her. She needed to think of ways to survive whatever awaited her until her husband came for her. Was this a plan of Lady Elizabeth's to whisk her away to the Lowlands? The woman would have to know that Noble would follow along with the Gallowglass. She could not be that foolish, and if that was so then it would mean Simmons betrayed her. Was he the spy in her clan and she never knew it? And who had he joined forces with?

There could be only one person—Hedley.

He could have escaped during the fighting and now would see Lady Elizabeth and her dead, then leave for the Lowlands, but never make it there. Noble would surely hunt him down. She was thinking too far ahead. She had to concentrate on surviving and escape.

Simmons hurried them behind the keep and from there into the woods. It was a disheveled Lady Elizabeth they came upon and her troop of men and mercenaries.

"Forgive this foolish, old woman, Leora," Lady Elizabeth begged. "I found that wealth truly can buy anything, and my wealth seems to have bought a mutiny."

Simmons pushed Leora toward Lady Elizabeth and Novice Angelica was quick to stop her from stumbling, and they walked together to the elderly woman.

"Have done with it and let's be on our way before the fighting ends," Simmons called out, impatiently.

"I want my revenge and there is no revenge or pleasure in ending it fast." Hedley stepped from behind a tree. "I want the old hag to suffer for what she's put me through. I want her to watch her granddaughter die slowly from the wounds I intend to inflict on her before I take her own life."

"And the novice?' Simmons asked.

Hedley grinned. "She can entertain the men on our journey home."

The men called out their pleasure at the news.

"Make jest all you will, for you will not be laughing when you reach the Lowlands and learn that Hedely will never get even a smidgen of my wealth," Lady Elizabeth shouted.

"She lies!" Hedley yelled. "Lies are the only thing she has left, and they will not help her. "There's no time to waste. We leave now and go deeper into the woods, but first—" Drawing his dagger from his belt, he walked toward Leora.

"Nay! Nay!" Lady Elizabeth cried out, hurrying to shield Leora.

Simmons shoved her away, Novice Angelica grabbing hold of her before she could take a tumble.

With nowhere to go, Leora stood her ground, ready to defend herself.

"Fearless, are you?" Hedley sneered.

"Will you be the same when you face my husband?" Leora challenged.

Hedley sliced her forearm quickly and the blood followed just as quickly. "I'll do the arms first, though I am eager to start on your face. Bit by bit, you will lose your beauty."

"How much of a coward are you that you wound my arms so I cannot defend myself against you?"

He raised his blade again, but this time Leora was quick and turned her face, the tip of his blade catching a small spot on her jaw near her ear.

"We'll see how brave you are when I cut out your tongue," he threatened and turned away from her. "We leave now. We have delayed long enough. Get them on horses."

***

Noble watched his warriors finish off the last of the mercenaries and wondered why the other troop hadn't attacked yet. Had Slayer's warriors taken care of them? Were they no longer a threat? Whatever the reason, he still had to keep his clan prepared to continue fighting no matter how exhausted some were or how many wounds were suffered.

He glanced at the aftermath of battle. Many of the enemy lay dead, some wounded beyond help. Weapons littered the ground along with shields and the stench of battle itself stung the nostrils, an odor all too familiar to him.

He shouted orders for discarded weapons to be gathered and weapons taken off the dead bodies. Clansmen saw to it while his warriors needed no orders to remove the dead bodies so they would not prove hazardous during another round of battle, a chore they had grown accustomed to doing.

It was a scene that Noble had seen repeatedly after battle, but this time it was different. This time it was his home he was defending, his clan, his wife. That Leora was safe in the keep and would remain there until he came for her allowed him to fight without worry. He would love to go to her now and hug her tightly, if only for a few moments, and feel her love for him but with another attack possibly imminent, he could not take the chance.

He turned his head quickly, hearing something. Men on horses. But there had been no warning, no sound of a horn from those in their tree perches.

"Weapons!" he shouted, so all would be prepared, not sure if friend or foe approached.

Everyone stopped what they were doing and those with weapons raised them ready to fight and those without grabbed the nearest weapon bracing for another fight. Tension was taut and though fatigue could be seen on many faces, so could a fierceness to defend their home.

Weapons were soon lowered, and smiles broke out in relief when Ross and his men emerged from the woods and entered the village.

Noble didn't smile. He saw the results of a hard-fought battle on Ross and his warriors. Dirt. Sweat. Blood. He surmised what had happened. They had run into the other troop of mercenaries.

Ross waited until he dismounted in front of Noble to speak. "My tracker warned of a nearby troop last night and in the opposite direction than the one you expected."

"I sent word as soon as I learned of the troop," Noble was quick to say.

"I got it a bit late, but it did not matter. When I learned of the size of the troop, I sent one of my men to divert Slayer's warriors to help us attack in the morning. I had no doubt you could handle the troop that would attack you, but this troop would have caused you difficulties and cost you a large loss of men. I sent warriors ahead to find Mother Abbess. They will return with word soon enough."

"I am grateful for your help," Noble said.

Ross rested his hand heavily on Noble's shoulder. "We are Gallowglass."

No more needed saying. Gallowglass always protected Gallowglass.

Noble turned his head slightly, thinking he heard Chief's puppy yap, but that couldn't be. The pup was safe in the keep with Leora. He heard it again, but closer this time. He turned to see Chief racing through the village, jumping and swerving to avoid fallen warriors and not once did he stumble over his own legs. When he spotted Calla trying to keep up with the pup, fear squeezed at his heart.

He ran toward Calla, Ross following along with him.

Chief reached him first and wouldn't stop barking.

"What happened?" Noble called out before reaching the young woman.

"Chief wouldn't stop barking. He wanted out of the keep and he would never leave the keep without Mistress Leora. I looked for her and could not find her. One of the young bairns told me she saw Mistress Leora and the novice leave the Great Hall with a man."

"Leora gave me her word she would stay in the keep until I came for her. She would have never left of her own accord," Noble said, his heart pounding violently in his chest.

"You should know, sir, that Mistress Leora was looking for Lady Elizabeth, who was nowhere to be found in the keep. And as you said, she gave you her word not to leave the keep so Novice Angelica offered to go find the elderly woman, but unfortunately failed to locate her."

Finley came rushing toward them. "Hedley is missing."

A fierce anger twisted Noble's fine features and everyone there took several steps away from him, fearful of what he might do.

"Get Lance, Finley. We go find my wife," Noble ordered.

Chapter Twenty-six

"You need to escape before he takes his blade to you again," Lady Elizabeth whispered. "Worry not about me or the novice, escape and get help."

Leora was thinking the same and was relieved when she and Lady Elizabeth had been forced to ride together, one of the mercenaries keeping a tight hold on their reins while Novice Angelica rode with Simmons, who kept her locked tight against him.

"He will not wait to cut you again and the blood loss you let drop from your arm as a trail to follow will weaken you if you do not stop it. You need to go before it is too late," Lady Elizabeth murmured. "The only thing that matters is that you stay alive. You must save yourself."

"You and the novice could suffer for it," Leora whispered.

"We will suffer either way. If you escape and get help, we have a chance of surviving," Lady Elizabeth encouraged. "We need a diversion so you can make your escape and, once free, no matter what you hear, you must keep going. Do not let anything stop you."

Leora understood what the older woman was trying to tell her. She had to ignore any threats and any horrific screams coming from her or the novice. She had to stay strong and make her escape no matter how others might suffer because of it. That would be difficult for Leora to do. She could not abide someone suffering because of her.

Lady Elizabeth gripped Leora's arm. "Do as I say. Let nothing stop you. It is our only chance. And know this, Leora, whether you are my granddaughter or not I would be proud to call you my granddaughter. You are a remarkable woman," —she chuckled low— "for a Highlander, that is."

"And you are not terribly bad, for a Lowlander, that is," Leora whispered, having grown fond of the woman.

Silence settled between them for a few moments, then Lady Elizabeth spoke. "I am going to pretend a faint and fall off the horse."

"You will hurt yourself."

"You can ease my fall some, keeping hold of my arm, as if trying to help me, until I am near the ground, then let go. Chaos will no doubt pursue. I have no doubt that Novice Angelica will fight Simmons to free herself and hurry to help me, and the fools will rush to gather around to see what happened since they are not an organized bunch. Hedley thinks highly of himself and would never consider that you would dare attempt an escape. He will make a show and push past the fools who gather to see what is happening and that is when you must make your escape. Back away easily so you don't draw attention to yourself, then run when you are clear of the chaos and don't stop running. You cannot ride out of there, that would cause attention and you would be stopped. Besides, on foot you can hide more easily. If it should go any other way, make a run for it. We are not that far from your clan and perhaps your husband is already on his way to find you."

"I pray it is so," Leora said, hoping that the possible miracle she and her husband often teased each other about would, in this situation, come true.

"Call out as I grow weak in your arms and tilt to the side to draw attention," Lady Elizabeth ordered and went limp.

Leora did not have to pretend, Lady Elizabeth delivering her performance without preamble and startling her. She called out her name with worry when she went completely limp in her arms and tilted precariously to the side. She grabbed the older woman's arm as she began to slide off the horse and frantically continued calling her name. She grew heavy to keep hold of as she tumbled off the horse and Leora was barely able to keep hold of her before she hit the ground. She hurried off her horse, and as Lady Elizabeth predicted, chaos soon ensued. Novice Angelica battled her way out of Simmons' arms and hurried to Lady Elizabeth. Everyone came to a stop and hurried off their horses, eager to see what had happened and Hedely shoved everyone out of his way to get to the core of the problem.

Leora took advantage just as Lady Elizabeth told her to and moved away as they all pressed forward, far too curious to pay her heed, not having given thought that she would dare make an escape. Once she was beyond the curious onlookers, Leora ran into the woods and again did as Lady Elizabeth advised… she did not stop running.

Surprisingly, she was able to run a distance before she heard the first roar of discovery. The next shout had her stopping.

"I will take great pleasure in making the old woman suffer if you do not return right now, Leora," Hedley yelled, his roar carrying loudly throughout the forest.

Let nothing stop you. Lady Elizabeth's warning rang in her head.

343

She started running again and halted when a bloodcurdling scream echoed through the woods.

"There will be nothing left of the old fool by the time I get done with her," Hedley bellowed angrily.

How did she let the old woman suffer? It wasn't right. She froze where she was uncertain as to what she should do. If she ran for help, Lady Elizabeth and the novice could be dead by the time she returned. If she didn't go for help, none of them would have a chance. Wasn't the choice easy?

A hand suddenly closed over her mouth and a strong arm circled her waist holding her tight. "Never hesitate. It gives your foe the advantage."

She did not recognize the voice nor the man's scent, potent and earthy. He was tall, the top of her head hitting his chin, and though his arms were lean, he had a powerful grip. She did, however, recognize the furious roar that suddenly ripped through the woods in the distance... it was her husband.

"Time to take our leave," the man whispered.

Her feet suddenly left the ground, and she was carried away and no amount of struggling would free her. His grip was far too strong. All she could do was listen in the distance to the sound of clashing swords and cries of pain as men met their death as her husband fought to rescue her.

***

Noble swung his battle axe with such anger and power that all moved out of his way, none daring to fight him. The fight was brief. The few men who hadn't

344

been felled by a Gallowglass sword laid down their weapons in surrender, especially after Noble got a hold of Hedley by the nape of his neck and swung him around like he held nothing more than a sack of feathers.

"Where is my wife?" he yelled in Hedley's face.

"She escaped," Hedley said and sneered. "And I wouldn't be surprised if another troop of mercenaries got hold of her. Lord William is generous with his coin, eager to have Clan MacMurray for his own."

"He will never get Clan MacMurray," Lady Elizabeth said, holding her injured arm and leaning heavily against Novice Angelica. "My granddaughter will inherit and rule the clan."

Hedley laughed. "A foolish old woman's wishful thinking."

"Who is the fool here, Hedley, since I am free, and you are about to meet your death?" Lady Elizabeth asked with a smile.

"Enough!" Noble yelled. "How long has it been since Leora escaped?"

"Not long," Lady Elizabeth assured him. "She had to have heard when Hedley had my arm nearly broken, I cried out in such pain. Leora has a good heart, and I would not be surprised if she stopped and considered returning so I would not continue to suffer, though I had warned her against it."

Noble didn't wait… he let loose with a roar. "LEORA!"

Everyone remained silent, listening for her response.

Noble shouted out again. "LEORA, ANSWER ME!"

His shout was met with silence."

"She might have fallen and gotten hurt," Finley suggested. "I'll have Lance track her."

"Nay," Noble said, "I will track her and this time I will find her. Lance can join me along with a small troop of men while you and the others finish up here and get the women back to the keep."

"You should know that Hedley sliced Leora on the arm and went to slice her face, but she turned in time to only suffer a slash near her ear," Lady Elizabeth said. "Hedley intended to keep slashing her until she finally succumbed to her wounds so I could watch her die before he killed me."

Noble walked over to Hedley, his anger flaring mightily.

Hedley went to step away, but Noble was quicker. He pulled his kirk from his belt and sliced Hedley on the face. The man let out a yell, his hand rushing to his bloody cheek. Noble slashed at him again, catching his arm and Hedley stumbled back.

"It would bring me great pleasure to do to you what you intended to do to my wife and give you the painful lingering death you deserve, but I have no time to spare for you. So, you will get a quick death."

Hedley went to speak, but never got the chance, Noble grabbed a handful of his hair, yanked his head back, and slit his throat. He let go of the man and he dropped to the ground dead.

He turned to see Lady Elizabeth and Novice Angelica staring at him.

"You need to return with my granddaughter to the Lowlands. No one would ever dare trouble Clan MacMurray with you as clan leader," Lady Elizabeth said while Novice Angelica whispered a prayer.

"I am tired of telling you that I'm a Highlander and always will be. Do not mention it again and if anything has happened to my wife, you will meet the same fate as your nephew," he warned, then turned to Finley and ordered. "Finish here. I will see you back at the keep."

Noble said not another word. He examined the ground at the edge of the worn path and found his wife's tracks, the familiar ones that had gotten him nowhere the first time he tracked her. But this time it was different. This time he would find her.

He followed the tracks into the woods intending to have his wife in his arms soon.

***

Lance said what Noble had surmised for himself when they reached a particular spot. "Someone took her, sir, and he had a troop of men with him."

Noble gave thought to his options as Lance wandered a bit deeper into the woods, searching the area. He could not chance losing the tracks and he could not chance returning to the keep, fearing how far his wife could get from him. He wasn't foolish enough to think he could defeat a troop of warriors on his own, but he could track them while Lance went for the Gallowglass.

"Sir," Lance said, rushing toward him just as he was about to call out to him. "They turned. Just a short distance away, they turned course."

"Where are they headed?" Noble asked anxiously.

Lance shook his head slowly. "If they hold a steady course, it looks to be toward the clan village."

Noble had to look for himself, thinking Lance was wrong, but he wasn't. The tracks did go toward the village.

"We follow," Noble ordered. "They could rear off somewhere along the way."

To Noble's surprise, the tracks stayed on course straight to the village.

It was when he heard the horn alert his clan of the troop's approach that he was sure of their destination.

"I am going to ride ahead to be there when the troop arrives. You follow from behind and alert me immediately if they should suddenly change course," Noble ordered Lance, taking no chances but knowing it was unlikely.

Noble turned and followed a different path that would get him to the village faster and he entered the village just as a troop of men approached and as Finley arrived. Penn had the Gallowglass waiting for them, weapons in hand and Ross at his side.

It didn't take long for him to spot his wife. She rode with the man who led them, and he grew angry at how she was tucked against him. Then he spotted her wagging her finger in the man's face and he had to smile.

Noble rode his horse straight for the man. He had good features, dark hair and eyes, and, though lean, one could see he had good strength to him. He sat his horse with confidence and held himself with even more confidence.

Noble kept his smile locked away when he heard his wife say, "That is my husband, just as I told you time and again until—"

"I grew tired of hearing it," the man snapped and brought his horse to a stop at Noble's approach. "Take her. Please take her."

"You are lucky you finally stopped being foolish and listened to me or my husband would have killed you by now," Leora scolded, her finger still wagging.

"It would have been a relief instead of listening to you endlessly harangue me," the man snapped again.

She turned to her husband and smiled. "As much of a foolish arse as he is, you should know that he tended to the wound on my arm and treated me well." She stretched her arms out to her husband.

Noble quickly hooked his arm around her waist, and her arms went around his neck as he lifted her off the man's horse and settled her in front of him on his horse. He wanted to hug her tight, kiss her, tell her how much he loved her and how happy and relieved he was to have her in his arms. But that was for later and he almost let loose his smile when she whispered, "Later."

"Who are you?" Noble demanded of the man after tucking his wife snug against him.

"He is Lord Drake, son of Lord Willian of Clan Braverman," Lady Elizabeth said as she approached on a horse with Novice Angelica. "You made the trip here for nothing. Your father's plan failed. Hedley is dead.

There is no one to wed your sister and unite Clan MacMurray with Clan Braverman."

"Aye, there is, and I came here to see it done so this senseless feud between my father and you can be brought to an end and two strong clans can form an even stronger alliance," Lord Drake said. "Unfortunately, your granddaughter is already wed, and she tells me she may not even be your granddaughter, which leaves your clan without an heir."

"There is someone here who may be able to confirm that Leora is my granddaughter," Lady Elizabeth said with a haughty lift of her chin.

Noble looked at Ross. "Mother Abbess is here?"

"Aye," Ross said with a nod. "She waits in the keep."

"Then we go to the keep and find out if Mother Abbess can finally solve this dilemma," Noble said and ordered Penn to see Lord Drake's men settled on the outskirts of the village while everyone else proceeded to the keep.

Noble kept a slow pace, lingering behind the others to have time to speak with his wife.

"You killed Hedley?" she asked.

"He deserved it," Noble said without remorse and wished his death had not been a swift one, seeing the exhaustion and pain in his wife's eyes and in the creases around them as she tried to hide her pain from him. "You are hurting."

"I think it best that Mother Abbess look at my arm."

That alarmed Noble and he saw that the cloth wrapped around her arm was stained with blood. He recalled her other wound and turned her head gently to look at it. He grew even angrier seeing the blood crusted there.

"It may leave a scar. The wound on my arm will definitely leave a scar," she said, seeing the fiery anger in his eyes.

"I don't care. All that matters is that you're safe and in my arms again." He couldn't wait, he had to kiss her. He took hold of her chin as he kissed her, and she returned it with the same overwhelming need.

Cheers rang out around them and shouts of praise for the chieftain and his wife.

"Light the fires and roast the meat. We celebrate our victory tonight!" Noble called out after reluctantly ending the kiss. Cheers echoed through the village, smiles lit faces, and all got busy preparing for the celebration.

Everyone waited at the keep's steps for Noble to arrive and take the lead. He kept a tight hold of his wife's hand as they climbed the stairs, making certain no one would whisk her away from him again.

Chief rushed at Leora when she entered the Great Hall, yapping and wagging his tale until she thought he would collapse from exhaustion.

Noble scooped him up so the pup could lavish kisses on Leora's face but wouldn't let her hold him. "Not until Mother Abbess tends to your arm."

Chief seemed to understand and remained close to her side when Noble placed him on the floor.

"You need to tend to my wife's wounds," Noble said as they reached the table where Mother Abbess sat.

"That can wait," Leora said, stepping in front of her husband. "Are you well, Mother Abbess? No one harmed you, did they?"

"I am good. Ross' men rescued me before anyone could do me harm," Mother Abbess assured her.

"Do you know if Leora is my granddaughter?" Lady Elizabeth called out as she hurried to the table.

Silence fell over the Great Hall, all present waiting anxiously to hear.

Mother Abbess smiled softly. "Aye, I do know, and Leora is not your granddaughter."

Lady Elizabeth's shoulders sagged, but her chin remained lifted as stubbornly as ever. "Were you told this? How can you be sure of another person's word?"

"I know without a doubt that Leora is not your daughter," Mother Abbess said gently.

"How? How can you be so sure?" Lady Elizabeth demanded.

Mother Abbess expelled a deep breath before saying, "I am sure because Leora is my daughter."

Chapter Twenty-seven

Noble's arm went around his wife, seeing her sway as if she might collapse at the news, and helped her to sit next to Mother Abbess. He took up a protective stance behind her, resting his hand firmly on her shoulder to let her know he was with her and not going anyplace.

Lord Drake took hold of Lady Elizabeth's arm and helped her to sit at the table opposite Mother Abbess, then remained standing behind her.

Novice Angelica went to stand behind Mother Abbess and rest her hand on her shoulder, offering what comfort she could while silence continued to reign in the room, all waiting for Mother Abbess to speak.

"Many years ago, Whitehall Abbey secretly took in unwanted bairns and sometimes women in dire need. The Abbess at the time was a woman of great courage. Against the church's belief, she took in unwanted bairns that unmarried women brought to the abbey or midwives who sought help for a newborn in danger. The abbess placed the newborns with parents willing to take them and protect them." She smiled at Leora. "Your parents were such a couple. They were generous, loving, and courageous. Elsie's true mum helped tremendously, even though her stay was short, when she arrived at the abbey with her daughter and was so brave when she had to part with not only Elsie but leave the abbey since she feared she had been followed and did not want to bring harm to the nuns."

Leora wiped away a tear that trickled down her cheek and was glad to feel her husband's strong hand squeeze her shoulder.

"I found myself in need of the abbey when I fell in love with a man my father did not approve of, but it mattered not to me or him. We had plans to run off together, but as fate would have it, he was killed in battle and, shortly afterwards, I discovered I was with child. I feared what my father would do but he unknowingly gave me the perfect escape. He ordered me to go to the abbey and pray for the strength to be a dutiful daughter and be ready to wed the man he chose for me. By the time my father arranged a marriage, I had given birth to you, and after holding you close and loving you for five days, you were taken away and given to the couple Mother Abbess assured me would love you and keep you safe, and she was right. I took my vows before my father could wed me since I could never be with another man. I loved your father far too much. It would have felt like I betrayed him. I have remained at the abbey ever since."

Leora reached for her husband's hand on her shoulder, and he took hold of it as Mother Abbess continued.

"Your father carved this cross for me," Mother Abbess said, hugging the wood cross lying on her chest. To keep me safe, he said, and it has kept me safe. He was a mighty warrior and a man so handsome it was difficult not to look upon him. You inherited his beauty," —she smiled— "and his tenacity. He was stubborn but never foolish, except when he fell in love with me." Her smile faded.

Noble recalled something. "The tapestry in your solar of the nun praying over the dying warrior—"

"I created it. I needed a way to work through my grief, a way to be with him when he needed me the most, a reminder that I would forever love him." Mother Abbess took another deep breath. "I never planned on telling you. It was a secret meant never to be revealed, but as danger grew for you, I began to see that it could remain a secret no longer. I planned on telling you the last time Noble summoned me here." Her smile returned. "You should also know that Clan Skirling is your true home. My brother died in a battle and my father took ill and died and without a direct heir, it passed to a distant relative who was not worthy to lead. My father and brother would be pleased to know that a rightful heir has returned to Clan Skirling."

Leora remained speechless, trying to digest the startling news and keeping a tight hold of her husband's hand.

"I had hoped, so hoped, you were my granddaughter," Lady Elizabeth said tearfully. "You and Noble would have done Clan MacMurray proud.

"This continues to create a problem between you and my father," Lord Drake said. "There is unrest in the Lowlands—"

"There is always unrest in the Lowlands," Noble said.

"You have your share of it as well," Lord Drake challenged.

"Caused by the Lowlanders claiming what they have no right to claim," Noble argued.

"Enough from the both of you," Lady Elizabeth admonished. "My journey is for naught. I go home without an heir."

"I confirmed that Leora was not your granddaughter. I did not say that I did not know about your granddaughter," Mother Abbess said, catching everyone's attention.

Lady Elizabeth's face brightened. "Tell me. Tell me she is still alive and not wed."

"She is alive and is not wed," Mother Abbess confirmed.

"Perfect," Lord Drake said. "We will go find her and I will wed her, uniting the two clans and settling the feud between you and my father and creating one of the most powerful clans in the Lowlands."

"How do I trust you or your father when he sent men here to kill my granddaughter?" Lady Elizabeth demanded.

"My father did not send men to kill your granddaughter," Lord Drake said, his brow wrinkling at her claim. "He sent men to prove there was no granddaughter. Hedley was the one who hired mercenaries and fed them lies, telling them Lord William ordered that your granddaughter was to die. When I returned home from a mission for the King, my father had only discovered Hedley's deceit and immediately sent me to rectify it. My father simply wanted proof that no granddaughter existed so Hedley would have a clear path to inherit Clan MacMurray. Now that there is a granddaughter the wisest thing is for me to wed her and unite the clans, and the sooner the better." He turned to Mother Abbess, his demeanor commanding. "Tell us where she is?"

"And I am to take you at your word?" Lady Elizabeth asked, preventing the Abbess from responding.

"You have known me since I was young. I was a friend to your son when others deserted him, and do you forget that day you told me you wished I was your son? I speak the truth and you know it, and I do what is best for both clans. Do not let your disappointment and anger prevent you from making a wise decision."

"I always make wise decisions," Lady Elizabeth said and straightened her sagging shoulders as she looked to Mother Abbess. "Tell us where we can find my granddaughter."

"It is her decision if she wishes to reveal herself. I cannot, nor will I make it for her," Mother Abbess said.

"That is nonsense," Lady Elizabeth argued. "A fortune awaits her as heir to Clan MacMurray."

"Also, a marriage she has not agreed to," Mother Abbess reminded. "You demand she give up her life here in the Highlands among family and friends and go to the Lowlands with complete strangers. That is a huge sacrifice for her to make."

"And her choice to make it," Lady Elizabeth said. "Wealth awaits her and will bring a freedom to her that most women never get to know, and of that I will make sure."

"So, she will be free to choose her own path?" Mother Abbess asked. "Pursue her own interests?"

"Within reason," Lord Drake said.

"She may do whatever she pleases," Lady Elizabeth corrected, and her glance shifted, "and on that, you have my word, Angelica."

The novice remained silent, gripping the Abbess' shoulder.

"I wondered when you might realize it," Mother Abbess said.

"I began to wonder when that sniveling weasel Hedley captured us." Lady Elizabeth smiled at Angelica. "You protected me, shielded me at times, and I saw something in your eyes that reminded me of your father. He could be a fool, but he was a fool who cared for me and there was a look he would give me at times, and I saw it in your eyes and wondered if it was simply wishful thinking."

"How long has she known?" Noble demanded.

Mother Abbess glanced up at Angelica. "Only moments before you entered the Great Hall. Her mum gave birth about a month after I did. She had no place to go and remained at the abbey with Angelica. Her mum was an exceptional healer, and it is why she comes by her skills so easily and why the nuns are learned healers. Angelica needs time to digest the news. I will not see her rushed into making such a life-altering decision."

"Let us find a place to talk, Angelica," Lady Elizabeth offered, "so that I may tell you of your inheritance and all it has to offer you."

Angelica looked to Mother Abbess.

"It is your choice to make, Angelica. Talk with the woman and then we will talk later," Mother Abbess said.

"We will go to the healing cottage to talk, so I may tend to your arm," Angelica said.

"I would like that," Lady Elizabeth said, smiling softly.

Lord Drake went to follow them.

"I will speak to my grandmother alone and know now, I am not a woman who takes well to orders," Angelica said, halting the man.

"Does she remind you of someone?" Noble whispered with a chuckle to his wife.

Leora jabbed him in the side with her elbow and winced.

"Her arm needs tending now," Noble commanded of Mother Abbess.

"May I use your solar?" Mother Abbess asked. "It will give Leora and I time alone to talk since I am sure she must have questions for me."

Leora answered for him, eager to speak with the Abbess… her mum. "My husband doesn't mind."

Noble was quick to disagree. "I do mind. I will see your wound tended to first, then you both may talk as long as you wish, though you will not miss today's celebration. It seems there is more than one victory to celebrate today."

***

Leora lay snug against her husband, her bandaged arm resting across his chest.

"You are not in pain?" he asked.

"Minor pain, no more, thanks to the brew Mother Abbess fixed for me."

"Mother Abbess took a chance revealing her secret. She could be banished from the church due to her deceit and the part she played in helping other women." He hugged her closely. "But I think it was more important to her that she let you know she was your mother, than worry about the church. I just wish she had told us sooner."

"She told me she was not sure if she should reveal the truth. There was the abbey to consider since it would reveal what the nuns had done there. But as she had said, after a while it became apparent that she had no other choice." She yawned again. "My heart broke when she spoke of my da. They loved each other so much and had only a short time together. I thought about you when she told me and how my heart would break if I had only a fleeting moment in time with you. It would devastate me."

He kissed her brow. "I thought the same when I discovered you were gone. That pup," —he nodded to Chief sleeping by the low burning hearth— "has good instinct and let me know you were in trouble. He will serve us well. But tell me how you feel about finding out Mother Abbess is your mum?"

"I don't how to feel. My parents, the ones who raised me, are still my parents to me, but Mother Abbess loved me enough to give me away to good people and to protect me from being rejected by her family and called a bastard child. She did not speak of my da's parents, but then I don't believe she ever met them since my mum and da kept their love for each other a secret. In time perhaps she will tell me more."

"You have time to get to know her, time to learn more about the past, about your da, about all she went through to keep you safe and loved."

Leora yawned again. "Aye. She said the same, that there was time for us to talk and she is eager to hear about my life with my parents." Another yawn slipped out. "I am annoyed. I had plans for us to make love—"

"You are too tired."

"I am, which is what annoys me. I promised myself that I would survive and that we would make love tonight, but my arm hurts and my body aches and I feel exhausted," she said, too tired to continue being annoyed.

"There is always tomorrow and the day after that and the day after that," he said and kissed her brow again."

"Promise?" she asked, sleep growing heavy in her eyes.

He had no chance to answer, her eyes closing in sleep, but he did anyway. "I promise, wife. We will love tomorrow and every day after, for I love you with all my heart and then some."

"I love you more," she said in barely a whisper.

He smiled and returned her whisper, "Impossible."

"Is that a challenge?" she asked, struggling to remain awake while her eyes remained heavy with sleep.

"I would not make it one since I never lose a challenge." He waited, wanting to hear the familiar words she had said repeatedly to him, and he had grown to favor since first meeting her.

"There is always a first time."

***

Lady Elizabeth hugged Leora tightly. "You will always hold a special spot in my heart."

"And you in mine," Leora said.

"Not so mine." Noble chuckled.

"You don't matter," Lady Elizabeth said dismissively. "But I do thank you for tolerating me, Highlander."

Leora elbowed her husband in the side, warning him to behave before asking Lady Elizabeth, "Do you think it will be a good marriage between them?"

The elderly woman looked to Lord Drake and Angelica, bickering in front of her horse and smiled. "I believe so since they remind me much of you two."

"Good luck, Lord Drake," Noble called out with a grin.

Lord Drake turned a scowl on him and raised his voice in annoyance. "And I thought your wife could not hold her tongue."

Lady Elizabeth chuckled. "This is going to be an interesting journey home with the newly wed couple." She nodded to Noble. "Thank you for alerting the Gallowglass that we are to be left unscathed and protected on our journey. That was kind of you."

"That was not my doing. That was Lord Slayer's doing. He wants you and yours out of the Highlands as much as I do."

"Noble!" Leora admonished.

"He tells the truth, dear, and that is refreshing. Good-bye, Highlander, and a good life to you and your wife, for we will no doubt never meet again."

Leora stood with Noble, watching them leave.

Noble slipped his arm around his wife's waist and tugged her close, a whiff of her freshly washed hair teasing his senses. "The week has been a busy one. I have barely had you to myself. Today is for you and me and your choice of what you would like to do, though somewhere in there I wouldn't mind if we spent some of it in our bedchamber."

She chuckled when he tickled her neck with playful nibbles. "I was thinking the same, though I wouldn't mind if we walked for a while and enjoyed this beautiful summer day, knowing we are safe to do so without worry."

Chief yapped as if agreeing.

"I would enjoy that very much," Noble said and took her hand, the pup running ahead as they walked.

"I cannot believe he has finally found the courage to talk with her," Noble said, glancing at Penn and Calla, the large warrior carrying a basket full of greens for her as they walked.

"I don't think she gave him a choice," Leora said, happy Calla's determined pursuit had succeeded.

Noble smiled, his chest expanding with pride as he said, "Just like I didn't give you a choice and you couldn't help but fall in love with me."

Leora laughed. "In what dreamworld was that? The choice was all mine to love you." She stopped abruptly. "You said that on purpose so I would admit—'"

Noble pulled his wife into his arms. "That I know you made the choice of your own free will to remain in our marriage to love me even though the marriage was forced upon you."

"Aye," she said softly, "but we weren't forced to love each other and that makes the difference."

Noble lowered his head to kiss his wife when his name was shouted and he mumbled several oaths before he looked to see Ross approaching them, an anxious pinch to his face.

"What's wrong?" Noble asked when Ross reached him.

"I received an urgent message from Lord Slayer that I was to return home immediately and that you and Cavell need to remain on alert and be ready if needed. If he requests both of your help, then I fear something is terribly amiss. I will let you know as soon as I find out. But remain on alert and ready for battle."

A dread settled in the pit of Leora's stomach as she watched Ross rush off. She didn't know how she knew, but she knew. She felt it in her roiling stomach and deep in her heart.

She turned to her husband. "It is Sky. Something has happened to Sky."

Visit donnafletcher.com to learn more about Donna and her books.

Printed in Great Britain
by Amazon